Return of the Hero

Hellhounds Series: Book 3

Theo Mann

The Invisible Publishing Company

Hellhounds Series

Contents

Chapter 1

C aptain Owen LeMaine wrestled his Imoliv fighter craft in every possible way, but the ship wouldn't obey him.

An Axichis laser shot had punched a hole through the fuselage, took out the controls, and blasted another perfectly round hole in the floor between LeMaine's feet. Only a miracle saved LeMaine from getting wiped out along with the ship.

The fighter wheeled wildly as it plummeted through the planet Aora's atmosphere. Wind pounded the hull and flipped the ship over and over itself, jerked it right side up, and then rolled it in somersaults again.

LeMaine had to concentrate hard to take his hands off the controls. He didn't know if this fighter craft had any eject function. The Imoliv didn't give their pilots emergency supplies. Maybe the Imoliv commanders didn't think to add an eject function, either.

Mountain ranges and rainforests cartwheeled in and out of view. The ship dropped straight down with no way to stop it.

Out of nowhere, three Axichis fighters shrieked from high orbit, ripped across the landscape, and lasers danced all over LeMaine's craft. The defenses went down along with the controls.

He hunkered low in his seat waiting for the shot that finally took him out. At least he wouldn't have to live through his ship crashing into the ground with him inside it.

A brutal shot slammed into the hull, and like magic, the cockpit cover blasted off, the pilot's seat ejected, and a parachute deployed right behind LeMaine's head.

The chute jerked him against his safety harness and then he started floating peacefully toward the ground. The surreal contrast between this and the sheer mortal terror of the last few seconds fogged LeMaine's brain for at least five minutes.

He stared around him at green, lush forests, blue lakes, and then his eye picked out more parachutes falling in the distance. Were the Hellhounds landing here, too.....or was someone else?

He couldn't decide whether he wanted the Hellhounds to land here or not. He didn't want his people stranded in the wilderness, especially not when they were so far away. LeMaine wouldn't be able to find them.

Then again, he didn't want them in the air, either, not with the Axichis hunting Elian Military craft everywhere.

The Hellhounds had gotten caught in a deadly campaign gone disastrously wrong. Flying around in either an Elian Military craft or an Imoliv fighter would be the most dangerous place for the Hellhounds to be.

The Hellhounds never shied away from danger, but LeMaine liked it better when he kept his people alive.

He couldn't do any of that right now, but at least he was going down on a populated Elian planet. He would be able to find some Elian citizens to help him.....eventually.

The chute lowered the pilot's seat to the ground at a gentle sloping trajectory. The whole package drifted toward one of the forests. That would create the problem of getting down from the canopy once the chute inevitably caught in the upper branches, but anything was better than getting shot down.

That thought barely crossed his mind when more Axichis fighters peeled out of the sky hunting Elian attack cruisers. The combatants thundered over the horizon, corkscrewed around each other trading shots, and then, out of LeMaine's worst nightmares, the skirmish veered toward him.

Axichis lasers punctured his chute and the gentle gliding descent came to an abrupt end. The pilot's seat ripped the torn chute out of the sky, the seat plummeted, and the whole chute crumpled and went with it.

LeMaine yelled at nothing, but fortunately for him, he was close enough to the forest that the landing didn't hurt him. The pilot's seat crashed through the branches, snapped twigs in his face, and would have hit the ground, but the branches caught the chute.

He slammed against his harness again and finally came to a stop with the seat swaying a hundred feet off the ground. Now he had the even bigger problem of getting out of the seat without breaking his neck.

He gave himself several minutes to just sit there and gasp and pant to get his heart to slow down. This wasn't how he planned to spend his morning.

He finally wilted in a combination of relief and exasperation. He had to do something. He couldn't stay here forever.

He stopped to think about how he was going to do this before he actually unclipped his harness. He had to be careful not to break any bones or hurt himself.

Sergeant Mason Kellogg, the Hellhounds' medic, wasn't here to save LeMaine's bacon if he got himself into a pickle—an even bigger pickle than he already was in.

He eventually made up his mind, unclipped the buckle, and slowly, slowly, eased himself out of the harness. He did it one painstaking step after another and kept a firm grip on the harness at all times. It was his only lifeline.

He twisted himself around, stuck his foot into the lower harness loops that had been around his legs, and hoisted himself up so that he stood right on top of the seat. From here, he could grab the lines that held the seat to the torn chute.

He considered working the lines back and forth and swinging himself to the nearest tree trunk. He could climb down from there, but he didn't want to risk the chute tearing out all the way. Then he really would fall.

The lines and the chute fabric were already supporting his weight, so he decided instead to climb the lines to the high branches. He could climb down from there.

He wrapped the lines around his hands, hoisted himself off the pilot's seat, and then used a combination of loop footholds to clamber the rest of the way up to where the chute lay tangled among the leaves.

He finally stepped off the lines onto a stout branch stiff enough to hold his weight. He scooted along the branch to the trunk, sank into a crook between branch and trunk, and at long last, he allowed himself to shut his eyes and gulp in every sacred breath.

He stayed there a lot longer this time. He was finally out of danger and the climb tired him out more than he expected. He wasn't as young as he used to be, but he could still pull it out when he needed to.

Now he could look forward to an indefinite stay on this planet until he either found his way to civilization or someone came to pick him up.

He had no idea when either of those would happen. He needed to use his resources. He still wore his backpack. He would never launch in any vessel ever again without that.

He didn't have a rifle, though. It wouldn't have fit in the seat, but he also had the chute, the lines, and the pilot's seat itself. They weren't much, but they were better than nothing.

He scooted back out onto the branch, pulled his tactical knife from his belt, and cut the lines holding the seat up. It landed hard on the ground and he busied himself freeing the rest of the chute and lines from their tangle.

He tossed everything to the ground and then got to work scaling down the tree. That turned out to be a hell of lot easier than climbing up those lines, and in a few minutes, he jumped down next to the seat and chute.

He wadded up the chute, put the fabric in his pack, coiled the lines into a bundle, lashed them to the outside, and then went over the seat.

He didn't see much here that he could use. He didn't want to take too much. It would only weigh him down, so he discarded the seat and started walking.

He'd gone down on Aora's northern continent and all the civilian habitations were near the planet's equator, so he headed south. It was still early in the afternoon, so he kept going until nightfall.

Axichis, Imoliv, and Elian fighter craft kept bursting through the atmosphere, whizzing across the landscape, and exchanging fire before they blasted off into space.

LeMaine didn't see the Imoliv and the Elians fighting each other anymore, so at least something good came from this campaign.

They both fought the Axichis, but LeMaine didn't see either the Imoliv or the Elians making any headway against the invaders. Neither army could do anything without the frequencies.

What a waste of time and effort that turned out to be, but at least LeMaine tried. If his efforts brought the Imoliv and the Elians together, if LeMaine giving the Imoliv the frequencies ended generations of hostility and isolation—then it was worth it.

He turned the problem over in his mind, but he came up with no solutions. Polasek might be able to work out a new set of frequencies, but who knew if *they* would work? They might fail at the most catastrophic time just like this set did.

The Axichis bombarded Aora several times during the day, but the enemy didn't come near the forest. LeMaine climbed into the branches to watch their battles, but they always stayed out on the planes toward the south. They better not be targeting civilian centers.

He couldn't do a thing to stop them if they did. He just had to keep moving and try to find a way to rejoin the Military.

He walked for hours until it started to get dark. He looked around for a place to spend the night when he heard a loud rip followed by a yell and then a deep thump as something hit the ground.

More yells followed and LeMaine recognized that voice. He ran toward the sound and found Kellogg still strapped to his pilot's seat. He had fallen to within a few feet of the ground with his chute wrapped around him in knots.

"Easy, son!" LeMaine had to yell to make himself heard over Kellogg's roars of frustration and confusion. "Take it easy!"

LeMaine pulled out his knife and sliced through the chute to free Kellogg from the seat. Kellogg frowned up at him. "Captain?"

LeMaine grinned back. "What are the odds—you dropping right in front of my nose? Come on. Let's get you out of that harness. Are you injured?"

"No, I'm just...." Kellogg gave another gasp of annoyance, released the buckle on his harness, and wriggled out of the seat onto the ground.

He finally dragged himself to his feet and dusted himself off. "That was not the way to make an entrance."

LeMaine laughed and clapped him on the shoulder. "I thought I was the only one out here. I didn't see you on my remote."

"That's because I wasn't on it. I just landed."

LeMaine spun around. "You did?"

"We've been in battle against the Axichis all this time. You got shot down first, and when we came to try to lift you off, they attacked us and drove us off. That's why all this...."

He paused while another series of booms and explosions rocked the atmosphere. Kellogg and LeMaine listened until the sound faded beyond the horizon.

"The Military and the Imoliv have been trying to get down here to find you ever since you crashed," Kellogg finished. "The Axichis keep interfering. Don't ask me how they know you're so important, but they sure do seem to be making an almighty effort to stop us from recovering you."

"How's the battle going?" LeMaine asked.

Kellogg grimaced and turned away. "Let's get out of here. We can talk about that later."

LeMaine didn't bring up the subject again. The battle must be going pretty badly if Kellogg didn't even answer.

Kellogg pulled off his pack and made a quick check that his supplies were all intact. He carried the bare minimum of emergency supplies. Medical supplies and equipment made up the rest of his pack weight.

LeMaine cut the rest of the Kellogg's chute free, added the fabric to his own pack, coiled up the lines with his own, and put his pack back on just as Kellogg was zipping up his own pack.

Kellogg straightened up and looked around more critically. "Where are we going, Sir?"

"I was going south to see if I can find any civilian habitation, but it's getting dark, so I was actually thinking about bunking down somewhere."

Kellogg snorted. "All right. Where did you plan to do that? This is a damn sight better than Kathopra, isn't it?"

"You got that right, but we still have to worry about the elements. I don't like lighting a fire with the Axichis still buzzing around. These chutes are silk. We can use them as blankets. Let's find a good spot, build a shelter, and bed down until daylight."

Chapter 2

LeMaine and Kellogg hiked another quarter of a mile before LeMaine spotted a fallen tree on a downward slope. He and Kellogg worked together to stuff the hollow underneath with leaves and grass.

Then they both wrapped themselves in their torn chutes, crawled inside, and stretched out side by side.

"It looks like you're stuck with me for tonight, Sergeant," LeMaine remarked.

Kellogg grinned at him. "You won't hear me complaining about the company."

"Aw, go on," LeMaine teased. "I'm sure you can think of plenty of girls back home you'd rather spend the night with alone in the wilderness."

Kellogg burst out laughing. "I wouldn't want to spend the night with them *here*. This is definitely not my idea of an ideal first date. Sorry, Sir. You're out of luck."

Now it was LeMaine's turn to laugh. He could think of a lot of people he'd like less to spend a night in the wilderness with than Mason Kellogg.

"I'm glad I found you," LeMaine went on. "It was getting mighty quiet without you Hellhounds making my ears bleed around the clock."

Kellogg chuckled to himself and worked himself deeper into his chute. "You love it. You know you do."

"I guess I do." LeMaine sighed. "I can't imagine doing anything else."

Kellogg glanced at him, and for some reason, that glance drew out longer and longer until it turned into a stare.

"What?" LeMaine asked. "Do I have dirt on my face or something?"

Kellogg laughed again and then got serious. "I was just thinking about that night we spent in the cave with those four Imoliv pilots."

"What about it? They were good guys. I guess I can't fault Lutov for hating us. He didn't know any better. He'd been taught to hate us all his life."

"That's what I'm saying. I can't think of anyone I've ever met or even anyone I've ever even heard of who would have done what you did. Not even Peterman wouldn't have done it."

"What are you talking about? What did I do that was so special?"

"You see?" Kellogg asked. "You don't even think you did anything special. You think what you did was just the normal thing to do. That's you. You always do it. You never think it's anything special."

"What?" LeMaine asked. "What did I do?"

"You saved those pilots' lives. You went out to them when they were stranded. You pulled them out of the line of fire and you took them back to the cave. You gave them shelter, even after Lutov insulted you to your face and called you filthy alien scum and told you not to touch him when you'd just saved his life."

LeMaine frowned. "Yeah, well....isn't that what anyone would do?"

"Not everyone."

"I bet you would have. I know Peterman would have. I bet any of the Hellhounds would have done it. You wouldn't have left those guys out there to freeze. No way. We don't do that. We just aren't made that way. That's what makes all of us special. I'm not the only one."

Kellogg paused for a second and then said, "None of us would have thought to withhold the frequencies from our own people and hand them instead to the Imoliv to make peace with them. Only you would think of that. You really don't belong in command of this squad. You should have been in some diplomatic post. You're too good for hanging out with a bunch of grunts like us."

LeMaine turned away, rolled onto his back, and stared at the shelter's ridgepole above his head. Kellogg was right. LeMaine didn't think giving the frequencies to the Imoliv was all that big a deal.

He'd like to think any of the Hellhounds would have done the same thing, but they didn't even suggest it. He was the one who thought of it. Not even Peterman thought of it.

LeMaine understood Kellogg's point. LeMaine didn't see it as special because it came naturally to him.

Kellogg squirmed deeper into his chute and sighed. He sounded like he was about to fall asleep.

LeMaine was tired. He wanted to sleep, too, but he couldn't let Kellogg's remarks go unanswered.

"I'll tell you one thing, though," he said. "Sehiri listened to me because I'm a grunt just like you. That's the only reason he trusted me. If I had been in some diplomatic post, he never would have listened to a word I said and we would all still be locked up on his ship right now."

"That only goes to show that I'm right," Kellogg replied. "He trusted you because you're trustworthy. You think doing this stuff for people is normal. He must have seen that in you and that's why he trusted you. I can't say I blame him. Everyone trusts you. You're a rock."

LeMaine left it at that. He didn't know if he was a rock. He was just a man doing his job and trying to save Elia while he was at it. He wasn't doing too spectacular of a job of it while he was downed on this planet, was he?

Kellogg closed his eyes, and in a minute, both he and LeMaine fell asleep.

LeMaine's eyes snapped wide open when he heard someone calling, "Captain! Captain LeMaine! Captain LeMaine!"

His head shot up. Someone outside was calling for him.

Kellogg jolted wide awake at the same moment and stared all around him with wide eyes. Then they both started scrambling to get out of their chutes.

LeMaine crawled outside to find Lutov standing outside the shelter. He held the same Imoliv rifle that Sehiri's security guards had used.

Lutov kept the weapon jammed into his shoulder the whole time, but he pointed it at the ground. He didn't threaten LeMaine or Kellogg.

"Oh, good! You're all right!" Lutov took a few steps forward and waved LeMaine away. You two have to come with me. We're lifting you off."

"Who's we?" Kellogg asked.

"Me, Galo, Tavon, and Sindra. Sehiri sent us down here to find you. He organized a flank of fighter craft to engage the Axichis so we could get down onto the ground. It took us all night just to land. We don't know how long the fighters can hold out before the Axichis break through and fire on....."

A fat laser crashed through the canopy, pulverized the forest floor less than fifteen feet from Lutov, and the blast knocked all three men off their feet.

LeMaine hit the dirt and pried his head up to see Axichis fighter craft engaged in an intense firefight against twenty Imoliv fighters.

The battle wheeled over the part of the forest where Kellogg and LeMaine had spent the night.

Lutov rocketed to his feet, lunged for LeMaine, grabbed him, and yanked him forward. "Come on! We gotta go now!"

Kellogg and LeMaine scrambled to retrieve their packs and then dashed after Lutov. He plunged into the woods running like hell, but he never took his weapon off his shoulder.

He wheeled it overhead and in all directions on the run and searched the skies for anyone who might threaten the three men.

Axichis fighters shrieked overhead and Imoliv craft pounded them with phase cannons, but the shots just deflected off. Dozens of shots hit the forest and split off heavy boughs that crashed all around the fleeing party.

LeMaine dodged a thick branch and barely tackled Kellogg out of the way of half a tree trunk collapsing twenty feet ahead. A laser severed the tree and the whole crown creaked off before it plummeted to the forest floor.

More lasers punched through the canopy striking the ground on all sides, but the three men never stopped running. Only their speed saved their lives.

They burst through the edge of the forest where Lutov waited for LeMaine and Kellogg to catch up, but continuous bombardments kept striking through the forest. Fighter craft from both sides battled back and forth overhead.

LeMaine approached Lutov from behind. LeMaine had been about to ask Lutov where the Imoliv's squad's craft was, but LeMaine could see for himself once he got clear of the trees.

A smallish Imoliv vessel somewhat bigger than a fighter sat on the downward slope beyond where the forest ended. Fighter craft from all three armies zoomed over the distant planes and hammered each other with gunfire.

Plenty of stray hits struck the ground across the open ground. Sinda, Tavon, and Galo marked the intervals between the three men and their only way off this planet. LeMaine and his men would have to run straight into that fire to get on board the vessel.

The three pilots stood armed and ready to defend the retreat, but that left all the ground to cover between here and the ship. LeMaine didn't want to think about the pounding the ship would take once it launched.

"Any ideas on how we do this, son?" LeMaine asked.

Lutov squinted across the planes and shrugged. "We run for it."

LeMaine nodded, and at that moment, Axichis lasers over the forest detonated one of the Imoliv fighters. It exploded right on top of the three men and the burning wreckage hurtled through the canopy toward where the three men stood.

"Go!" LeMaine bellowed and pushed Lutov into the open.

The three men burst out from under the trees. Now nothing protected them from the bombardment, but at least they didn't have to worry about falling trees anymore. That was the only thing they didn't have to worry about.

LeMaine kept a firm grip on Kellogg so they stayed together, but Kellogg didn't have any trouble keeping up. Explosions kept going off all around LeMaine. He didn't dare to look up to see what was happening in the air.

A blast pounded the terrain on Kellogg's left and he staggered into LeMaine. "Are you all right?!" LeMaine hollered.

"Keep going!!" Kellogg yelled back.

The three men drew level with Galo. He trained his rifle to the skies—as if he could do anything against the Axichis with that. He wheeled as they passed him, joined the fugitive, and they all took off running for the next pilot, Tavon.

The ship got bigger and bigger as the squad approached, but the bombardment drew nearer to the ship at the same time. Escape hovered just beyond LeMaine's grasp, but he dreaded some stray cannonshot hitting the ship. That would be disastrous.

The squad drew level with Sindra. He herded everyone toward the ship and behind it to board through the rear hatch. Sindra raced to the cockpit and Galo shut the hatch to close everyone inside.

He waved to two rows of seats on either side. "Buckle up, Captain! We have some serious flying to do!"

"Get up here now!" Sindra bellowed from the cockpit. He barely got the words out when a brutal smash struck the ship.

Galo staggered forward, vanished into the cockpit, and didn't come back. Lutov and Tavon strapped in with LeMaine and Kellogg. LeMaine didn't like riding as a passenger while someone else fought his battles for him, but he had to leave this one to the two pilots.

He tucked his chin into his chest, braced himself for one hell of a bumpy ride, and it didn't disappoint him. He heard Sindra and Galo yelling at each other as the ship launched.

More hammer blows rocked the ship from side to side. The ship barely made it twenty feet off the ground before another punishing strike smacked the ship down hard.

It didn't crash to the ground, though, and the next minute, the engines shrieked to their highest pitch. Blue sky streaked past the cockpit window, stayed blue for a split second, and then turned black as the ship blasted into space.

That didn't help anybody, though, as the vessel flew straight into the air battle between the Axichis invaders, the Imoliv defense force, and the Elian Military all going at it tooth and nail.

The ship vibrated with cannon fire and Sindra definitely could have given Buca a run for the Intergalactic Lunatic Pilot Awards.

Sindra dodged Axichis fighters taking hellish fire on the ship's hull. Galo's body kept wheeling and pivoting in and out of view through the cockpit opening as he swung his cannons in all directions to return fire.

Another bone-crushing laser strike slapped the ship's tail downward. The nose flipped up and then another vicious assault slapped the ship from the side. It hit the cockpit and sent the ship tumbling off course.

Sindra fought the helm to correct and then glanced toward Galo's cannon station. "Someone get up here! Galo's hit! We need someone on the cannons now!"

Kellogg sprang out of his seat in a heartbeat, lunged into the cockpit, and started working overtime to unhook Galo from his harness. Kellogg hauled him into the back just as LeMaine got there to help lay Galo's unconscious body on the floor.

"Go!" Kellogg yelled to LeMaine. "Get up front! I'll deal with him!"

LeMaine's instincts reacted to that order and he sprang for the cockpit, dropped into Galo's seat, and grabbed the cannon controls.

Sindra gave him one glance. "Do you know how to work that thing?"

A shivering boom made the ship tremble as an Imoliv destroyer exploded not far away. The shockwave hit the Sindra's vessel. "I'll figure it out!" LeMaine yelled back and concentrated hard on figuring it out real quick.

This vessel's weapons system had the same layout as the fighters LeMaine had flown. More Axichis fighters came within range, so he swung his cannon that way and peppered them with phase shots.

"Where are we going?!" he yelled over his shoulder to Sindra.

"I was just about to ask you the same thing! Where should we take you?"

"Who sent you to find me?"

"Sehiri ordered us to retrieve you. We deployed from that ship that just blew up, so we can't go back there."

LeMaine grimaced over his shoulder. "Not helpful."

"We should take you to an Elian center. It will be closer." Sindra scanned the area of space around them. "You know this system better than I do. Where should we go?"

LeMaine stopped shooting long enough to survey the battlefield. I didn't give him a hopeful feeling at all.

Ten ragged-ass Elian bombers remained to defend the system from certain doom. The rest of the Elian fleet had scattered throughout the system fighting side by side with what remained of the Imoliv defense force.

"Was that battlecraft Sehiri's ship?" LeMaine asked.

"No, he's still in command of the defensive line."

Sindra indicated a group of Imoliv destroyers bunched up near Ar'el. They hadn't made much progress to get inside Elia since the failed surprise attack, but maybe Sehiri didn't want to make any progress.

His objective had always been to defend Imoliv's border with Elia. He probably wanted to stay near the border in case the Axichis made a play to invade Imoliv, too. LeMaine couldn't fault him for that.

LeMaine pointed to the gathered destroyers. "Let's go there."

"Are you sure you want to take the chance of going back into Imoliv custody?" Sindra asked.

LeMaine made another face over his shoulder. "I think we're way past that now, don't you?"

"I could take you to any Elian outpost and then I could go back to Sehiri."

"I don't know of any Elian outpost where I could rejoin the Military. Most of the Elian centers are still under bombardment. Just take me back to Sehiri and we'll figure it out from there."

Chapter 3

Sindra's vessel drifted into the hold of Sehiri's destroyer, but this hold wasn't an empty, cavernous prison like the one where Sehiri held the Elian personnel as his prisoners.

Mechanics, technicians, and pilots swarmed over fighter craft of different sizes. None of the Imoliv looked sideways at LeMaine and Kellogg when they disembarked with the four Imoliv pilots.

"Follow me, Captain," Sindra told LeMaine. "You, too, Kellogg. I'll take you to see Sehiri."

"Are you sure that's wise?" Kellogg asked.

Sindra shrugged. "He'll have to be informed either way that you're here. He'll be the one to decide what to do with you."

Kellogg snorted. "I can't wait."

"Don't worry. He won't harm or mistreat you. He thinks very highly of you, Captain."

"He does?"

"Of course," Sindra replied. "He wouldn't have given the Elians the time of day if not for you."

"Why does he think I'm so special?" LeMaine asked.

"He trusts you, which is more than he can say for most of his own generals and attaches."

LeMaine halted in his tracks as the puzzle pieces clicked together. "So he's more than just the commander of the border defense. I knew it."

"He's one of five top admirals who run the Imoliv Defense Force. He *is* the commander of the border defense. It's one of the most important posts in our military."

LeMaine took that in while he followed Sindra out of the hold. They took the destroyer's many corridors back to the bridge.

"How do you know Sehiri trusts me?" LeMaine asked Sindra on their way there.

"He told me."

"When did he tell you that?"

"In our quarters that first night after you and the Hellhounds brought me back from the Kathopra." Sindra glanced at LeMaine and his eyes glowed with a strange light. "He's my father."

LeMaine actually forgot to keep walking. He froze with those words ringing in his ears and then corrected himself a second later to catch up with Sindra.

Sehiri didn't look old enough to be anyone's father. Sehiri must be extremely dedicated to the cause of protecting his people if he sent his own son to fight in this war.

Why should that surprise LeMaine so much? Plenty of Elian fathers and sons followed in each other's footsteps to join the Military. Commander Russel Lodge's father had been a colonel before him and Jimmy Hurst had three brothers in the service.

The news about Sindra and Sehiri jolted LeMaine, though. He'd always thought of Sehiri as some kind of snow king—cold, distant, unfeeling, and aloof from all the fighting.

LeMaine imagined Sehiri standing in his ice tower watching all the insects scurrying around fighting the war for him. Sehiri couldn't possibly think that if one of the insects was his own son.

Sehiri obviously didn't give his son any special treatment or consideration. Sehiri didn't hesitate to send Sindra into danger. Sindra could handle danger just fine, but still.

LeMaine would have given anything to be a fly on the wall in their quarters when Sindra told his father about everything that happened on Kathopra and afterward.

Did that conversation have anything to do with Sehiri deciding to trust LeMaine—because LeMaine saved his son's life?

LeMaine doubted it somehow. LeMaine was starting to get a clearer picture of who Sehiri was behind the glacial exterior.

He'd been telling the truth when he said he had a strong ability to sense people's personalities. He could detect when someone was being sincere and when they had an agenda to pursue.

Some forgotten instinct told LeMaine that Sindra must be right. Sehiri wouldn't have looked sideways at LeMaine if Sehiri hadn't already gotten the sense that he could trust LeMaine.

Sehiri had already told LeMaine that long before LeMaine and Sindra ever set foot on Kathopra. Saving Sindra's life might have meant something, but not enough to overcome

Sehiri's gut feeling that LeMaine was his man—the man he needed to turn this campaign the way Sehiri wanted to turn it.

Sindra led the rest of the squad onto the bridge where they found Sehiri in conversation with a bunch of other Imoliv officers. His sharp eyes darted from one pilot to the next and then they snapped first to LeMaine and then to Kellogg.

"We brought Captain LeMaine back as you ordered, Sir," Sindra began. "This is Sergeant Mason Kellogg. He's the medic that saved my life—and Lutov's life."

Sehiri sauntered over to them. He examined LeMaine with that nonchalant intensity Sehiri used when he inspected one of his insignificant insect minions.

"I told you to deliver him to the Elian Military—not to bring him here," Sehiri countered

"I asked him to bring me here," LeMaine interjected. "The battle is still going on—as you can see. Most of the Elian centers are still under bombardment. An Imoliv vessel approaching an Elian bomber might have been seen as a threat. I thought this would be the best way....since you're still here inside our system. It isn't like I'm your prisoner anymore, is it?"

Sehiri jolted ever so slightly when LeMaine answered on Sindra's behalf. Then Sehiri relaxed. "I see. Well, since you're here, Captain, perhaps you'd be interested in liaising for me again. I wish to contact your Command. It would be much more convenient if I had an Elian do it for me. You could assure them that I'm not holding you as a prisoner and perhaps you could communicate Imoliv's intentions in this matter."

"I'd love to. What exactly are your intentions?"

"Just what we discussed before. You can tell them that we organized this surprise attack to transmit the frequencies to them under the most favorable possible conditions—not to infiltrate our fleet into your system. You can assure them that we have no intention of conquering Elia—only to defeat the Axichis before they breach our border next."

LeMaine nodded. "I can do that....but there's a high chance Colonel Nicholson and Commander Lodge have already communicated that to Elian Military Command."

"I prefer not to take any chances. My first attempt at communicating with your Command would be much less likely to end in another catastrophe if you liaise for me and...." Sehiri waved his hand at nothing. "Let's put it politely and say that you would speak for me. You would be my mouthpiece. Your Command would be able to hear those words much better coming from you.....the same way Nicholson and Lodge heard my plan better from you."

"I understand," LeMaine replied. "And yes, I agree to liaise for you."

"Excellent. In the meantime, I have some logistical matters to attend to. Sindra will show you and Sergeant Kellogg to quarters where you can stay. I'm sure you'll find them comfortable—much more comfortable than your last accommodation."

"Thank you," LeMaine replied. "Not to put too fine a point on it, I would appreciate it if you housed us together. I don't mean to imply anything, but if you're concerned about us being comfortable, I would appreciate it if you didn't separate us."

"As you wish, Captain." Sehiri waved to Sindra to dismiss everyone. Sindra stepped forward, but at that moment, an alarm went off somewhere on the bridge.

One of the bridge staff called out, "Elian Command is contacting us, Sir. They're requesting parlay."

"Parlay for what?" Sehiri asked. "We aren't at war against them."

"They don't know that," LeMaine chimed in. "Accept their request and I'll talk to them now."

Sehiri scanned LeMaine up and down. "You aren't exactly presentable."

"They've seen worse. Trust me. Just accept their request. They'll feel a lot less threatened if they see me with you."

Sehiri nodded and signaled his crewman to accept the request. The schematic of the Elian system displayed on the big bridge screen disappeared and Colonel Nicholson's face took its place.

He opened his mouth to say something and faltered ever so slightly when he saw LeMaine and Kellogg standing on the Imoliv bridge with Sehiri.

Then, just as quickly, Colonel Nicholson's eyebrows came together in a black scowl. "I sure as hell hope you aren't holding Captain LeMaine hostage. We would consider that an act of blatant aggression against Elia."

"I'm not being held as hostage or prisoner or anything like that, Colonel," LeMaine replied. "These men retrieved me from Aora and I asked them to bring me here. They wanted to deliver me and Kellogg somewhere inside Elia, but the Military was still tied up with the Axichis. I didn't think it was safe either for us or the pilots that rescued us."

"The Imoliv better not be holding you against your will," Colonel Nicholson snarled. "We've all seen enough of that for the rest of eternity."

"The Imoliv wish to communicate to you and the rest of Command that they have no hostile intentions toward Elia at all," LeMaine began.

"No hostile intentions!" Colonel Nicholson blurted out. "Is that what you call firing on our craft, invading our territory, and attacking us in the middle of a war against another species?! The Imoliv have devastated our fleet and left us crippled against the Axichis......and you call that no hostile intentions?! Don't even get me started on them capturing the *Excursion* and the *Lucidity*. If those incidents don't signal hostile intentions, I don't know what does."

"The first shots fired between Elia and Imoliv were accidental," LeMaine went on. "It was purely accidental that the *Excursion* and the *Lucidity* crossed the border. The Imoliv are concerned about the Axichis breaching their border and we were the first to do it. Then it was also accidental that Imoliv fighter craft got blown back over our border and fired upon by the Elian fleet. All the hostilities between our peoples have been the result of misunderstanding and miscommunication. You know this as well as I do, Colonel. You also know that the Imoliv's intentions were friendly when they helped us launch this surprise attack. It isn't their fault the frequencies didn't work."

Colonel Nicholson only frowned more deeply. "What do you want from us? What do *they* want from us?"

LeMaine glanced at Sehiri. They hadn't gotten that far in their conversation. "Well, Sir, I'd say they want to do whatever it takes to stop the Axichis from reaching Imoliv territory. The Axichis have already crossed over and attacked the Imoliv system. The Imoliv are inside Elian space right now to push the Axichis back into their own system. The Imoliv need us just as much as we need them. Neither of us can defeat the Axichis alone, so we have to work together. We all have to put aside our resentments and figure this thing out. We started well by launching the surprise attack. Maybe....." LeMaine thought fast. "Maybe we could work out a different set of frequencies—ones that actually work."

Colonel Nicholson shook his head. "We already have the entire Elian Science Corps working on it, but no one can come up with anything. Not even Lieutenant Polasek can figure out why the last set didn't work."

LeMaine startled. "Polasek! He's there? Is he all right? Are the rest of the Hellhounds there, too?"

Colonel Nicholson made a face. "They're here and they won't leave me alone. They've been nagging me day and night to get you back. You know what they're like where you're concerned, Owen—you and Kellogg both. I knew they were dedicated to you, but I had no idea they were so fond of Kellogg. A few of them have even broken into my office to threaten me with dire consequences if I didn't get on the horn and find out what the Imoliv were doing to you two."

LeMaine experienced such an overflow of affection and gratitude toward the Hell-hounds that he couldn't speak for a minute. He knew they were dedicated to him. He should have known they would have been on the warpath about getting him back.

He glanced over at Kellogg and read the same thing in Kellogg's eyes. Of course the Hellhounds adored Kellogg. They just showed it by giving him non-stop shit around the clock. That was their way of adoring him. They would never want to do without him.

"Anyway, I'll have to take this up with Command," Colonel Nicholson went on. "We'll need to discuss a way forward with the Imoliv. None of us wants to trust them...." He glanced toward Sehiri. "I don't mind telling you this, Owen, but you know how it is. These people did attack us and leave us weakened. I don't know if Command can come back from that to see their way to working with the Imoliv."

"I understand, Sir. No one in Elia knows this, but the Imoliv have quite a deep-seated prejudice against Elia, too. That's why they've never allowed diplomatic relations. The Imoliv are willing to put aside their old resentments and prejudices to bring about the result we both want. It will take compromise on both sides, but isn't it worth it if we can defeat the Axichis and make sure they don't threaten either of our systems again?"

"I'll do my best, Owen." Colonel Nicholson shot Sehiri another look. It wasn't the nicest look, either. "Are you going to be okay over there? If you aren't, we'll come and get you. Don't you worry about that."

"You don't need to do that. I'm here of my own choosing and I'm fine. Don't risk any of the Military's resources on me. Save them for the real war. I've been telling the Imoliv all this time that Elia isn't their enemy. The Axichis are and the same goes for Elia. The Imoliv are not our enemies. We should be working together."

"I'll see what I can do, Owen. You and Kellogg take care of yourselves."

"Thank you, Sir. We will."

Chapter 4

The communications feed went dead and LeMaine lost sight of Colonel Nicholson. LeMaine turned away from the screen. He didn't realize until after the fact how hard it would be to see Colonel Nicholson without being able to go back to Elia himself.

LeMaine really wanted to see the Hellhounds again. He wanted to assure them that he was all right, but more than that, he wanted to assure himself that they were all right.

Colonel Nicholson's words left LeMaine in no doubt that they were just fine. They must be if they were threatening the Command staff over LeMaine's safety.

Life wasn't the same without them, though. He wanted to go home. He'd worked himself into another pickle and now he had to stay here.

He turned to Kellogg. Kellogg remained standing in the same place staring at the blank screen. The bridge staff had returned the display to a chart of the Elian system. The image only made the distance seem that much more agonizing. Kellogg and LeMaine were a long way from home.

LeMaine bumped Kellogg's arm to get his attention. "Come on, son. Let's get out of here."

Kellogg blinked and turned away, but he was still a million miles out in space—over there in Elia where he belonged. Neither he nor LeMaine would ever feel comfortable until they made it home, no matter what accommodation the Imoliv gave them.

LeMaine and Kellogg followed Sindra off the bridge and back down many winding corridors. LeMaine didn't keep track of where he was or where he was going. It didn't matter.

Nothing would matter until he and Kellogg rejoined the Hellhounds. The squad wouldn't even be the Hellhounds without the two of them.

Sindra escorted them into a very nice cabin that had been set up like a small apartment. It had three bedrooms, a food dispenser on the wall, and everything else the two men might need.

"Do you need anything else?" Sindra asked.

LeMaine faced him and only noticed then that Galo, Tavon, and even Lutov had all come with them. The other three pilots stood out in the corridor looking into the apartment as though it wouldn't be good enough for LeMaine and Kellogg.

"We're fine, son," LeMaine replied. "Thank you for speaking up for us on the bridge."

"Of course. I've been telling Sehiri about you from the beginning." Sindra pointed to a panel near the food dispenser. "This is the communications system. When you activate it, a mechanized voice will ask you who you wish to speak to. It will put you through to me anywhere I am on the ship. Don't hesitate to let me know if I can do anything for you."

"Thank you," LeMaine glanced at the other three. "All of you. Thank you for coming to get us. We're very grateful."

"It was our pleasure, Captain," Sindra replied and he and the other pilots left—all except Lutov.

He stood out in the hall. He'd acted civil or at least professional toward LeMaine ever since the four pilots showed up on Aora this morning.

Now Lutov scowled at LeMaine with plenty of the old hostility from the cave on Kathopra. The sight of Lutov's expression made LeMaine stiffen. "What can I do for you, son?"

Lutov didn't respond for a second and then he squared his shoulders. "I'd like a word, Captain—with both of you."

"Do you want to come inside or do you want to stand out in the hall and shout your word across the threshold?" LeMaine asked. He didn't try to make his tone nice and welcoming. He had no desire to make it easy on this kid. Lutov better not be about to spout a bunch of insults again.

Lutov waited another minute while he made up his mind and then stepped across the threshold. The door hissed shut automatically behind him.

Lutov halted there. He didn't relax his shoulders. He pulled himself up even straighter to confront LeMaine. Kellogg was already sitting down on a bench seat across the room.

"Well?" LeMaine asked. "What's on your mind?"

"I...." Lutov began. "I....regret....what I said.....in the cave. I'd like to apologize. I *do* apologize....."

"Did Sindra or Sehiri send you here to apologize?" Kellogg asked from his place. "You don't have to do that. We understand you were only saying what you'd been taught about Elians."

"That's no excuse. Galo and Sindra didn't." Lutov lowered his eyes. "I apologize. I regret it deeply...especially after what you did for me.....both of you.....and then.....when you brought the frequencies to Sehiri......" He choked on the words. "I don't know what to say. I've always been taught to hate aliens—that they can't be trusted and that they mean us no good. I never considered." He waved his hand at nothing. "But Galo and Sindra obviously did. I should have realized. I should have known better.....and now I can't take back what I said."

"You just did, son." LeMaine squeezed the young pilot's shoulder. "Consider your apology accepted."

"I should have told you on the planet just now," Lutov blurted out. "I should have apologized to you in the cave. I should have apologized to your whole team. That would have been the right thing to do."

"I'll tell them," LeMaine replied. "I'm sure they'll understand. The Hellhounds are good that way, especially when they find out that you were the one who came to get us from Aora."

Lutov didn't answer. He compressed his lips and then seemed to come to another decision. He strode out of the room and the door shut behind him.

"Wow," Kellogg breathed as soon as he left. "I never thought I'd live to see the day."

"It would appear the Imoliv aren't as stuck in their backward ways as we thought." LeMaine crossed the room, sat down next to Kellogg, and surveyed the apartment. "This isn't half bad. I could get used to this."

"Don't," Kellogg told him. "We'll be going home soon."

"What makes you say that?"

"Command will be too eager to join forces with the Imoliv. They'll make a truce and fight together."

"How can you be so sure?" LeMaine asked. "Command might decide to tell the Imoliv to shove it."

"They won't do that. You saw the state of the fleet when we were on our way over here. The Elian Military can't fight the Axichis anymore—not with firepower. Command won't have any choice but to accept help from anywhere they can get it. The Imoliv are the only people offering that help. It's a no-brainer."

LeMaine laughed and clapped Kellogg on the shoulder. "You're the one who should have been in the diplomatic corps, son. You could give old Peterman a run for his money if you keep thinking like that."

Kellogg blushed and they both reclined back on the couch. LeMaine couldn't see anything outside this apartment, but the state of battle kept repeating in his mind.

Kellogg was right. Elia was on the ropes. Elia was worse than on the ropes. It was on the canvas and down for the count. The fleet couldn't hold it together much longer. The Imoliv were Elia's only hope now.

Chapter 5

LeMaine and Kellogg stood on the bridge of a much smaller Imoliv spacecraft. It was much bigger than the one Sindra and his men used to get LeMaine off of Aora, but much smaller than Sehiri's destroyer.

Sindra, Tavon, Sehiri, and all of Sehiri's entourage clustered around LeMaine and Kellogg as the ship drifted down to dock at Elian Command.

The building had been partially destroyed by Axichis bombardment. This was the first time LeMaine had returned to Elia since he and the Hellhounds first deployed to Ziea to find Lulara. The squad had been fighting nonstop ever since.

LeMaine barely recognized his home planet. All the stately buildings, hangars, and control towers that made Elia so inviting and civilized—they were all gone.

The only spacecraft parked outside the main Command compound had been so wrecked in the war that they would probably never fly again. Anything space-worthy enough to leave orbit was already out there fighting the Axichis.

LeMaine gulped as the Imoliv vessel touched down and he saw the rest of Maenides, the Elian capital city. It used to sparkle like the jewel of the cosmos. The Military Command compound, its acres of polished spacecraft, the Academy of Sciences, the Elian Assembly Consortium Building—they all used to gleam in the sunshine.

Seeing that city when he returned from deployment had been one of the great joys of LeMaine's life. The city used to give him hope and inspiration. All those lofty institutions showed him what he was fighting for.

He fought to preserve this city and all the people who made it such a prosperous hub of life, diplomacy, government, and commerce. He gladly dedicated his life to making that city as safe as he could for them. It was his mission in life and a mission he was glad to fulfill.

Now the city lay in ruins. The Axichis must have targeted Maenides even more than the Command compound. The Elian fleet hadn't been able to stop the Axichis from devastating any of it.

The sight turned LeMaine's horror to rage. He wanted to kill the Axichis for this. How dare they target a civilian center? They didn't have to bomb innocent civilians when they could have just hit the Command compound instead.

He already knew the answer to that. The Elian Assembly Consortium Building was in Maenides. All of Elia's other political decision-making centers were there, too. The Axichis destroyed the city to conquer Elia.

None of this made any sense. The Axichis already had a free trade agreement with Elia. Why throw that away? What did the Axichis hope to gain by completely obliterating Elian society?

That didn't matter. Only defeating the Axichis mattered, and for that, Elia needed the Imoliv.

A chill went through the Imoliv party when Sehiri and his entourage saw the city lying flattened to rubble before their eyes.

If the Axichis succeeded, they would do the same thing to Imoliv next. Elia was Imoliv's only hope now, too. Neither system had a choice about joining forces. Kellogg was dead right about that.

The vessel's rear hatch hissed open, folded down to the ground, Sehiri led the Imoliv party outside, and everyone turned toward the Command compound.

Colonel Nicholson, Commander Lodge, and all the other members of the Command staff came out to greet the Imoliv envoys.

LeMaine and Kellogg stayed in place on the Imoliv side. This would be the first time since the *Lucidity's* capture that Sehiri and Colonel Nicholson had exchanged words without LeMaine liaising between them.

The two parties halted facing each other down and Colonel Nicholson nodded stiffly to Sehiri. "Thank you for coming."

"Thank *you* for coming," Sehiri returned, but he kept his tone even. He didn't use the dismissive drawl he'd used on board his destroyer. "It's in our mutual best interest to put our differences aside and face this threat together."

Colonel Nicholson nodded again. "Yes, I think we can all agree on that. Come inside. We have a lot to discuss."

Sehiri bowed his head very slightly and shut his eyes. "Thank you."

Colonel Nicholson's gaze shot to LeMaine. "You and Kellogg are dismissed, Owen."

"But...." LeMaine glanced at Sehiri. "Don't you want me to come with you?"

"That won't be necessary. We all appreciate your assistance in this matter. The rest of the negotiations will be between the Imoliv and Command. You and Kellogg get over to the enlisted mess. There are some people there who want to see you....and after that, you can both consider yourselves off duty until further notice."

LeMaine straightened up and saluted. "Yes, Sir."

Colonel Nicholson saluted him back and then, amazingly, the rest of the Command staff saluted LeMaine, too.

They snapped their arms down and then did exactly the same thing to salute Kellogg.

Everyone turned away at the same moment. Colonel Nicholson rotated over to walk at Sehiri's side. Both parties headed off for the Command compound together as though they really might be friends.

That left LeMaine and Kellogg with no option but to leave in the opposite direction. LeMaine kept glancing over his shoulder until the Command staff and the Imoliv delegation vanished inside the building.

Kellogg cut in on LeMaine's thoughts. "They should have let you go with them."

"I'm not worried about that. I'm just damn curious to hear what they're going to say to each other." Kellogg laughed and LeMaine couldn't help but grin. "I suppose I should feel lucky that I'm *not* getting involved with all that. No one will be able to hold me responsible if it all goes wrong later."

"It sure looks like they're holding you responsible for it all going right. The whole Command staff saluted you. I've never seen that before. I've never even heard of it."

"They saluted you, too." LeMaine hooked his arm around Kellogg's neck and gave him a rough noogie on the head. "If this works, it will be all thanks to you."

"Cut it out!" Kellogg fought his way out of LeMaine's grip, but they both laughed the rest of the way to the enlisted mess. It sure felt good to be off duty for a change.

They walked in and LeMaine spotted the Hellhounds seated at a table across the main room. They all sat with their heads together like they were planning another assault on Colonel Nicholson's office. Even Polasek was with them.

They all shot off their benches when they saw LeMaine and Kellogg. The Hellhounds surrounded the two men all talking, laughing, and shouting.

They jostled and hugged LeMaine and rumpled Kellogg's hair. Everyone wanted to know everything about LeMaine's crash on Aora and the events after that.

LeMaine sat down at the table with them. "What's the word around here?" he asked. "I hear you kids have been giving Colonel Nicholson a hard time."

"He's been giving *us* a hard time," Heckler growled. "He wouldn't tell us shit."

"That's because he didn't know shit," Kellogg replied.

"He never does and he still doesn't," Lemon fired back. "He's got nothing but shit between his ears."

"Take it easy on the man," LeMaine interjected. "He's doing the best he can under nightmarish circumstances. Anyway, I'm back now."

"Please tell me you brought that asshole Sehiri's head back on a spike," Nunn chimed in.

"Nope," LeMaine replied. "He's over at the Command compound now, hobnobbing with the senior staff. They're all the best of friends now."

"Why do you want his head on a spike anyway?" Kellogg asked. "He's the one who made this alliance happen."

"Some alliance," Lemon fired back. "Those damn frequencies didn't even work. How do we know he didn't sabotage them to screw with us?"

"Because Imoliv stands to lose as much as Elia does if the Axichis win," Peterman pointed out. "Besides, Sehiri is the one who loaded the frequencies onto the *Excursion,* the *Lucidity,* and all those Elian attack cruisers. Imoliv craft wound up in just as much danger as we did when the frequencies failed. He wouldn't have endangered his own people."

"He might be some kind of psychopath who doesn't care who he hurts," Monk suggested. "Maybe he wanted to get Elia that badly that he'd risk his own people into the bargain."

"If he's the one who loaded them onto Elian craft, then he could have sabotaged us then," Lemon added. "He led us into a trap."

"His own son was flying one of those fighters," LeMaine interjected. "Sehiri wouldn't let Sindra go into battle without working frequencies if he had them."

A gasp went through the squad. "Sindra is Sehiri's son?" Nunn murmured.

"Yeah, and those four guys from the cave have been working their tails off behind the scenes to make the Imoliv our allies. There are a lot of good people among the Imoliv."

No one answered for a second until Polasek chimed in. "There was something wrong with those frequencies. I'm certain of it now."

"How can you be sure there was anything wrong with them?" Peterman asked. "Maybe the Axichis found a way to block them even before we deployed them. That makes more sense to me."

"I don't know what's wrong with them," Polasek replied, "but I'm damn well gonna figure it out. There has to be a way to defeat these assholes."

"If anyone can figure it out, you can," O'Hara told him. "You've been locked in the communications center since we got here." He turned to LeMaine. "You really need to tell this boy to take some time off. He's been burning the candle at both ends."

"Is that true, Lieutenant?" LeMaine asked.

"Can you blame me?" Polasek countered. "Shooting at the Axichis does nothing. We need to come up with a different way to neutralize them. That's the only way we're going to get rid of them. Not even the Imoliv can help us beat the Axichis in battle. We have to use our brains."

"That's right, genius," Nunn added. "Throw your big brain at them. That will send them running for their burrows faster than anything."

Laughter broke out and LeMaine let it wash over him like the sweetest music as the Hellhounds fired jokes and rude remarks back and forth.

They gave Kellogg a much rougher time than they usually did, but he only beamed at them and gave back as good as he got. They were all enjoying themselves too much to care about anything else.

Chapter 6

LeMaine and Peterman stepped into Colonel Nicholson's office. LeMaine stiffened when he found Sehiri there along with Commander Lodge.

LeMaine pulled up in front of Colonel Nicholson's desk and LeMaine and Peterman both saluted. "You asked to see me, Sir?" LeMaine asked.

"Yes, I did. At ease, Owen. You, too Peterman. I hope you don't mind Sehiri joining u s."

LeMaine and Sehiri exchanged glances, but LeMaine didn't say anything. That was just Colonel Nicholson being polite. Sehiri wouldn't leave if LeMaine did have any objection to Sehiri joining them.

"Here's the situation, Owen," Colonel Nicholson began. "The Axichis have pretty much secured most of the system, so we need to launch another counteroffensive against them."

"How do you plan to do that without the frequencies, Sir?" Peterman asked.

"That's the sticky part. The Imoliv have been studying the Axichis' technology. The Imoliv technicians think they can modify their phase cannons to produce the same effect as the first batch of frequencies."

"Polasek says he and the other Elian techs still haven't been able to do anything about the frequencies," LeMaine remarked. "That will leave what's left of the Elian fleet with no weapons to speak off—none that are effective, at least. We might as well let the Imoliv go after the Axichis alone—assuming an adjustment to the phase cannons actually works."

"Anyway, none of this bears on the Hellhounds," Peterman added. "You wouldn't call us in here if you only meant to deploy us with the rest of the counteroffensive."

"Right, Lieutenant. I have a different mission for your squad. We have intelligence from the outer planets that the Axichis have set up a command center on an Elian planet. They're coordinating their invasion from there, which means they'll be using this command center as a launching point to invade Imoliv. We want the Hellhounds to go

in, take out the command center, and weaken as many attack craft and warships as you ca
n."

"Which planet are they on?" LeMaine asked.

"Ziea," Colonel Nicholson replied.

LeMaine froze and then spun around to stare at Peterman. Peterman gaped back at
LeMaine with huge eyes. Ziea. The Axichis were on Ziea.

That name brought up so many memories—good ones and bad ones. The Hellhounds
came closer to losing some of their best members on Ziea. The Hellhounds got Buca on
Ziea and they also got Lulara there before the Hellhounds lost her on Iumia.

"I see you understand the importance of this mission, but you don't understand just
how important it is." Colonel pulled up a chart of Ziea on his desk. "The Axichis have
set up their command center here, at the Nulia Compound where you first met Lulara. It
appears from our reconnaissance flights that the Axichis are holding the resident Cezians
as captives. Heaven only knows how the Axichis are treating them."

LeMaine swallowed hard, but he didn't trust himself to answer. This was bad.

Colonel Nicholson pointed to another part of the same area of the planet. "This is
their airfield. They keep all their fighter craft and warships here when they aren't in battle
against us. You need to get down on the planet, free the Cezians, and weaken the Axichis
as much as you can. If we aren't actually in battle against them at the time, you might be
able to take out a sizeable portion of their fleet."

LeMaine cleared his throat with difficulty. "Yes, Sir. I understand."

"If this mission is a little too close to home for your Maczhi Hellhound, tell him he's
free to stay behind and fight with the regular Military. I know how he feels about his home
planet. He doesn't have to go back if he doesn't want to."

LeMaine only nodded. He had no clue how Buca would react to the news that the
squad was going back to Ziea. Would Buca decide to sit the mission out? LeMaine
couldn't imagine Buca sitting out any mission, even if it meant going back to Ziea.

Colonel Nicholson scrolled to a different part of the charts. "The only problem with
this plan is dropping you Hellhounds onto Ziea in the first place. We'll launch our counteroffensive and you can use the battle as cover to break through to the outer planets."

"The outer rim will be crawling with Axichis," Peterman pointed out. "We'd be fighting our way alone through their entire invasion force."

"I realize that, Lieutenant," Colonel Nicholson replied. "That's why I'm bringing in
you badasses. If you can't do it, it can't be done."

LeMaine passed his hand across his mouth and immediately put it down. He didn't mean to let any of these men see him this disturbed by the news.

Elia needed the Hellhounds back on Ziea, so that's what he would do. God only knew how he would do it, but he would just have to find a way. There was no other option.

All the details of this job raced through his mind trying to fit into some sensible order, but it didn't work out too well.

Like most missions, he would just have to throw himself and his squad out there into the shit storm and see what happened. It wasn't much of a plan, but what else could he do? He'd be launching into another unwinnable battle.

In fact, it was no plan at all. Landing on Ziea to weaken the Axichis and free the Cezians was no plan at all, either, kind of like landing on Ziea to find an unknown diplomat no one had ever heard of or had ever even seen. The planet was turning into LeMaine's worst nightmare.

He somehow managed to stand at attention while Colonel Nicholson went over the battle plan for the counteroffensive. LeMaine did his best to pretend to pay attention, but whatever battle plan Command came up with wouldn't mean anything to the Hellhounds, either.

It would all go down the gurgler the instant the Hellhounds got into the air. Peterman was right. Even after the Hellhounds got through the battle, they would have to run a deadly gauntlet of Axichis ships just to get near Ziea. It was a disaster in the making.

LeMaine somehow got out of Colonel Nicholson's office without making a fool of himself or passing out on the floor. That would have been unthinkable.

He stopped in the hall outside to catch his breath and try to reorient himself to reality. "This is not good," Peterman breathed.

"Jesus Christ!" LeMaine whispered. "Please Sweet Jesus tell me I dreamed all that and I'm gonna wake up in a few minutes. Please tell me I ate something wrong at the mess and this is all a terrible hallucination or something."

Peterman laughed nervously. "Are you gonna give Buca the option to sit this one out?"

"Hell no!" LeMaine countered. "I wouldn't insult him like that."

Peterman nodded. "I thought not."

"Do you honestly think he would have joined in the first place if he planned to sit out every time he didn't like the mission? He'll deal with it the same way the rest of us will." LeMaine pointed at Peterman. "What about you? Would you sit out just because of what happened to you there?"

"No, of course not," Peterman replied. "Never. I'm sure the others won't, either."

"Of course they won't." LeMaine turned away. "Come on. Let's get this over with."

They returned to the enlisted quarters where they found the Hellhounds goofing around in the dorm. They were the only ones in there, thank God. LeMaine wouldn't want to discuss this mission in front of anyone else. Telling the Hellhounds to go anywhere else would only tip them off that the shit was about to go down big time.

Monk and Nunn sat on one cot while Kellogg and Heckler sat on the cot right next door to them. Each of the four of them had hold of one of O'Hara's wrists or ankles and they held him suspended off the floor with his limbs spread out in a four-pointed star.

"Higher!" Nunn ordered. "Lift him higher!"

"All right! All right!" O'Hara shrieked. "I'll tell you where the buried treasure is! I'll tell you who's working for Prince Torquemada! I'll tell you anything you want to know! Just let me go! PLEASE!!!"

Lemon stood across the room with her shoulder propped against the wall and her arms crossed over her chest while she laughed at the other Hellhounds' antics.

Buca sat alone on a different cot some distance away. He smiled at them, but he obviously didn't get the joke well enough to laugh.

Polasek sat in the corner with a pair of headphones over his ears and a tablet computer propped on his knees. He worked over it, totally oblivious to everything going on around him.

"Drop him," LeMaine told the four on the cots.

"NO!!" O'Hara shrieked as the others let him drop right onto the floor. He gave another blood-curdling scream that made everyone laugh.

"Thanks a lot, Captain," O'Hara complained. "You've killed the prisoner."

"Good. He was never gonna give up the intel anyway. Sit up, Sergeant. We got work to d o."

O'Hara cocked his head. "Does it involve shooting people?"

"Yes, it does. The rest of you Hellhounds gather around. We have a new mission."

LeMaine went over to Polasek, tapped him on the shoulder, and waved him over to join the others. Polasek put his headphones away, but he sure looked disappointed about it.

Buca stayed on the same cot. He could hear everything perfectly well from there and LeMaine didn't insist on him moving.

"What's the mission, Sir?" Nunn asked.

"I'm glad you asked. As you all know, the Axichis have the run of the whole system now. Neither the Military nor the Imoliv have the firepower to stop them, not even if we join forces. Command is planning a new counteroffensive and the Imoliv think they can modify their phase cannons to produce an effect similar to the frequencies."

"Will that work?" Polasek scratched his head. "I never thought of that."

"No one knows if it will work. That's the problem. It's a total crap shoot that could wind up backfiring on us—again."

"So what's our mission? Sing and dance in front of the Axichis until they get so sick of us that they run home crying to their mamas?" O'Hara asked.

"Only you could pull off a stunt like that, you dope," Lemon muttered.

"We aren't part of the counteroffensive," LeMaine replied. "Not that way, at least. We're going to launch into the middle of the battle and use the confusion to punch through to the outer planets. The Axichis have a new center of operations out there that Command wants us to hit."

"If we punch through to the outer planets," Monk interjected, "that will put us right in the sights of all their ships that are using this center of operations."

"You got that right, champ," Peterman chimed in. "Exactly."

Monk rubbed his chin. "What's the point of going out there, then?"

"Command wants us to weaken their center of operations—hit as many of their ships as we can while they're on the ground and not defending themselves. Also, the Axichis have set up their center in a civilian installation. They're holding the residents hostage, so we have to free them."

"Which installation is it?" Kellogg frowned. "I can't think of any civilian installations out there except for.....?"

He trailed off and his jaw dropped as he realized what LeMaine was suggesting.

"We're going back to Ziea," LeMaine announced. "The Axichis have taken over the Nulia Compound. They're holding the Cezian residents as prisoners, so we gotta free them into the bargain."

No one said anything for a minute and then everyone glanced over at Buca. He listened to LeMaine's speech in silence and didn't react to the news. Buca didn't even react when everyone turned around to stare at him.

"Anyway," LeMaine finished. "That's the mission. Any questions?"

Some of the crew frowned. Others raised their eyebrows and puffed out their cheeks taking it all in.

"So...." LeMaine went on. "I'm just waiting to hear from Command when we deploy. I'm sure they'll give us another ship and we'll be on our way."

He nodded at nothing and walked out of the room. The squad would discuss the so-called mission behind his back, but he already knew none of them would talk to Buca about it. None of them would ask him how he felt about returning to his home planet after leaving it so decisively.

Buca never talked about that. The whole squad respected his privacy, but LeMaine couldn't help but burn with curiosity.

Buca would handle this mission. He would handle it the same way he handled everything else. He never acted in any way other than with the utmost professionalism. He was by far the most professional Hellhound ever to join the squad.

That made him so different from all the other wise-asses under LeMaine's command, but it also made Buca one of them. They all respected him implicitly because he always handled himself.

He handled everything no matter what it was. He would handle this, too. LeMaine would be very surprised if Buca showed even the slightest hint of emotion on Ziea. He never did and he wouldn't then, either. He would just execute.

LeMaine and Peterman went back to the officer's mess and talked about the mission, but there wasn't much to talk about. "I guess we just go and deal with it," Peterman finished.

"Yep. That's about the size of it."

"At least we don't have to stick around and watch the Elian Military get its living ass kicked again during the counteroffensive."

LeMaine made a face. "You said it, not me."

"You don't really believe that shit about adjusting the phase cannons to make them behave like the frequencies, do you? It's a propaganda stunt if I've ever heard one. I don't see Sehiri being foolhardy enough to float a dopey idea like that. He's too practical. It had to come from Command. They don't want to spook the troops by saying outright that this is a suicide mission. It's a Hail Mary because we got exactly nothin' left in the tank."

LeMaine winced. He didn't like to think those things, much less say them out loud.

"Anyway, it's like you said," LeMaine countered. "We won't be around to find out if it works or not. We'll be lightyears away."

"Getting *our* asses kicked by the Axichis," Peterman finished. "I can't wait."

"The good news is that, once we get down on Ziea, we can go underground and sneak up on them by stealth. We won't be under bombardment the whole time."

"That's what you're hoping happens. If the Axichis see us coming in, they'll know exactly where we are. They'll know an Elian team is trying to infiltrate their operations center. The Axichis will send ground troops to scour the countryside until they find us. We won't get anywhere near the Nulia Compound."

"What's gotten into you?" LeMaine countered. "Why are you spouting all this doomsday prophesy? It isn't like you at all."

Peterman looked away. "I'm just telling it like it is."

LeMaine studied him for a while. After a few minutes of looking at the wall, Peterman glanced over and noticed LeMaine watching him. "What?" Peterman asked. "What's wrong?"

LeMaine shrugged. Now he was the one who looked away. "Nothing."

Peterman jumped. His eyes popped and he pointed at LeMaine. "You have a plan, don't you?! You have a way for us to get down on the planet without the Axichis coming after us. Tell me what it is."

"I don't have a plan," LeMaine replied.

"Liar! Spill it! I'm not leaving you alone until you tell me."

LeMaine stood up and crossed the mess to the refrigerator. "I don't know what you're talking about. I don't have a plan. I just agreed with you that we just have to go and see what happens."

"I don't believe you," Peterman countered. "I've served under you for years. I know every facial expression of yours and that one....." He pointed in LeMaine's face. "That's your I-have-a-plan face."

LeMaine laughed, but he couldn't stop his cheeks from flushing.

Peterman dogged him over to the fridge and stood way too close while LeMaine pretended to look for something to eat. "So? What is it?"

"I told you I don't have a plan."

"Aw, come on, man!" Peterman exclaimed. "Don't leave a brother hanging. You know I won't tell anyone."

"You won't tell anyone because there is no plan."

"Will you stop it? How the hell do you expect me to sleep between now and then if I have to wonder the whole time?"

LeMaine groaned, and since he couldn't shake Peterman off, LeMaine went back to the couch and sprawled on it. "You won't be able to sleep if I *do* tell you."

"HA!!" Peterman pounced on that and pointed at LeMaine again. "I knew it!! Tell me. Tell me now."

LeMaine hesitated. "You won't like it."

"I'll like it a hell of a lot better than not knowing."

"That's what you think. Be careful what you wish for."

Peterman sat down on the next couch over, leaned forward, propped his elbows on his knees, and his eyes flashed with excitement. "So.....what is it?"

"Well," LeMaine began. "The only way to get through the Axichis force and land on the planet is to make them think we aren't there—or to make them forget about us. For that, we would have to completely disappear off the map."

Peterman frowned trying to understand. "I don't get it."

"Forget it." LeMaine stood up. "You don't want to know. Trust me."

"I do!" Peterman sprang to his feet, too. "You aren't walking out on me like this!"

LeMaine turned around slowly. "Stuart....drop it."

Peterman's face fell. "Do I have to?"

"You're asking too much." Peterman's expression crumpled so badly that LeMaine caved. "Fine. I'll tell you, but you have to promise not to say a word to any of the rest of the squad."

Peterman perked up right away. "I promise!"

"I mean not even by your facial expressions. You can't get all despondent and mopey about it. You have to continue to act like you don't know. Understand?"

Peterman frowned. "Is it that bad?"

"You're the one who wanted to know. I said you wouldn't like it."

Peterman thought about it and then squared his shoulders. "All right. I do want to know. I'm ready."

"Well, for the Axichis to give up looking for us, they would have to think we were dead. They would have to shoot down the ship and see it crash and burn in flames on the planet. We wouldn't be able to drop from the atmosphere or they would know there was a team on the surface. They would have to see the ship crash with no survivors escaping."

Peterman's countenance drained of all color and a look of true horror glazed his eyes. "You.....your plan....is to crash the ship.....with no survivors?"

"There have to be survivors or we wouldn't accomplish our mission, but crash the ship—yes. That's my plan. Now do you think you can keep your promise and not let on by word or deed that you know all that?"

Peterman gulped and then pulled himself together. "Yes, Sir. Thank you for telling me."

LeMaine clapped him on the shoulder. "Now if you can help me figure out how to do that without getting us all killed, I'll be in your debt for life."

Peterman tried to laugh it off, but it came out more as a grimace of pain. Should LeMaine have told him the plan? Should LeMaine tell the rest of the Hellhounds?

He discarded that notion right away. They would be agitated enough over this mission without him making it worse.

Chapter 7

The Hellhounds milled around their new ship and examined it from all sides. It was another heavily armed Hunter-class attack frigate like the *Renown*.

"*Mirage,*" Monk growled. "I don't like the name."

"I think it's a perfect name," LeMaine countered. "It's all about deception and subterfuge. That's exactly what we need on this mission."

"She looks alright," O'Hara remarked. "She'll do."

"Well, you aren't the one that has to fly her, are you?" Monk countered. "She isn't the *Renown.*"

"Nothing is the *Renown*, son." LeMaine clapped Monk on the shoulder. "I can get Buca to fly us in if you want me to."

"No!!" Monk roared. "I'm flying and that's final."

"All right," LeMaine replied. "Why don't you go on board and get familiar with her? She might grow on you."

Monk humphed under his breath. He'd been flying the *Renown* for so long. He didn't let anyone see his private pain after the ship got destroyed on Iumia, but LeMaine knew it was there. That pain was bound to come to the surface the minute the squad got a new ship.

Fortunately, Monk wouldn't get too much of a chance to bond with the *Mirage*. He would fly her once and that was it.

The others studied the ship from all sides. Buca did the same. "What do you think?" Nunn asked him.

He shrugged. "She looks very good."

"Did you want to go see the cockpit, too?"

"Why would I do that? She'll fly the same as the *Renown*. I don't have to familiarize myself with the controls."

"I was just wondering....in case....." She trailed off and then left to go talk to her other squad mates.

LeMaine didn't see the other Hellhounds talking to Buca as much since the word came down that they were going back to Ziea.

He showed no sign that the mission meant a single thing to him. His utter lack of emotional reaction, good or bad, unsettled the rest of the crew even more than if he'd been downright hysterical about it.

The others went inside and came out. There wasn't a lot to see that they hadn't already seen a million times before on the *Renown*.

"So when do we deploy, Sir?" Kellogg asked. "When does this big glorious counteroffensive get underway?"

"I should find out later today." LeMaine broke off when a young female lieutenant approached him from the Command compound.

She crossed the landing zone and handed LeMaine a folded piece of paper. "This is for you, Sir. It's from Colonel Nicholson."

"Thank you," he replied and they both saluted.

She hurried away and he unfolded the note. "Why is Colonel Nicholson sending you hand-written notes?" Polasek asked. "He could have just told you in person."

"Haven't you heard?" O'Hara called out. "It's my pleasure to announce that Captain Owen LeMaine and Colonel Elias Nicholson have announced their engagement to be married on the fifteenth of....." He trailed off when he saw LeMaine staring at the paper.

"What is it?" Peterman murmured.

"It's tonight. We're launching tonight—2300 hours."

"That's....like....the middle of the night," Lemon countered. "Why so late?"

"There is no middle of the night in space," Kellogg pointed out. "The middle of the night on Elia could be the middle of the afternoon on Ziea."

"It will be just before noon on Ziea," Buca interjected.

Everyone froze and stared at him. They were the first words he'd spoken about the mission apart from his comments about the *Mirage*. LeMaine had started to wonder if Buca even realized the gravity of the mission yet.

He must have been thinking about it the entire time. How could he not be?

His words cast a chill over the rest of the squad—all except for Monk who was in the cockpit and didn't hear.

The others turned away from the *Mirage* grimacing in disgust. "I'm going back to the mess," Heckler growled. "Who's coming with me?"

"Me," Lemon replied and the others all followed Heckler away.

Monk came out a few minutes later looking much more chipper. "She'll do just fine, Sir. She's a mighty fine ship."

"I'm glad you think so because we're leaving tonight at 2300," LeMaine informed him.

Monk stopped dead in his tracks and his eyes bugged out of their sockets, but a second later, he shrugged it off. "Oh, well. No time like the present, right?"

"Right, Corporal."

Monk left for the mess, too. LeMaine went back to the officer's quarters where he stretched out on his bunk and went over his whole plan.

Getting the Axichis to shoot down the *Mirage* would be the easy part. Getting the ship down on the planet without any of the squad losing lives and convincing the Axichis that the squad was all dead—that was completely different kettle of fish.

He didn't sleep at all. He stayed awake staring at the ceiling until 2230. Then he got up, put on his fatigues, checked his backpack, and went down to the hangar where the squad had left the *Mirage*.

The whole squad was already there in full drop gear and they were all armed to the teeth. He recognized instantly that none of them had gotten any sleep, either.

Now wasn't the time to worry about whether they'd be too fatigued to handle the mission. They would all be way too keyed up for anything as mundane as lost sleep to break their focus. They would be pumping with adrenaline for however long this mission lasted.

He sliced his forefinger at them. "Load up, Hellhounds."

They filed into the back of the ship and ducked into their cannon placements—all except Monk, who went to the cockpit and fired up the engines.

LeMaine went forward, strapped in next to Monk, and ran through his checks on the ship's systems. The Hellhounds sat in their usual places the same way they did on the *Renown,* but none of them laughed or joked around.

They exchanged information and encouragement, but they sounded way too subdued and Buca didn't talk at all.

The launch signal came down from Command and Monk lifted off. The *Mirage's* floodlights illuminated the Command compound for a second. The Hellhounds were the only people moving around on the whole landing zone.

Then the ship rocketed into the atmosphere. There were no other ships around. LeMaine found out why when the *Mirage* climbed to high orbit. Every other Elian vessel was already up there. They formed ranks in a dense cloud all facing the outer planets.

An even bigger force of Imoliv destroyers stood off to one side. A swarm of fighter craft hovered around the destroyers waiting for the word to attack.

The Axichis had obviously noticed the counteroffensive forming. They launched dozens of warships from the outer planets, but the Axichis force didn't look nearly as intimidating as LeMaine expected.

Maybe the Axichis didn't think much from these attackers....and they would be right. LeMaine didn't hold out any more hope than Peterman did that the Imoliv's adjustments would make a lick of difference.

"Join the Elian ranks, Monk," LeMaine ordered. "You can choose where."

"Yes, Sir," Monk replied and steered the *Mirage* into line with expert ease. He must have bonded with the ship and now they were best friends—for as long as the *Mirage* lasted.

"Here's what I don't understand," O'Hara began in his old chipper tone.

"You don't understand how your mother and your father could stand to be in the same room with you long enough for you to be conceived—not to mention to raise you to adulthood?" Lemon interrupted and everyone laughed, but not as loudly as they used to.

O'Hara ignored the crack. "If the Imoliv did adjust their phase cannons to work against the Axichis, why not share that technology with the Military? Why keep it to themselves and leave us defenseless?"

"Because we don't use phase cannons, you muppet," Kellogg pointed out. "We couldn't exactly retrofit the whole fleet in such a short time frame."

"But why not share it?" O'Hara asked. "Why are they holding out on us?"

"Don't think so hard," Nunn told him. "Then you wouldn't smoke the ship out with all that burning rubber and stripped gears."

More laughter answered her until Lemon spoke up. "Here's what *I* don't understand. Why would the Axichis take over the Nulia Compound? The Cezians are one of the toughest species around. If the Axichis wanted to take Elian captives, they should have gone for the Maczhi....right?"

A moment of tense silence echoed through the *Mirage* and then the conversation broke out at last. The squad had been sitting on this long enough. It was bound to come to the surface eventually.

"The Axichis must have wanted the compound," Kellogg pointed out. "They're keeping all the Cezians locked up inside the building. That explains why. They would need a strong place to keep the Cezians incarcerated."

"They don't need the Nulia Compound," Peterman pointed out. "Look at the base they built on Toreon. They built that in the middle of nowhere in record time. They could have done the same thing on Ziea. They didn't take the Nulia Compound to house the Cezians and I don't believe they went after the Cezians in particular. They'd have to be truly stupid to do that and the Axichis aren't stupid."

"They wouldn't need any strong place to keep the Maczhi incarcerated," Buca cut in. "The Maczhi are weak and submissive. They would give up without a fight. The Maczhi would walk into any holding pen the Axichis pointed them toward. The Axichis wouldn't even need to aim a weapon at the Maczhi to get them to bow to whatever the Axichis wanted them to do."

"But didn't the Maczhi become weak and submissive when the colonists stole their food and medical supplies?" Nunn asked. "They couldn't do anything to stop it."

"They became weak and submissive long before that," Buca replied. "They used to be powerful. They could have stopped the colonists from taking their supplies if the Maczhi had only fought back. That's what the Cezians did. The Maczhi just gave up. They abandoned their warrior ways to become animals for another species to kick around. If the Axichis rounded them up and locked them in a prison, they would deserve nothing less. The Cezians are strong. They fight for what's theirs. The Maczhi will never be like that again. They'll fade away....and they deserve to. I went into the mountains to follow the warrior's path the way our ancestors intended. That's why I'm here while they're there starving and whimpering in fear every time a ship lands on the planet."

He said it with such bitter resentment and disgust that no one answered. So this was what had been going through his mind all this time. No wonder he kept it to himself.

No one made a joke out of this, and a second later, the launch signal raced down the Elian line. "We're away!" Monk hollered and punched the throttle just as the whole Elian fleet erupted out of position.

Chapter 8

"Arm your cannons, Hellhounds!" LeMaine ordered. "Stand by to spit some lead."

"Standing by!" Heckler replied.

"Come to papa!" O'Hara gloated. "It's about time we racked up some points."

"I say we team up against Buca," Nunn suggested.

"He can beat all of us put together with one hand tied behind his back," Peterman called back.

"Don't tempt me," Buca replied and the whole squad howled in delight.

"He made a joke!" Kellogg yelled. "Did you hear that, Sir? Buca made a joke."

"We'll loosen that boy up come Hell or high water," Heckler added. "Who's on Team Beat-Buca?"

The others all yelled in agreement.

"Pay attention back there!" LeMaine ordered. "Prepare to engage! The Imoliv are making their move!"

The Imoliv destroyers veered out of line and advanced on the Axichis from the port flank. The Axichis seemed to realize that their enemies weren't screwing around for once. Maybe they thought the Elian-Imoliv alliance wouldn't send out such an impressive fleet if they didn't have some trick up their sleeve.

The Axichis shrank farther away toward the outer rim, tightened their formation, and bunched together watching all those ships close in.

"You better run, ya bitches!" O'Hara sneered.

"If this works, there might not be any Axichis on Ziea when we get there," Peterman pointed out.

LeMaine turned his scanners toward the planet. "They'll be there. They're holding back half their force."

"Maybe....." Nunn began, but at that moment, the Imoliv line unleashed a brutal wave of phase cannon fire. Dozens of destroyers fired in unison.

Their shots crackled through space and smashed the Axichis line apart.

"Holy guacamole, Batman!" Kellogg hollered. "It's working! The phase adjustment is working!"

"Gun it, Monk!" LeMaine ordered. "Pinpoint that spot and get us through!"

Monk clenched his jaws, clamped his meaty fingers on the throttle, and hit it hard. The *Mirage* rocketed away and burst through the Elian front line.

"Fire at will!" LeMaine ordered and all the cannon positions exploded. They couldn't do any damage against the Axichis, but that didn't matter. The Hellhounds weren't here to fight the Axichis. The squad just had to make it look like they wanted to fight while the Imoliv did the real damage.

All those assembled Imoliv fighters streaked in at a wicked pace, overtook the *Mirage,* and the Imoliv force attacked in fury.

The phase cannons worked better than anyone dared to hope. LeMaine didn't think anyone on the Elian side hoped they would work at all, but man! They sure sent the Axichis packing!

The destroyers' first strike blasted four warships. They detonated right on top of each other and the combined fireball flared outward to consume the warships on either flank.

Monk smashed himself back in his seat and locked his arms training the helm on that spot alone. The Imoliv fighters whirled around the *Mirage* bombarding every Axichis vessel in sight.

The *Mirage's* cannons scattered shots in all directions and then Monk plunged nose first into the inferno. Fire enveloped the cockpit and then the *Mirage* burst through into empty space behind the Axichis line.

The Elian Military and the Imoliv fleet showed up just in time to stop any Axichis from turning back to tail the *Mirage*.

"Hold your fire and get out of your cannon placements!" LeMaine ordered. "Suit up for drop!"

"Are we dropping, Sir?" Lemon asked. "Won't that tip off the Axichis that we're on the planet?"

"Do as you're told Corporal," LeMaine snapped. "Get us into orbit, Monk!"

Monk hauled the helm toward Ziea and LeMaine laid hold of the cockpit cannon controls. His would be the last active cannon. He had to make a good show to convince the Axichis that the *Mirage* was still returning fire.

Monk skirted the planet Zukion and Ziea came in sight at the solar system's very outermost edge. LeMaine didn't see anything at first and then a giant torrent of ships erupted off the planet.

"Shit!" Monk whispered.

"Get us into orbit, Monk!" LeMaine roared. "Don't think about anything else!"

LeMaine glanced into the back. The other Hellhounds stood around grasping their anchor lines for support against the ship's movements.

All the Hellhounds had pulled up the hoods of their drop suits to protect them from the fire when the ship went down in flames. LeMaine couldn't be as certain about anyone surviving the impact.

A smash of laser fire on the *Mirage's* hull brought LeMaine's attention back to the front as Axichis fighter craft surrounded the *Mirage* on all sides.

LeMaine slammed his cannon to starboard and unloaded on the fighters. They buzzed so closely to the *Mirage* that he didn't have to try too hard to hit them.

They didn't have to try too hard to hit the *Mirage*, either. The ship wobbled dangerously under continuous bombardment from all sides.

"Get in the back, Monk!" LeMaine ordered over the noise.

"But Sir....."

"Get in the back, Monk!" LeMaine bellowed. "I'll take it from here. Suit up and prepare to drop."

Monk gulped and struggled out of the cockpit. That left LeMaine alone to carry out his plan. He adjusted his grip on the cannon controls so he could keep shooting and steering the ship with his other hand.

He moved his hand to another button on the *Mirage's* dashboard. This was a really good ship. Too bad she wouldn't last.

He waited until the Axichis hammered the ship from port again and he pushed the button. The explosives he planted in Heckler's cannon placement exploded and the shock hurled the *Mirage* hard into the Axichis on the starboard side.

He pushed the button twice more and two more cannon placements erupted in massive explosions. Fire consumed the ship and the hull started to radiate heat through the wall by LeMaine's shoulder.

He fought the helm just enough to make sure the *Mirage* held her course. She would crash close enough to the Nulia Compound for the squad to make it there.

The Axichis backed off a little and then they all charged in at once. They fired again and again and LeMaine blew three more cannon placements. Deafening booms rocked the ship and then a brutal laser sheared off the cockpit window.

He ducked as broken glass sprayed in his face. He narrowly missed becoming the first casualty on this mission.

He hit the floor and scrambled into the back yanking his drop suit hood over his head. "Mask up!" he bellowed. "Curl up for protection from the fire!"

The Hellhounds obeyed instantly, dropped to the floor, pulled their masks over their faces, and curled into balls. Their drop suits protected them from the heat of entry into the atmosphere. The suits would protect the squad from this, but maybe not the crash itself.

The Axichis kept pounding the ship all over even as it plummeted in flames through the atmosphere. They batted it back and forth between them. They were just playing with it now.

LeMaine curled up between Nunn and Polasek, covered his face, and curled up as tightly as he could. The rush of flames licked through the walls just as he shut his eyes.

The suit deflected most of the heat, but he still felt waves of heat flashing all over him and then a sudden powerful whoosh of cool air swept all that heat away.

He opened his eyes, raised his head without meaning to, and saw that the Axichis had completely blasted off the *Mirage's* upper fuselage. He stared through the breach at blue sky above.

The flames didn't surround the ship anymore. They trailed out behind it. "Hold onto something!" he bellowed. "Brace for impact!"

The Hellhounds crawled to the walls. Kellogg, Heckler, and Buca managed to wriggle into their seats and slip into their harnesses. Peterman and Lemon just held onto the straps.

LeMaine caught a glimpse of mountain peaks whipping past the breach. "Curl up now! Cover up!"

The whole squad curled up as quickly as they could just as the ship careened through the last few inches of atmosphere and slammed into the ground. An almighty explosion consumed the cockpit and enveloped the rest of the ship.

Searing heat burned LeMaine through his suit as the fire enveloped the *Mirage*. That part of the plan worked. The ship crashed and burned on the planet's surface. Any Axichis watching from the atmosphere would think the crew had perished in the crash.

He stayed in that position for a long time. After waiting an eternity, he felt another gust of cool breeze and untucked his head.

He glanced around to find Polasek and Monk both looking at him. They were fine.

LeMaine uncurled and picked himself up. Most of the *Mirage's* hull had been reduced to cinders and twisted, blackened metal frames. The grass around the ship still burned, but the ship had burned herself out.

Peterman straightened up and looked around. "My God! It actually worked! Remind me never to doubt you again, Captain."

"Have you ever doubted me before?" LeMaine asked.

"Actually, no," Peterman replied and chuckled.

"I'll give you a pass this time, then."

They both stood up and looked around. "Welp!" Peterman exclaimed. "I guess that's the end of that ship."

The others uncoiled themselves and Kellogg, Buca, and Heckler got out of their harnesses. "Is anyone hurt?" Kellogg asked.

"I think I am," Polasek croaked.

He lay flat on his back near the rear hatch. He hadn't been curled up and he didn't move.

Kellogg went over to him, dropped on his knees, pulled open his pack, and started working on Polasek. LeMaine didn't go over there to find out what was wrong with him. Kellogg would take care of Polasek.

LeMaine checked his remote. The ship had crashed in the same mountains where the Hellhounds first dropped on their mission to find Lulara. He located the Nulia Compound.

"How far out is it?" Peterman asked.

"About five hours' walk. We better get rolling as soon as Polasek is okay." LeMaine made sure all the other Hellhounds were up and moving around. They took off their drop suits and checked their weapons.

"What's the situation, Sergeant?" LeMaine asked Kellogg.

"Just a few broken vertebrae. I'll have him on his feet in a few minutes."

LeMaine turned to Polasek. "You'll be all right, son."

"I tried to curl up in time...." Polasek struggled to control his lips.

"Don't worry about it, Lieutenant. You did real good. This is the best result I could have hoped for—just one Hellhound injured. You can put this on your tab."

Polasek started to laugh and grimaced in pain, but right at that moment, Kellogg fired the bone electrolyzer and knocked him out.

LeMaine went back to the other Hellhounds, pulled off his own drop suit, put it in his pack, and checked his carbine. He checked his remote several more times and frowned at the readings.

It showed him at least three hundred Cezians imprisoned in at Nulia along with about a hundred Axichis guarding the prisoners.

LeMaine didn't much care for those odds, and even as he watched, dozens of Axichis craft of all sizes returned to the planet from the battle. They landed on the flat ground Colonel Nicholson had pointed out to LeMaine on Elia.

All those pilots and crews unloaded and went into the compound. By the time they all returned to the facility, the Axichis outnumbered the Cezians by two to one. No wonder the Cezians hadn't tried to break out yet.

The Axichis would have disarmed the Cezians right off the bat. The Cezians would like nothing better than to help the Hellhounds finish off the Axichis. The question was how to release the Cezians, arm them, and communicate a plan to them without tipping off the Axichis in the process.

Polasek came over to LeMaine. He was fine now. "What's wrong?"

"Nothing," LeMaine replied. "Let's move out. We have a long way to walk."

The squad left the Mirage wreck smoldering on the planes. LeMaine scanned the skies, but he didn't see any other Axichis ships flying around. They were all back at the compound. They would all be there when the Hellhounds showed up.

Chapter 9

L eMaine crawled forward a few feet and stuck his eyes up over the hilltop. O'Hara peered through his scope, but the other Hellhounds could see the situation at the Nulia Compound with their naked eyes.

"Holy Mother of God!" Heckler breathed. "Look at them all! I've never seen so many Axichis in one place."

"You should have brought more explosives, Nunn," Kellogg added. "You would never be able to blow all those ships."

LeMaine barely glanced at the airfield beyond the compound. Whoever Colonel Nicholson had gotten his intelligence from had been dead right. The Axichis had set up a full base here.

They already controlled most of the Elian solar system. They could only be gathering this force to take on the Imoliv system next.

LeMaine concentrated on the compound and nudged O'Hara. "Do you see any Cezians?"

"Nope. Not a single one."

"They're all inside," Peterman replied. "Just check your remote. You can see them all in there."

"Remember what happened when we trusted our remotes the last time we were on this planet?" Lemon countered. "I don't believe anything until I see it with my own eyes."

"You're smart, Corporal," LeMaine replied. "I don't, either. Our remotes have been too unreliable lately."

"The Axichis have access to Elian technology," Polasek pointed out. "They might have found a way to interfere with the remotes' signal."

"How does that help us, Lieutenant?" O'Hara asked.

"Cut the lip," LeMaine ordered to no one in particular. "We're falling back."

"To where?" Nunn asked.

"To anywhere but here. We need to think about how we're going to do this. There are too many Axichis down there and too many ships. We need to change our strategy."

"What was our strategy to begin with?" Monk asked.

"Whatever it was, it's changed now. Fall back. We'll find a place to camp for the night and make another foray in the morning."

"How will it look different in the morning?" Buca asked.

He'd spoken so little since this mission started that every word out of his mouth rang with a kind of finality. His words dropped into a well of silence and meaning that LeMaine didn't like to think about.

He steered the Hellhounds away from the compound and they set off overland in the direction from which they'd come. The squad had spent half the day walking here and it was starting to get dark.

LeMaine moved forward to Buca's side. "Do you know anywhere near here where we can camp?"

"I might know a place."

"Good. Take us there."

Buca only nodded. He seemed to be a million miles away. His sharp eyes kept tracing the horizon for something that wasn't there.

LeMaine's remote showed him the local Maczhi camped far out in the mountains to the north. They hadn't moved since the Hellhounds came here last time.

The Maczhi packed together in camps and their life sign readings on LeMaine's remote seemed even weaker than they had been on the Hellhounds' last visit.

LeMaine tried to put that out of his mind, but Buca's behavior only brought it back. Buca didn't check his remote even once. He rarely did even on strange planets.

This wasn't a strange planet. It was his homeworld. He seemed to sense every detail of the landscape through his skin. LeMaine couldn't imagine everything Buca could pick up without even thinking about it.

He led the squad into a draw between two mountains. They hiked up it in the dark and then Buca ducked into a cave.

This one started as a crack between two cliffs, narrowed, and then widened out to form a large room. He squatted down, pulled over some dried sticks that he must have left here for the purpose, and lighted them with the striker from his pack.

Heckler dropped his pack and folded into a sitting position next to the flames. "Man! Could Command have dropped us into a bigger briar patch? I thought finding Lulara was gonna be tough—but this?"

The other Hellhounds gathered around and O'Hara took his ration bars out of his pack. "I don't care what mission Command sends us on as long as I have these. I can handle anything else."

"Don't eat them all now," Kellogg told him. "Then you'll have none for tomorrow."

"Do you have to rain on my parade by being so practical?" O'Hara fired back. "Just let me enjoy the illusion of abundance."

"So you can be an insufferable pig tomorrow while you bore us all with your fantasies about what you're going to eat when you get home?" Lemon asked.

O'Hara pointed at her. "Exactly. Bingo. I'm glad someone understands me. I might just have found my dream girl."

Lemon snorted. "You can dream about me kicking your ass, shithead."

LeMaine let himself drift over to the fire, but he didn't want to join their conversation. He had too much on his mind.

Peterman and Polasek kept throwing worried glances in LeMaine's direction. They kept waiting for him to come to some decision about how the Hellhounds could defeat such an impossibly large enemy force.

He sat down with the rest of the squad, but he didn't lean forward to make himself one of them. He rested his back against the rock. His silence infected the rest of the squad and they didn't talk as cheerfully as usual until Kellogg broke the ice.

"What's the grand plan this time, Sir?"

"Maybe you folks can help me out," LeMaine replied. "Who's got an idea for me? How about you, Heckler? Get the old grey matter pumping."

"Not me, Sir," Heckler growled. "That's why you get paid the big money."

The others laughed some. "Whatever we do," LeMaine went on, "we have to do it now and we have to do it here. We can't let this force go out against the Imoliv."

"Or the Elians," Nunn added.

"They just did," Peterman pointed out. "The Imoliv might have bloodied the Axichis' noses in that battle just now and we would never know."

"The Axichis wouldn't have all their ships lined up ready for another assault if the Imoliv bloodied their noses," Lemon pointed out. "Whatever the Imoliv did to them during that battle, it wasn't enough to stop the invasion."

"We could pull another trick like we did on Nainia," Polasek suggested. "We could sneak on board some Axichis warships, turn them on the fleet, and destroy all their ships so they can't launch."

"How would we free the Cezians?" Kellogg asked. "We couldn't exactly open fire on the compound."

Polasek frowned. "Oh. Right."

"How much explosives did you bring?" O'Hara asked Nunn.

"Nowhere near enough. I should have brought the whole Command warehouse for this job."

"That would definitely blow our cover," Heckler pointed out.

No one said anything for a minute and then Kellogg turned back to LeMaine. "It looks like this one is all on you, Sir. You're in charge."

"Thanks for reminding me, Sergeant."

"So what's the solution?" Monk asked. "Don't tell me you don't at least have an idea. You always have some idea on how to do the impossible."

"If it was impossible, he wouldn't be able to do it," Nunn countered. "That's what the word, 'impossible' means."

"Did you replace some of your explosives with a dictionary?" Monk returned. "Is that going to be your new job on this squad—telling us all what words mean?"

That shut her up. "We can't take the compound by ourselves," LeMaine mused. "We need more people."

"We don't have any more people," Kellogg pointed out. "We're alone on this planet. We're the only ones here."

"We aren't the only people here—not by a mile," LeMaine replied. "There are several thousand other people here. The Maczhi are camped right on the other side of those mountains."

Dead silence answered him. The fire crackled in the night and a few Hellhounds shifted nervously in their seats. Then Nunn glanced over at Buca.

"What do you say?" LeMaine asked him. "We could recruit the Maczhi to help us. They're Elian citizens and they have the numbers to take the compound."

"Are you making a joke out of me?" Buca snapped back with so much venom that LeMaine froze to his seat. "Is this your idea of a joke?"

"Of course not," LeMaine exclaimed. "I would never....."

"You don't know anything about the Maczhi," Buca spat with undisguised hatred and murderous fury. "Do you think you can drop out of the sky and change the Maczhi overnight? Do you have any clue how many years I spent trying to convince them to fight back? Do you have any clue what it cost me?"

"How could I know when you've never told me?" LeMaine replied, but he found himself cringing before Buca's fury.

Buca had always been so measured and reserved. LeMaine never dreamed Buca could be hiding this depth of rage and resentment.

"I lost my entire family trying to get them to follow the old ways," he snarled through gritted teeth. "I begged and pleaded and threatened them to make them fight back against the colonists. I told the Maczhi they were all dying of starvation and disease while the colonists stole the food and medicine my people needed. No one listened and they turned against ME!! They attacked ME and drove me out for trying to help them."

LeMaine trembled before this onslaught. He didn't dare to answer back. He had no idea that was what caused the rift between Buca and his family.

LeMaine kicked himself for not realizing this sooner. He could have asked. He could have questioned Buca more closely about why he was so enthusiastic about leaving Ziea to join the Hellhounds. LeMaine could have demanded that Buca explain why he refused to represent the Maczhi in negotiations between the Cezians and the Elian Command.

LeMaine gulped trying to decide what to say. He wanted to apologize for bringing it up, but he wasn't sorry. He should have found out long before now, but now he knew and he wasn't sorry about that.

No one made a sound for a long time. LeMaine didn't break the silence and neither did anyone else.

After a long, uncomfortable wait, Buca got up, left the cave, and came back with an armload of firewood. He dropped it on the floor by the fire, left again, and he didn't come back.

No one said a word after that. Hours passed—or it felt like it. Finally, Heckler sighed, stretched himself out on the ground, and curled up to go to sleep. The others stayed awake for a while, but one by one, they did the same thing.

Chapter 10

Peterman and Polasek stayed up talking much longer than the other Hellhounds, but both lieutenants eventually gave in and crashed, too.

LeMaine should have slept, but he couldn't stop his brain from churning. He ought to just drop the subject of recruiting the Maczhi to help with this mission, but he found it impossible to put the idea out of his mind.

They were right here. There had to be a way to turn their fighting spirit back on. It couldn't be completely dead. They were the only way to crack the Nulia Compound to save the Cezians. LeMaine couldn't think of any other solution.

He made it his job to keep the fire going to keep his squad warm. The cave blocked the light so no searching Axichis would find them.

He used up the last of the wood and got to his feet to go outside to get some more. He stepped out of the cave and froze again when he spotted Buca squatting on a rock next to the cave mouth.

LeMaine should have known Buca wouldn't leave the squad unguarded here. He wanted to be alone, so he chose that spot to keep watch over his squad mates.

LeMaine walked off into the darkness. The moon gave him enough light to see where he was going. He gathered another armload of wood, took it back to the cave, and put it down quietly on the floor.

He made sure the fire was burning well and then he went back outside. He had to make up with Buca before morning. LeMaine couldn't let this yawning chasm remain between him and one of his subordinates, especially not this one.

LeMaine sat down on the rock next to him. "I'm sorry that happened to you. You're right. I don't know anything about the Maczhi. Maybe you can tell me."

"They're pathetic worms," Buca snarled low. "They deserve to die."

"Don't say that. Something must have happened to rob them of their spirit."

"If it did, it happened before I was born. My parents' generation moved into the camp and gave up the old ways. My grandparents told me about the way it used to be. That's the only way I found out."

"How did you become a warrior with no one to teach you?" LeMaine asked.

"I taught myself. Once I realized what a disaster they were heading for, I went out into the mountains and I learned. I questioned my grandfather about certain things. The rest I learned by trying different things and failing miserably."

"It's too bad they didn't listen to you," LeMaine remarked. "Their lives could have been so different if they followed you and took you as their leader."

Buca snorted. "That will never happen."

LeMaine thought it over. Buca must be right. He must have tried so hard to convince them, but they'd already taken the life in the camps. They'd abandoned their warrior tradition to become weak, docile, and easily manipulated.

LeMaine would probably never find out what caused that change. If something didn't change them back, the Maczhi would likely die out just like Buca said. Then Buca would die and the Maczhi would go extinct.

No wonder Buca resented them so much. It must have been eating away at him every day. This disaster would swallow him along with them. All his efforts to change things would come to nothing.

"I don't blame you for leaving," LeMaine finally told him. "I'm glad the Hellhounds could give you a place, even if it's a poor substitute for the real thing."

"The Hellhounds are all I have left," Buca murmured and his voice cracked. "These people....and you.....you're the only true warriors I've ever known. You're the only people alive who understand me and who I understand. This squad is the only place I have ever belonged. I hate this planet!"

He spat the last words and cast a menacing glare at the hills around him. For the first time, LeMaine questioned if he should have left Buca behind on Elia, but he changed his mind immediately.

Buca wouldn't want to be anywhere but with the Hellhounds no matter where they went. He would even rather come back to Ziea if it meant being with them—being one of them.

LeMaine turned back to the problem of the compound. "How would you feel if I approached the Maczhi? Would that bother you?"

"It won't do any good," Buca muttered.

"You might be surprised. They might listen to me in ways they didn't listen to you."

Buca's head snapped up. "Why would they? I'm Maczhi. I'm one of them."

"That's exactly why they didn't listen to you. You're their kid brother and son. What would you know? They probably resented you for trying to buck the system when they wanted you to conform to what everyone else was doing."

Buca snorted again and turned away. "That's exactly what they wanted me to do."

"It would be different with me. I'm an authority figure. I'm an officer in the Elian Military. I could order them to take up arms against the Axichis. I could strongarm them by pointing out that they have an obligation as Elian citizens to defend the system from the enemies that threaten us all."

"That might work, but you would be foolish to take the Maczhi into battle against anyone, especially an enemy as powerful as the Axichis. You might be able to stick a carbine in every Maczhi hand—if you could find that many carbines. The moment the Maczhi came face to face with the Axichis, the Maczhi would crumble and fall to the Axichis. The Maczhi would never even raise their weapons. The Axichis would gun them down and probably kill the Cezians into the bargain just to punish us for trying."

LeMaine flinched. "You're right."

They sat in silence for a long time. Buca's point drove the last nail in LeMaine's coffin.

He might be able to recruit the Maczhi. In fact, he knew he could, but they wouldn't be able to help him complete this mission. They were so weak they would probably make matters worse.

"Thank you for telling me," he finally went on. "I'm sorry I didn't make more of an effort to find out the truth sooner. That was wrong of me. I should have found out what you needed."

"You are what I need. This whole squad is. I don't need anything else. I don't need you or anyone to know why."

"You might not have needed us to know why, but *we* needed to know why. We need to know you. We've left you alone all this time, but we can't anymore. Now we know and it will bring us closer. You'll see. Telling us will turn out to be a good thing."

"I'm glad I didn't say anything before," Buca murmured. "I couldn't."

"I understand. Maybe there's a way to recruit the Maczhi without turning them into cannon fodder. They have the numbers. Maybe they could get involved another way."

Buca remained silent.

LeMaine waited for him to say something else. "What do you say? Would you help me recruit them if we could do it in a way that didn't get them all killed?"

"Why do you ask me that *now*?" Buca's voice started to rise again. "You defended me against the Military when I said I wouldn't negotiate with the Maczhi. You said it was my choice."

"Things were different then. The whole system is in jeopardy now. You took a pledge to defend Elia against its enemies. Now you have a job to do. We need the Maczhi to take this compound and I need you to get them to do it. You could be saving all their lives by doing this. Wouldn't that be worth at least trying?"

Buca still didn't say anything. He stared off into the dark. LeMaine couldn't tell if Buca was simmering with resentment or just thinking.

"The Maczhi saving Cezian lives could be the turning point that brings the Maczhi and the Cezians together," LeMaine went on. "*You* could be that turning point. It isn't too late for you to turn your people around. Do it for Lulara."

The instant LeMaine said that name, Buca shot to his feet, stalked off alone into the darkness, and vanished.

LeMaine waited, but Buca didn't come back. What if he never came back? What if he disappeared into the mountains and never rejoined the Hellhounds because of this?

He wouldn't do that. He'd just told LeMaine that the Hellhounds were all he had. Buca said he hated Ziea. He wouldn't stay here.

LeMaine couldn't think of how to repair the breach between them and he couldn't repair it until Buca came back.

LeMaine sighed and went back into the cave. The others were all still asleep. He sat down in the same place and tended the fire. He didn't want to sleep now. So he considered the assault instead.

It sure did look hopeless without a much larger force to attack the compound and the airfield. The Maczhi were his only option.

Without Buca, LeMaine would have to approach the Maczhi himself. Buca's absence would make the job of convincing them a thousand times more difficult.

He checked his remote. There had to be at least ten thousand Maczhi living in the camps. At least some of them had to have some gumption left. They couldn't all be as pathetically submissive and cringing as Buca made them out to be.....could they?

Who would know better than he did just how far they had fallen? LeMaine had nothing to go on apart from Buca's word.

LeMaine didn't know anything about the Maczhi, but their vital signs didn't look good. The only other Maczhi he'd ever met besides Buca had been sickly and starving. They wouldn't have been good for much, especially not fighting.

He groaned and eventually shut his eyes. He had to come up with something, but the more he thought about it, the more nothing kept coming up. If he really couldn't use the Maczhi, then he had no choice but to assault the compound with just his squad.

That was bound to turn into another catastrophe and he didn't need that. He would rather not assault the compound at all, but he had no choice. He had to do it for Elia.

Chapter 11

LeMaine stood up, stretched his shoulders, and pulled a ration bar out of his pack. The other Hellhounds were already sitting up, drinking their water, scratching their heads, and readying their gear for the day.

"Where's Buca?" Nunn asked.

"He went for a walk last night," LeMaine replied. "It looks like he hasn't come back yet."

She blinked at him and then exchanged glances with her squad mates. "Does that mean....he isn't coming back?"

"I don't know where he is or what he's doing. I suppose he'll catch up with us eventually."

"What if he can't find us?" O'Hara asked.

"He'll find us," Heckler growled. "That dude could find a needle in a haystack. One thing I know about that guy—he always knows where *we* are. We might not know where he is, but he always knows where we are. You can bet on that."

"What are we doing about the compound?" Monk asked.

"Good question," LeMaine replied.

"So what's the answer?" Polasek asked.

"I'm still not sure. We need to figure out a way to locate some more resources—more people, more explosives—something to tip the balance in our favor. The compound is a suicide mission as it stands right now."

"What about the Nanov Outpost?" Kellogg asked. "The colonists might have some supplies we could use."

"That's too far away," Peterman replied. "It would take too long to get there and we might not find anything when we got there."

"Do you still plan to recruit the Maczhi?" Polasek asked. "What did Buca say about it?"

"He doesn't want to, obviously," LeMaine replied. "They're a big question mark anyway. Even if they were willing, they might be too unhealthy to participate. I'm not sure what to do about them. Let's pack up, go back to the compound, and scout the terrain. We can get a clearer picture of the situation. After that, if we still haven't come up with anything, we'll go see the Maczhi. They're our only other resource at this point."

The Hellhounds went back to what they were doing, put their packs on, and headed for the cave exit. LeMaine kicked the cold embers apart just to make sure the fire was all the way out. The squad might be coming back here tonight.

The squad didn't feel the same without Buca. How did such a quiet, reserved guy make himself such a fundamental part of this squad so quickly?

The rest of the squad seemed to feel the same way. They talked in low tones and didn't joke around. The gravity of the situation hung heavily over them all.

LeMaine left the cave and stood outside observing the grey dawn as the other Hellhounds stepped out behind him. They gathered around the entrance adjusting their packs and narrowing their eyes at the surroundings.

LeMaine waited for them all to assemble. He turned to head down the draw when he heard running footsteps somewhere in the trees. They came from on top of the high cliffs behind the cave and approached at high speed.

He grabbed his carbine, but before he could raise it, something burst through the undergrowth and Buca hurtled off the highest cliff.

He landed right in front of LeMaine, rushed up to him, grabbed LeMaine's sleeve, and tugged him forward breathing heavily. "You have to come with me now, Captain! Come on! It's critical! You have to come with me right now! I have to show you something!"

"What is it?" LeMaine asked. "Where have you been all night?"

"I can't explain right now!" Buca panted. "You'll understand everything when you see, but you have to come right now! Come on, Captain! Hurry! The whole assault depends on you coming with me right now!"

LeMaine resisted. He didn't want to go anywhere without some explanation, but the prospect of carrying out this mission the way it was didn't tempt him.

He glanced behind him at Polasek and Peterman. The whole squad watched and listened to see what would happen.

LeMaine softened and took a step forward. Buca didn't let go of LeMaine's sleeve. "We have to hurry! You Hellhounds stay here," Buca told them. "Don't go near the compound—not yet. I'll bring the captain back soon. Just stay here. Come on, Captain! We have to hurry."

He let go of LeMaine's arm, ran off down the draw, and paused thirty yards away to wait for LeMaine.

LeMaine hesitated a second longer and then went after him. LeMaine started off walking, but when Buca burst into another run, LeMaine had to run to keep up.

Buca shot away straight up the mountain. Running over this rough country meant nothing to him and he covered the ground easily. LeMaine was no slouch, but he couldn't keep up with Buca's speed.

Buca had to stop and wait for him, but Buca didn't seem to mind that. He just kept insisting that LeMaine hurry and that whatever Buca had to show LeMaine was important enough to put the whole mission on hold until LeMaine saw it.

They scaled the mountain to the very top. LeMaine stopped there, propped his hands on his knees to catch his breath, and wiped his sweaty face on his sleeve. "Whatever it is you want to show me better be something pretty good."

"It is," Buca replied. "You'll see."

"How much farther do we have to go?" LeMaine asked and tried not to make it sound too much like he was complaining.

"It isn't far and we can run on the level ridgetop now." Buca headed sideways following the mountaintop to the west.

LeMaine prepared himself for another torturous ordeal, but Buca stopped less than a quarter of a mile from the peak where they'd first paused.

He stepped out onto a rock outcropping and squatted down where he could peer into a steep canyon below him. Scraggly trees dotted the sandy bottom and a small stream flowed down the canyon to forests leading to the planes.

"Look down there, Captain," Buca murmured in a hushed, reverent tone. "Just look at them all!"

LeMaine went over to him, squatted down, and followed Buca's gaze to the bottom of the canyon. A large camp sprawled between the trees with handsewn tents, women cooking over fires, and armed men standing guard.

LeMaine froze at the sight of them. They were all Maczhi, but they weren't weak or sickly. They all walked upright and they all looked very muscular and incredibly tough.

"They're following the old ways," Buca breathed. "I visited them last night. They've broken away from the Maczhi in the camps. These people moved up here to reclaim our warrior traditions. Even the females are fighters. They have weapons, explosives, training—everything we need. They're perfect!"

His voice quavered with suppressed emotion. That sound set LeMaine's hair on end. It didn't seem possible that such an excellent fighting force could have fallen right into his lap.

Even as he and Buca watched, armed sentries appeared on the rocks opposite where the two men crouched. The sentries squinted at the visitors until Buca raised his hand to wave at them. The sentries waved back and went back to patrolling the area.

"They've been stealing supplies from the Axichis," Buca went on. "They've sent out raiding parties to the airfield, pulled down ships, and taken weapons and anything else they can lay their hands on. Most of their weapons are Axichis."

LeMaine didn't know what to say. He gripped Buca's shoulder once. "Come on. Let's get down there and talk to them."

"I already did. I talked to them last night. They want to fight. They didn't know about the wider war, but they want to do anything to drive the Axichis off the planet."

Buca turned around to look at LeMaine. LeMaine couldn't remember Buca's eyes ever burning as brightly as this.

"These people know about the Cezians being held as prisoners," Buca told LeMaine. "These Maczhi want to free the Cezians from the Axichis. They're angry that alien invaders came here imprisoning people these Maczhi consider their neighbors. These Maczhi want relations with the Cezians. They consider the Cezians their brothers. The Maczhi just don't know how to organize an assault. They can coordinate with the Hellhounds. We can do this!"

"Come on," LeMaine repeated. "We gotta get down there. You can introduce me to them."

They left the clifftop, and this time, they walked down the mountain. Buca entered the canyon half a mile downstream from the Maczhi camp.

LeMaine slowed his pace as he approached the first tents. The women around the fires straightened up to glare at him. They looked as ferocious and warlike as the men. Domesticity didn't soften them at all.

More Maczhi gathered around as Buca and LeMaine made their appearance. Armed men gathered and they didn't relax when they saw Buca.

Buca and LeMaine kept walking through the camp as more and more Maczhi assembled and surrounded the two men in a large crowd. No one said a word until Buca led the way to one of the tents.

Three huge Maczhi stepped out of it and planted themselves in front of Buca and LeMaine. LeMaine never dreamed the Maczhi could get this big. These three bulged with muscle and their long hair and fierce attitude made them look so much bigger somehow.

They glared mostly at LeMaine and then all three stepped aside as a different man emerged from the tent. He wasn't as big as the others, but he carried himself with such superiority that he had to be these Maczhi's leader.

He nodded to Buca and then scrutinized LeMaine. "So you're the Special Forces captain Buca has been telling us about. Captain LeMaine is your name, is that correct?"

LeMaine nodded. "My squad is camped over by the Nulia Compound, but I guess Buca probably told you all about that and our mission here." LeMaine gave the guy a hard look. "Who are you?"

"My name is Zonoth. These are my brothers, Rolmo, Sunus, and Linau." He waved to the three hulks. "We all lived in the camps when Buca was thrown out. We all heard him arguing with the elders to get them to change their ways. We grew up hearing his claims that he was out here hunting to feed himself and defending himself alone against the colonists. We were too young then to go with him, but after he left, we determined to follow his example. We built this camp in the hope that we could be like him. We never imagined he would ever come back to Ziea."

"He's an exceptional man," LeMaine replied. "I've rarely met anyone like him. He's given everything to help the Maczhi."

Zonoth nodded back. "So when can we assault the compound? We were making overtures of friendship to the Cezians when this happened. The Cezians may not be our friends yet, but they are our neighbors on this planet. No alien invaders from another system are going to move in and start abusing the Cezians as long as we can do something to stop it."

"Hold up," LeMaine replied. "We can't assault the compound until I know how many of your people are ready to help us."

Zonoth blinked once, glanced at Buca, and then squared his shoulders. "All of them are ready to help you. We all want to fight the Axichis. We've trained for years for this moment. We won't disappoint you, Captain. Just give us a chance. We want to be a part of the Elian community. This is our best chance."

"I understand and I'm very grateful for your help." LeMaine glanced around him.

It really did look like all the Maczhi were standing around. They crowded too closely and hung on every word as though they really were ready to go out and fight the Axichis this very instant.

Buca caught LeMaine's eye. Buca remained at LeMaine's elbow through the whole exchange and didn't interject once.

LeMaine's head spun with all the possibilities. Buca. All these people looked up to him.

"I'll tell you what," LeMaine began. "How would you all feel about me putting Buca in charge of you? He can coordinate your movements with our squad and I can communicate with him through his remote."

"That will be perfect," Zonoth replied. "We would all love to have him command us on behalf of the Elian Military."

LeMaine turned to Buca. "Are you okay with that?"

Buca dipped one quick nod. "Of course."

"Okay. I want you to go through the whole camp and do an inventory of all your supplies, your personnel numbers, weapons, ammo—the whole kit. I'm going back up to the cave to send the Hellhounds down here. I'll take Peterman and Polasek back to the compound. I need to see the place again, now that I know we have these resources."

"Take one of us with you," someone called from the back of the crowd.

LeMaine turned around. He didn't see who'd spoken out. They all looked just as eager to get involved and to go with him to the compound.

They did know more about this planet than he did, so he told Zonoth, "You can assign someone to go with us. You know your people the best."

"Guza can go with you," Zonoth replied. "He knows the Nulia Compound well."

A tall, wiry Maczhi elbowed out of the crowd to approach LeMaine. Guza looked much younger than Buca, but just as capable and alert. LeMaine didn't put anything past these people.

"Okay," LeMaine said again. "I'll be back in a little while."

He met Buca's eye one more time. Buca definitely shone with a very different light. He didn't hold himself back anymore. He was in his element and all his old resentment and reserve disappeared.

LeMaine tore himself away with difficulty. He would have loved to stick around and watch Buca take charge of these Maczhi, but he wouldn't be able to do that with LeMaine watching.

That story Zonoth told about Buca changed everything. He'd influenced a whole generation of young Maczhi without even realizing it.

"Do you remember Buca from the camps?" LeMaine asked Guza on their way back up the mountain.

"Of course," Guza replied. "We all remember him. We couldn't miss him back then."

"What do you mean?"

"He announced his opinions to the whole camp. He started by trying to convince his parents. His grandparents kept the old ways, but they abandoned the warrior's path when they entered the camps. Buca tried to get his grandfather to speak out to the other Maczhi. When that failed, Buca went through the whole camp telling everyone that they should leave it and return to the mountains. He spoke in front of the whole population and told what he was doing out here by himself. He pointed to himself and to all of us. He told us we could be as strong and healthy as he was if we only abandoned the camp and returned to our traditions."

"Wow," LeMaine breathed. "That must have been something else."

"No one would listen to him....except the young people, of course, but we were too young to act then. Zonoth got in trouble with his parents for trying to influence his brothers to leave the camp. Zonoth wanted the four of them to go join Buca, but their parents punished them and even confined them to the camp to stop them."

"So what happened?" LeMaine asked. "What finally turned the tide and made you all leave the camp?"

"I suppose we all just got old enough and disgusted enough with life in the camp. Zonoth and his brothers got big enough that no one could stop them. Zonoth was the one who went around to all the other young people and encouraged us to follow him up here. Our health improved immediately. Our battalion has only gotten stronger since then."

"Battalion?" LeMaine repeated. "Is that what you call yourselves?"

"Yes," Guza dipped his chin. "Of course."

LeMaine didn't ask any more questions. How interesting that these Maczhi considered themselves a fighting force before anything else. They didn't consider themselves a village or a society or an enclave.

They were a battalion. Fighting was their lifeblood. They just needed a battle to fight and an enemy to attack.

Chapter 12

LeMaine, Polasek, Peterman, and Guza lay behind the hill overlooking the Nulia Compound again. "All the Axichis are still there," Polasek reported. "They aren't running any campaign."

"I wonder if that means the Military and the Imoliv have retired," Peterman replied.

"It doesn't matter," LeMaine cut in. "We're attacking this compound. That's all there is to it. We just need to strike quickly so we take out both the compound and the ships on the airfield at the same time."

"That shouldn't be hard," Polasek suggested. "Nunn can mine those ships while we overrun the compound. She can arrange that all the ships blow at the same time. Then the Axichis won't be able to escape."

"If you'll excuse me, Captain," Guza interrupted. "I have a different idea."

"Please," LeMaine replied. "That's why you're here. You have information I don't."

"The Maczhi battalion can take those ships and use them against the Axichis. We've attacked enough of them before. We know how to fly them. They'll be more useful in our own hands. You don't have to blow them up."

"What would you do with them once you got them?" Peterman asked. "The only other target is the compound and you couldn't target that without putting the Cezians in danger."

"I disagree," Guza replied and pointed to the compound's outer walls. "The Axichis are holding the Cezians at the very center of the compound in an underground bunker protected from strikes from the air."

"How do you know that?" Polasek asked. "You can't see inside the compound."

"Do you remember, Captain? Zonoth and his brothers have made contact with the Cezians and offered to form an alliance with them. The Maczhi battalion was in communication with the Cezians when the Axichis took over the compound. Zonoth and his brothers have all been inside it along with several other Maczhi. We know the layout."

"That doesn't explain how you know where the Axichis are holding the Cezians," Peterman pointed out.

"It's the only logical place the Axichis would be holding them. The Axichis wouldn't hold the Cezians anywhere near the outer walls. The Cezians are a powerful people. The Axichis will want to keep them far away from anything that might give the Cezians an idea to escape."

"All right," LeMaine interjected. "I'm willing to take your word for it, so what's your plan?"

"We capture as many Axichis vessels as we can and use them to bombard the outer walls. Your explosives technician can mine the walls and the Hellhounds and the Maczhi battalion can invade the compound to free the Cezians."

LeMaine glanced at Peterman and Polasek. Polasek frowned and rubbed his chin. "I guess that could work."

"It's a great idea," LeMaine replied.

"It's better than wasting our explosives on the Axichis spacecraft," Guza added. "After the battle is over, we'll have possession of these craft. We can use them against the Axichis later."

LeMaine laughed. "I don't even want to think about how deadly the Maczhi battalion will be with stolen Axichis spacecraft at their disposal. Let's fall back and regroup. We need to organize the whole assault, now that we know what we're doing."

The four men left for the Maczhi camp. Peterman and Polasek grilled Guza all the way about Buca and how the Maczhi battalion came to exist.

LeMaine didn't join in. He'd heard enough. The story staggered his mind. It didn't seem possible that one man could change his whole species' fortunes so quickly and so completely.

Now Buca was in charge of these people. They were realizing their fondest wish by following his command.

LeMaine didn't dare to let himself think about what that meant and how it all might play out. He was too happy for Buca even to speculate on the future.

They returned to the camp close to sundown. The Hellhounds were scattered all over the place helping the battalion inventory their equipment and organizing everyone into smaller squads.

LeMaine returned to Zonoth's tent to find him up to his neck in discussions with Buca and the rest of Zonoth's entourage about the preparations. They were all thrilled with

Guza's suggestion to steal Axichis fighter craft, not just to raid them for supplies, but to actually steal the craft themselves and keep them.

LeMaine tried to stay out of it, but he didn't have to try too hard. The Maczhi addressed all their comments to Buca and agreed with practically everything he said and every suggestion he made. Even Zonoth asked him what they should do about certain aspects of the campaign.

As soon as the meeting ended, Zonoth came up to LeMaine and threw his arm around LeMaine's shoulders. "You and your squad must all come and have dinner with us tonight. I insist."

"If you insist, then I guess I have no choice."

Zonoth laughed loudly. He didn't act like a Maczhi at all. LeMaine was too used to being around Buca who hardly ever laughed.

The rest of Zonoth's entourage were just as loud and jovial as he was, especially his giant brothers. The whole group trooped to another tent next door. It was already packed with both Maczhi and the Hellhounds.

Everyone sat on the floor around a fire burning in the middle. The Maczhi passed roasted meat back and forth to each other and to the Hellhounds, along with sewn leather flasks of some intoxicating beverage.

Zonoth planted LeMaine on one side of Buca while Zonoth sat on Buca's other side. Zonoth regaled Buca through the whole evening about everything the battalion had done since they left the camps.

Buca listened in silence except when Zonoth's tale absolutely required that Buca respond. Zonoth got progressively louder and more excited as he recounted all the battalion's successes.

LeMaine watched from Buca's other side and experienced another stab of painful pride in Buca's accomplishments. Zonoth obviously wanted Buca to realize that all the battalion's success had been Buca's doing. Zonoth wanted Buca to be proud of the battalion for following so faithfully in Buca's footsteps.

Buca only nodded and murmured his responses in his usual reserved way. He was too humble and quiet to blow himself up or feel proud of himself for essentially saving these people from starvation and extinction.

He definitely got the message, though, and he became more silent and brooding as Zonoth became more animated and enthusiastic.

Zonoth launched into all his plans to expand the battalion, recruit more young Maczhi from the camps, and hopefully, in time, get all the Maczhi into the mountains where they belonged. It was Zonoth's cherished dream to completely abolish the camps so that no Maczhi remained there.

"You can help us," he told Buca. "More people will listen to us when they realize you're with us. You're a legend to the traditionalists."

Buca only murmured, "We'll see."

Zonoth didn't react to that. He just went right on describing all his future plans and how much more assured their success would be, now that Buca had returned and joined the battalion.

The evening wore on and everyone became much more relaxed until all formality went out the window. The Maczhi reclined around the fire and several people fell asleep right there on the floor.

They sprawled over each other while others curled up in each other's arms. No one seemed in too big a hurry to go sleep anywhere else.

LeMaine tried to stay awake, but his vigil last night made him tired. The food, drink, fire, and the relaxed company made him even sleepier. He couldn't keep his eyes open much longer.

Then the Hellhounds stretched out and went to sleep followed by Zonoth and his party.

LeMaine was just deciding to do the same thing when Buca turned in his direction. It was the first time Buca had faced LeMaine all evening. "What do you think, Captain?"

"About what?"

"About all of this. About everything the battalion is doing."

"I think it's spectacular. I think it's so fitting that you should be the one who caused all this. You're a hero to your people. You should be very proud of yourself."

Buca cast his eyes down at his hands. "I'm not."

"Why shouldn't you be? You saved these people's lives. It's thanks to you that we have a chance to save not just the Cezians but the rest of Elia into the bargain. What is there not to be proud of?"

"We haven't done it yet. The battalion doesn't have any combat experience....."

"That isn't true. They've raided the Axichis before. They've attacked Axichis ships, pulled them down, and overrun them. I can't think of any other Elian species that would be able to do that."

"I mean they've never fought in a campaign like this before. They aren't regular Military."

"You weren't regular Military before you joined the Hellhounds. That didn't make any difference. You were just as capable as any of us. You can't convince me these people aren't capable."

"I just worry about them." Buca cast a heartfelt glance over the sleeping Maczhi nearest him. "I guess that's what it comes down to. I don't want them to get hurt.....or killed. There are so few of them."

LeMaine couldn't stand seeing Buca like this. LeMaine gripped his shoulder. "Listen to me, man. What makes these people great is that they're fighters. They want to fight. They wouldn't be great if they didn't want to fight and they weren't capable of fighting. They are. They're as capable as any of the Hellhounds if not more so. You know this. Trying to save them from the danger would make them less than what they are. You love them because they are this way. Don't wish for them to be any different."

"I know. I just want to protect them. I want to protect everything they're doing." Buca choked on his next words. "I should have been here. I should have been here to meet them when they left the camps. I should have been here to help them establish themselves. I could have taught them things. I could have made it easier for them. I never should have l eft."

LeMaine's throat constricted. He couldn't think of any words to express the irony of this moment.

"I don't think I can walk away from these people, Captain," Buca husked. "I don't think I can leave Ziea when this mission is over. I have to stay with them. I have to help them and make up for the lost time. I have to go back to the camps with them. There might be other young people I can save."

"I know," LeMaine replied, "and I understand. You should stay."

Buca shook his head. "I made a commitment to the Hellhounds. I hate letting you down....."

"You aren't letting me down. You're a great man. You belong with your people. They need you a hell of lot more than we do. You obviously belong here. You should stay."

His assurance didn't cheer Buca up. "It doesn't seem right to leave the squad. I don't know how I could ever face the others."

"I wouldn't worry too much about them. You just said that, if you'd known it would turn out this way, you never would have left."

"Of course I wouldn't have. I would have stayed forever if I'd known even one person was going to leave."

"There you go," LeMaine returned. "You leaving Ziea and joining the Hellhounds was a.....Well, I won't call it a mistake because it wasn't that. You made that decision based on incomplete information. How long were you out here on your own before you left?"

"Eight years."

"There. You see? Your people threw you out. You couldn't possibly know this battalion movement was simmering under the surface. You made a decision based on eight years or more of information about what they were going to do. All the evidence led you to believe they would never change. You didn't know. You couldn't have known. Give yourself a b reak."

Buca wouldn't look at him. "You're the best man I've ever known, Captain. All these people look up to me, but it's you I hope I can be like. I hope I can be a commander like you someday."

"You already are, son," LeMaine breathed. "Did you see the way Zonoth was talking to you before? Do you have any idea what you mean to these people? You already are that for them. You've given them the greatest gift anyone could possibly ask for. You've given them something worth a thousand times more than anything I could ever give you. You deserve this. You all do."

Buca didn't answer and LeMaine didn't say anything else. The weight of Buca's decision weighed on him too heavily, but that was what made him such an outstanding person. He took his commitment to the Hellhounds seriously. He hated to break that commitment, even for something so much more important.

LeMaine decided to break the tension by lying down. He shut his eyes and exhaustion took him.

Buca remained sitting up in the same place. He gazed at all the Maczhi asleep around him. Emotion twisted his face despite his best efforts to control his features.

His whole life had changed in a single day. He started this mission by saying that he hated Ziea and that the Maczhi deserved to die. Now he was planning to stay with them and pull them even farther out of the darkness than he already had.

That was the kind of man LeMaine called a leader. Buca was exactly the leader the Maczhi needed right now.

Chapter 13

LeMaine, Polasek, Peterman, Buca, Zonoth, Guza, and the rest of Zonoth's entourage filed out of Zonoth's tent. The other Hellhounds and the Maczhi battalion waited for them outside.

Buca stepped forward. "All you squads know what you have to do. Squad 9 will circle the airfield and approach from the north where the trees offer the most cover. When Guza gives the signal from the northern mountaintop, Squad 9 will sneak onto the airfield, neutralize as many Axichis as necessary to keep our cover, and get on board the Axichis vessels. Break up so you get an even mix of warships and fighter craft."

A group of thirty Maczhi on the lefthand flank of the assembly nodded.

"Nunn, you'll take Squad 4 to the south. O'Hara, you and the sniper team will take out the guards on that side of the compound so Nunn and Squad 4 can approach and mine the outer walls on the south side."

"Not a problem," Nunn replied. "We're on it."

"Guza will give the second signal and you'll blow your charges," Buca went on. "As soon as Squad 9 hears the explosion, you'll launch and turn your guns on the compound. Restrict your fire to the northern walls and take out any Axichis that leave the compound to stop you."

Buca turned to LeMaine. "Captain, you'll take Squad 7 battalion to the draw east of the compound. Zonoth will take Squad 5 to the west and I'll take Squads 3 and 5 to the southwest. As soon as the walls come down, all our squads will rush the compound and take out any other Axichis standing guard. If this works, we should have the Cezians out of there before the Axichis can mount a response."

"What about reinforcements?" someone in the crowd asked. "What if the Axichis call in more of their forces from off the planet?"

"O'Hara and his team will shoot out the Axichis' communications array when he takes out the guards. As soon as we get inside, our first job will be to capture any communications equipment the Axichis might use to call for help. Polasek will monitor all communications coming and going from the planet. That will help us figure out if the Axichis have another base set up somewhere that we don't know about. Any other questions?"

LeMaine hesitated to ask anything in front of the whole company. He didn't want to call Buca's authority into question.

This issue had been becoming more and more obvious over the last few days as the Maczhi battalion prepared to go to full-scale war against the Axichis. LeMaine didn't like to question or contradict anything Buca said.

The Hellhounds in particular had been becoming increasingly agitated by Buca telling them what to do. More than once, the Hellhounds waited until they were out of any Maczhi's earshot before confirming an order or plan with LeMaine.

It had also been becoming increasingly clear just how much the Maczhi idolized Buca. None of the Maczhi would hear a word against him. They even attacked their own people for daring even to ask for clarification on anything he said.

LeMaine waited until Buca dismissed the battalion. The squads left in different directions to go to their stations before the battle. Buca had to discuss a few more things with Zonoth's party before that group broke up, too.

Buca headed off to join his own squad and LeMaine took the chance to hustle over to catch up with him. "Can I make a suggestion?"

"What is it?" Buca asked over his shoulder.

"You're sending fifteen guys on Squad 9 to capture Axichis craft—warships and fighters."

"Yeah?" Buca asked. "So?"

"Don't you think this might be a perfect opportunity to capture more of them? You're sending these guys in undercover. You could send a lot more—like a *lot* more. You could take thirty or fifty or even a hundred ships. The original Squad 9 could blow out the compound while the others launch into the atmosphere. They could secure the whole planet and make sure no Axichis come around to interfere with us. Then the battalion would have all those ships in their own private fighting force for later. You could hold Ziea through the whole war. The Axichis would never get a toehold here again."

Buca spun around so fast that LeMaine thought Buca might be angry at him for even mentioning this plan.

Buca's eyes flickered with some unknowable light and he inclined his head to one side. "And where would I get a hundred men to send onto the airfield? They're all assigned to other flanks."

LeMaine shrugged. "Send them from my squad. I don't care. We already have enough people invading the compound. This is more important....don't you think?"

Buca studied him for a minute and then a rare smile twisted across his face. It was unlike any other smile LeMaine had ever seen from him. Buca actually grinned in mischievous, boyish delight.

"You're right, Captain. It is more important and we can spare the men. You can go reassign the men under your command. Send them to Squad 9 and give them their orders." He thumped LeMaine on the shoulder. "Good idea, Captain."

Buca walked off alone and LeMaine raced back to Squad 7 to give the order.

He found them waiting for him at the bottom end of the canyon. They were all loaded with weapons and at least half their number were female Maczhi just as strapped up and prepared as the men.

Lemon and Heckler were with them. Those two fit right in with these people. "Are we moving out now, Sir?" Heckler asked.

"Hold up." LeMaine cast a glance over the rest of the group. Buca had divided up the remaining Maczhi and assigned two hundred and fifty fighters to each squad. "Which of you badasses knows how to fly Axichis craft—including warships?"

Almost everyone raised their hands. LeMaine sectioned off eighty people at random and reassigned them to Squad 9. A ripple of excitement went through the group when LeMaine explained what he wanted them to do.

"Don't stick around on the surface," he ordered. "As soon as Squad 9 opens fire on the compound, you folks get in the air and set up a patrol around the planet. No one comes in or out that isn't regular Elian Military. Understand? Guard the planet and make sure no Axichis come down to reinforce their friends. If any other Axichis craft take off, blow them to kingdom come."

"Yes, Sir," they all replied and then laughter broke out in the ranks.

"These ships are going to be the Maczhi battalion's new air force," LeMaine told them. "You're gonna hold Ziea against all comers. I know you'll do Elia proud. You can go."

The pilots hurried away and left Squad 7 vastly depleted, but LeMaine didn't care. A hundred Axichis ships in orbit would be way more helpful to the wider war than another hundred Maczhi getting inside the Nulia Compound.

He led the way out of the canyon. The Maczhi talked on their way into the mountains, but they all fell silent when they reached the peaks.

They fell into a single-file line with LeMaine, Heckler, and Lemon dotted amongst the Maczhi. They hiked through the forests and eventually came to the edge of the trees overlooking the compound.

Two hundred yards of open ground separated the group from their destination. LeMaine checked the situation on his remote.

Plenty of Axichis sentries and gunmen stood guard on this side of the compound. Squad 7 would never get across those fields without covering fire from the stolen Axichis fighter craft.

The Maczhi settled down to wait. The other squads would take time to get into position. Guza wouldn't give the first signal until close to noon. That was an hour away.

The Maczhi got comfortable, but no one spoke above a whisper. LeMaine stayed where he was and kept an eye on the compound.

If this didn't work, the compound probably couldn't be taken by any means. He definitely wouldn't even consider taking it if Buca hadn't handed him the Maczhi battalion on a silver platter.

Heckler strode up behind LeMaine. "Anything moving out there?"

"Nothing. If we're lucky, we won't see a thing until it all goes up in smoke."

"These people are something else, aren't they?" Heckler remarked. "I never thought I'd ever meet a whole culture of Hellhounds all living in one place."

LeMaine chuckled and finally tore his eyes away from the compound. He couldn't stand here staring at it for the whole hour.

Lemon sat among the trees talking in low tones with the Maczhi. Heckler was right. The Hellhounds blended right in with these people. They spoke each other's language. The Hellhounds almost seemed like they'd been here all along and would always be here.

LeMaine shook those thoughts out of his head. His conversation with Buca that first night disturbed LeMaine more than he wanted to admit.

LeMaine didn't want to leave Buca behind, but leading these people was Buca's destiny. It had always been his role to be their guiding star even when he wasn't around to do it in person.

LeMaine didn't want to let Buca go. LeMaine couldn't imagine the Hellhounds without him. He didn't talk as much as the others, but he'd made himself so indispensable that LeMaine felt his loss even before Buca actually left.

He'd been so steady, reliable, and always, always ready for anything. He was a true Hellhound, but in a way, he never had been.

He'd been the first Maczhi to reclaim the old ways. He'd been the first Maczhi to become a Hellhound and now he'd be creating a whole society of Hellhounds—a society he created by his example.

He'd been moving farther and farther away from the other Hellhounds the longer he stayed with the other Maczhi. He spent all his time with them and LeMaine noticed Buca investing his attention and knowledge with them, too.

He spoke to them and responded to them more than he'd ever spoken or responded to the Hellhounds. He took every opportunity to interact with them and share their company.

Groups of Maczhi followed him everywhere he went. He expressed more emotion when he talked and obviously appreciated everything they said to him.

LeMaine paced up and down for a while, tried sitting down, and got up again. He went back to the edge of the trees and peered out just as an alarm went off on his remote.

Lemon and Heckler both looked up at the same time. "That's the first signal," Heckler announced and all the rest of the Maczhi got to their feet, too.

They migrated to the edge of the trees where the undergrowth hid them from view. Squad 7 gazed out across the fields just as a whole bunch of tiny black specks darted out of another block of trees to the north.

They raced across open ground in groups of two and three, sprinted onto the airfield, and vanished around the landing gear of hundreds of Axichis craft. Hardly any Axichis pilots or mechanics worked out there.

The few that were there got pulled down and killed by the stealthy Maczhi. Then Squad 9 fanned out with one Maczhi going to each craft. They vanished inside and the whole scene went back to being as silent, deserted, and peaceful as before.

Someone chuckled low in the back. "I can't believe we're going to have our own space force! The Maczhi battalion really is becoming a battalion."

"We won't have any trouble recruiting out of the camps now," someone else remarked. "Everyone will want to join us."

"They'll need to get their health back first," a third person pointed out.

"How long do we have to wait for the second signal?" Heckler asked.

"There's no way to know," LeMaine replied. "It just depends on when Nunn finishes laying her charges."

No one spoke for a minute, but the whole squad stayed where they were and held their breath watching for any sign. It was all quiet.

LeMaine glanced over his shoulder, but he couldn't see the mountaintop where Guza was giving signals to the different squads. LeMaine could only hope and pray that O'Hara's snipers took out enough guards for Nunn and her bomb squad to get near the walls.

Rustling noises shattered the stillness behind him. "This could take hours," Heckler growled and turned away.

The instant he said it, a ground-shaking boom went off as the compound's southern wall evaporated in a towering column of dust and rubble.

All the remaining Axichis guards jumped, spun in that direction, and raised their weapons, but they couldn't go to guard the breach against intrusion without leaving their posts.

Five more devastating explosions went off one after another. They detonated down the compound walls dissolving all protection on that side.

"Arm up!" LeMaine ordered. "Get ready to move as soon as the......"

He didn't get a chance to finish his sentence before a shriek set his hair on end. Everyone rushed to the edge of the trees in time to see a hundred Axichis craft launch from the airfield.

That sight struck fear into LeMaine's heart. He had to remind himself that the Maczhi were piloting these craft.

They sure knew what the hell they were doing. They whizzed across the airfield, trained their laser cannons on the compound, and opened fire.

The sentries on the walls froze trying to figure out why their own craft were targeting them and then lasers shattered the compound to smithereens.

Chapter 14

Twenty Axichis fighter craft surrounded the Nulia Compound and unloaded on the walls all around the structure. The rest of the fighters and warships skyrocketed into the atmosphere and vanished behind the clouds. The Maczhi battalion was away.

"Go!" LeMaine ordered and pushed Heckler into the open. "Get inside the compound!"

Hundreds of Maczhi poured from every direction converging on the walls as they crumbled before the Maczhi onslaught. LeMaine's group raced to the west side just as the other squads showed up from their positions.

LeMaine spotted different Hellhounds embedded in the Maczhi force and then a torrent of lasers erupted from behind the smoke screen.

Buca strode from one squad to the next giving orders. "Spread out! Squad 5—flank them from the south! Squad 1—take the east!"

Maczhi vanished into the haze. The dust scattered the lasers and gave a perfect pinpoint location where every Axichis was hiding.

"Where's O'Hara?!" Buca yelled. "O'Hara! Get over here!"

"Right here, boss," O'Hara called and hustled over to Buca.

Buca positioned O'Hara behind a wall and O'Hara set up his carbine on top of it. "Get ready to take them out as soon as they open fire," Buca ordered.

"You got it," O'Hara replied and glued his eye to his scope.

Buca stayed next to O'Hara and didn't move. Buca kept his sharp eyes on the smoke where the lasers were coming from.

"Squad 5—report!!" Buca yelled.

A disembodied voice drifted out of the murk. "Squad 5 in position!"

"Squad 1!!" Buca yelled.

Another voice came from a different direction. "Squad 1 in position and standing by!"

Buca glanced around. "Squad 7—stand by to attack on my command."

"Standing by," LeMaine replied.

Buca waited for a long, tense moment. LeMaine couldn't tell what he was waiting for, but LeMaine didn't interrupt. This was Buca's operation. The Hellhounds were just along for the ride.

Without warning, he bellowed. "NOW!!"

Gunfire exploded from everywhere at once. Lasers from the Maczhi's stolen Axichis rifles erupted from deep in the smoke. They shot toward the center with another bunch of lasers firing outward toward where Buca, O'Hara, and the Squad 7 waited.

O'Hara unloaded directly on the source of those lasers and they cut out instantly. "Squad 7—move in!" Buca ordered.

LeMaine charged forward with the rest of Squad 7 right with him. They rushed into the smoke, but no more Axichis lasers came from beyond the curtain.

The squad burst through into a destroyed corridor. LeMaine recognized it from his first visit to Ziea. Dead Axichis lay all over the place.

The Maczhi went from body to body taking weapons and anything else of value. They spread out searching rooms and gunning down any Axichis they could find.

Buca strode up the corridor behind LeMaine. "All you squads—get down to the bunker. The Axichis are bound to have guards around the Cezians. Squad 7—take the north stairwell. Squad 5—take the south stairwell. Squad 1—take the east."

People out called, "Yes, Sir," and the squads hustled away.

LeMaine didn't know where any bunker was, so he followed his own squad. All the Maczhi seemed to know where they were supposed to go and they took him to a stairway leading underground, but the Maczhi didn't go down right away.

They hid behind the door frame, darted out, and swept the stairs with their guns before anyone dared to enter. When they did, they crept down one stair at a time covering every possible corner to make sure no Axichis got the jump on them.

The Maczhi acted so jumpy that they put LeMaine on edge. Buca was right. The Axichis would have the bulk of their forces around the Cezians. More Axichis would have fallen back to the bunker as soon as the Maczhi attacked.

The first Maczhi made it to the bottom of the stairwell. One man pressed his ear to the door to listen before he cracked it open.

He squinted through the gap, and when he still didn't see or hear any threat, he pulled the door open.

The squad went through the same process of hiding behind the door frame, darting out to sweep the corridor beyond, and then pivoting back out of sight.

LeMaine marveled at how well-trained they all were. They must have been training day and night for years, but he already knew that. He just didn't expect them to be so well-versed in urban warfare.

The first man stuck his head out and the corridor beyond instantly exploded in a shower of lasers. They bombarded the door frame and scattered rubble and debris over the Maczhi standing behind him.

"Fall back!" he hollered, but it was too late.

Lasers punched through the walls and cut off any retreat. "Get into the corridor!" LeMaine roared. "Get out there and return fire! It's our only way out!"

He tried to push the Maczhi ahead of him, but it took him at least a minute to make himself heard over the noise.

The Maczhi responded instantly. The first guy dragged the torn door the rest of the way open and held it. Five others gathered behind him and jammed their rifles into their shoulders. The Maczhi nodded to each other and then the whole squad burst out of the stairwell.

They charged straight into the path of the Axichis laser fire, but the Maczhi opened fire with their own guns so fast that it didn't make any difference. A handful of Axichis shots crackled down the corridor only to be answered by a shower of return fire from the Maczhi.

Three Maczhi went down and the enemy fire cut out. The rest of the squad streamed into the corridor and met up with Squad 5 coming from another stairwell.

LeMaine knelt down by the three wounded Maczhi. "Hold tight. We'll get a medic down here to take care of you."

The first man who'd been under fire in the stairwell grabbed LeMaine's arm. "Don't let Buca take me out of the campaign! Don't let him take me out off duty! Please!"

LeMaine had to smile down at him. "The campaign's over, son. We'll all be off duty after this. Now just sit tight. There's nothing shameful about getting shot in combat. It happens to the best of us."

The guy pinched his lips, clamped his eyes shut, and looked away. He acted devastated that he wouldn't be able to fight with his people. These Maczhi really were the hardest badasses LeMaine had met in his life.

Kellogg showed up a second later and started working on the wounded. Squad 1 had wounded, too, and Kellogg gave orders for the Maczhi to carry all the wounded upstairs to the hospital ward where the Hellhounds had stayed last time.

LeMaine strode through the combined Maczhi force. "We gotta find the Cezians."

"We know where they are," one of the Maczhi told him.

"Where are they?"

The guy almost answered, but he shut his mouth real quick when Buca and Zonoth showed up.

Buca surveyed the walls and doors. He waited until Kellogg finished clearing out the wounded and then Buca waved to Zonoth. "Let's go."

Zonoth led the way down the corridor to a different door. This one had been constructed of heavy steel with three massive reinforced rods locking it in place.

Zonoth gave orders and several Maczhi got to work rolling the rods back. Zonoth signaled everyone to get out of the way before the door creaked open.

Laser fire exploded from inside. "Hold your fire!!" Buca yelled. "Don't return fire!! We don't want to hit the Cezians!!"

The Maczhi flattened themselves against the walls as lasers sprayed from beyond the door. The battalion cowered for any scrap of protection, but all of a sudden, the laser fire died to nothing.

Pounding thumps and vicious, animal snarls echoed from behind the door. The Maczhi crept forward and peered inside.

Everyone halted on the threshold watching the Cezian prisoners beat the last remaining Axichis to the floor, kick in their heads, and snap their necks one after another. The Cezians went into such a rage that they didn't see the Maczhi standing there.

After the Cezians reduced their enemies to a bloody pulp, one youngish male happened to glance up. He blinked through a film of blood at Buca, Zonoth, LeMaine, and all other Hellhounds and Maczhi watching from out in the corridor.

The guy straightened up, sniffed, shook some of the blood off his fist, and cleared his throat. "Zonoth.....thank you for coming."

"Are you and your people all right, Vulo?" Zonoth asked.

Vulo blinked again and glanced around like he had to think about it before he answered. "We're fine. We weren't expecting you."

Zonoth strode into what turned out to be a very cramped basement crypt. All the Cezian prisoners had been jammed in shoulder to shoulder.

"Do your people need medical treatment?" Zonoth asked. "We have an Elian medic upstairs. He's taking charge of all the wounded."

"We don't need medical treatment." Vulo surveyed the assembled Maczhi and then noticed LeMaine. "Captain LeMaine, isn't it? I recognize you from when you were here last time. You were the one who negotiated with Lulara."

"I recognize you, too." LeMaine stuck out his hand. "It's a pleasure to see you again."

"Are you in charge of this operation?" Vulo asked. "Is the Elian Military here to free us?"

"I'm not in charge," LeMaine waved to Buca. "Buca is in command of the Maczhi battalion. My squad is under his authority."

Vulo glanced at Buca and froze. "I recognize you, too."

"I recognize you as well," Buca growled.

"That's all in the past," Zonoth interrupted. "We're all friends here. Come upstairs with us, Vulo. An Elian communications expert is taking charge of your transmission array. We can monitor the situation and find out if there are any other Axichis on the planet."

Vulo nodded and everyone headed for the stairs. LeMaine hung back and pulled Heckler, Lemon, and the other Hellhounds back with him. They let the Maczhi accompany the Cezians alone.

The freed Cezians streamed upstairs and spread out through the compound. They all commented on the damage and then they departed in different directions to resume their normal lives.

LeMaine hung back, but eventually, he made his way to the communications center where Polasek sat in front of a large bank of electronics.

The Cezians had repaired their transmission array with help from the Elian Assembly.

"The new air force is signaling that all's quiet in the atmosphere," Polasek told Buca, Zonoth, and Vulo, who all stood behind him looking over his shoulders. "They're reading Axichis life signs in three locations. One of them is the Nanov Outpost."

"Where are the other two?" Buca asked.

"It looks like the Axichis have set up their own bases at two other locations. The pilots are triangulating their coordinates now."

"Do the Axichis have any other aircraft there?" Buca asked.

Polasek cocked his head studying his controls. "The pilots are reading forty warships at, but none of the warships are coming to interfere with us. There aren't any craft at all at the Nanov Outpost. There are five hundred Axichis life signs there........" Polasek glanced over his shoulder to meet Buca's eye. "And two thousand human colonists."

"Bastards!" Vulo growled. "The Axichis are using the colonists as human shields."

"We'll deal with that later," Buca replied. "How many craft at the other bases?"

"None," Polasek asked. "They're all in the air."

"Where in the air?"

Polasek took a second to answer. "They're launching for open space. They're trying to rejoin the Axichis fleet in other parts of the system."

"Signal our air force to stop them," Buca ordered. "Down them all before they leave orbit.....and then tell them to vaporize the two bases. Tell the pilots not to touch the Nanov Outpost until I give the word."

"Yes, Sir," Polasek replied and got onto his controls in a whirlwind.

LeMaine stood back and watched the air battle ensue, but the Maczhi ended it after only a few minutes. They outnumbered the Axichis by at least four to one and the stolen Maczhi craft could do plenty of damage against the Axichis' own ships.

Then they went after the two bases and erased them completely off the map. The bases were defenseless without their spacecraft to counteract the Maczhi space force's firepower. The pilots left nothing but two round smoking craters where the bases had been.

"We should have thought of this before," Buca muttered to no one in particular. "We should have thought of stealing their vessels and using them against the Axichis. We shouldn't have spent so much time buzzing around trying to shoot at them when it didn't do any good."

"What are you going to do?" Vulo asked. "If you go after the Nanov outpost, you'd leave this compound undefended."

"We won't leave you undefended," Buca replied. "We'll arm the Cezians with all the guns you need to hold the compound, but we'll need a Cezian fighting force to help us assault the outpost. We need to wipe the Axichis off Ziea once and for all. We need to reclaim this planet and send a message to the Axichis never to set foot here again."

Cheers broke out among the Maczhi listening in the background. Vulo eyed Buca and then nodded. "You can count on the Cezians. We'll work together to take possession of our planet. We'll make a stand here and your fleet will ensure that no one comes near us again without our permission."

Buca's eyes flashed again and then he and Vulo shook hands. LeMaine took that opportunity to slip out of the room. His presence was no longer needed here.

Chapter 15

L eMaine entered a conference room in the Nulia Compound.

The ruling Cezian Council that had taken over this colony after Lulara left, including Vulo, two of his brothers, and three of his cousins, already stood across the table from Buca, Zonoth, Zonoth's brothers, and five other high-ranking Maczhi from the battalion.

These men had been in constant conversation with each other for the last week since the Maczhi had liberated the Cezian prisoners.

LeMaine had made a point of staying in the background. In fact, Buca hadn't even invited LeMaine to any of the meetings between the Cezians and the Maczhi. They'd organized the assault on the Nanov compound without any Elian input at all.

That was just fine with LeMaine. The farther Buca moved away from the Hellhounds now, the easier the transition would be once the Hellhounds left Ziea.

Buca *had* invited LeMaine to this meeting. LeMaine was the only human in the room.

The Maczhi occupied one side of the long table while the Cezians sat opposite them. It was a repeat of the negotiations that took place under Lulara's diplomatic guidance with two glaring differences.

First, there were no other Elians in the room besides LeMaine and he was only here in a ceremonial capacity. None of the Elian brass or Assembly members were here to offer any opinions on how the Maczhi and the Cezians conducted their relationship.

The other startling difference was the demeanor and condition of the Maczhi at the table. The previous delegation had been cringing, submissive, and barely able to speak on their own behalf.

These men glared across the table at their Cezian counterparts and the Cezians glared right back—not in hostility, but in matched ferocity and intensity. The Cezians had a reputation as being one of the toughest, fiercest species around, but they had finally met their match.

Buca stood at the head of the table on one side. Vulo stood opposite him. They'd both left the actually head seat empty to signify that neither of them was truly in charge.

LeMaine slipped into the seat at the very end of the table nearest the door. It wasn't exactly a place of shame, but it was without a doubt the lowest-ranked position in the room. He was nothing but a token—a gesture of politeness to the Elian Military.

He'd barely said a word during the last negotiations between the Cezians and the Maczhi. This meeting was looking like it would be going the same way. None of these people wanted him involved at all because he wasn't.

Buca straightened up, narrowed his eyes, and dipped his chin at Vulo. "Vulo...Zon oth....all you assembled warriors.....we are gathered here today to sign a formal treaty of friendship and mutual aid between the Maczhi battalion and the Cezian Council. Our stated mission will be the defense of Ziea against all invaders, no matter their origin or species, as well as to offer any assistance possible to the wider Elian community. Our mission will be to strengthen both our colonies by mutual assistance, joint military operations, sharing of resources, and open communication between our peoples. How say you?"

Everyone at the table called out at the same time. Several warriors on both sides raised their fists in support.

Vulo spoke next. "In recognition of the Maczhi battalion's aid to the Cezian community in our time of need, the Council proposes an additional amendment to our treaty. The Cezian Council proposes developing a special Defense Squadron of Cezian volunteers to assist the Maczhi battalion in its efforts to defend the planet. This squadron would be subordinate to the Maczhi battalion. The Cezian Council will provide the Maczhi battalion free access to any weapons, artillery, and other resources we have to strengthen the Maczhi battalion as much as possible. We would be honored to accept any training you can give us to bring us up to defensive readiness so that we can be of the most usefulness to you the next time the battalion is called upon to defend our lives."

Buca shut his eyes and bowed his head. "I'm truly grateful for your consideration and your help. The Maczhi and the Cezians have been antagonistic to each other for too long. It's high time we all put aside our old hostilities to fight our common enemy."

"I agree," Vulo replied. "If the Maczhi followed their traditional path of strength and self-reliance, we might have come to respect and regard each other long ago."

He extended his hand across the table and Buca shook it. The tension broke and all the other warriors started talking to each other.

Buca and Vulo both sat down and started passing their written treaty back and forth. They both signed it and then the paper made its way down the table as all the Maczhi and all the Cezians present added their signatures.

The meeting dissolved into a casual conversation. The men from both sides stood up, milled around, talked about everything, and rubbed elbows as though they'd known each other all their lives.

LeMaine joined their conversations, but he didn't expect much to come from this. He wasn't even really a part of this anymore. The Hellhounds were just another squad in the Maczhi battalion. None of these people cared about LeMaine's opinions anymore, so he didn't offer them—about anything.

The gathering broke up with plenty of handshakes and pats on the back all around. LeMaine left them still hobnobbing with each other and went back to the enlisted quarters where the Cezians had housed the Hellhounds after the campaign.

LeMaine heard the squad talking in the common room they all shared. He went there to join them, but when he got to the threshold, Buca came up to LeMaine out of nowhere.

LeMaine knew better than anyone how fast Buca could move, but he really must have burned rubber to get here from the conference room in time to intercept LeMaine.

"I'd like to speak to you in private, Captain," Buca began.

He'd developed a very flinty way of talking. He remained as formal as ever with LeMaine and the Hellhounds. If Buca softened up with the Maczhi battalion, he did it when LeMaine and the Hellhounds weren't around to see.

"Of course," LeMaine replied. "Where would you like to talk?"

"Follow me, if you don't mind." Buca turned away and walked off down the corridor. He waited only long enough for LeMaine to join him.

"Is anything wrong?" LeMaine asked on their way to.....wherever it was they were going. "I thought that treaty negotiation went very well. Vulo offering to make his squadron subordinate to the battalion was a massive gesture."

"I'm aware of that," Buca replied.

LeMaine struggled to come up with some other way to break the ice. He hardly recognized Buca anymore. LeMaine was just starting to worry that he'd made some terrible diplomatic blunder when Buca turned off into a random room somewhere deep in the Nulia Compound. This room was a small office with a table and a few chairs.

"What's up?" LeMaine asked again. "Did I do something to offend you?"

"No, nothing like that. I want you to go on a mission for me—just you and the Hellhounds."

LeMaine's eyes popped. *You*....want to send....the Hellhounds....on a mission?"

"Isn't that what we came here for—to eliminate the Axichis threat to the rest of the solar system?"

"Yes, and we've done that," LeMaine replied. "We freed the Cezians and weakened the Axichis fleet."

"Not entirely. The Axichis still have a presence on this planet at the Nanov Outpost. Our mission now is to eliminate them completely. Once we do that, we'll have secured Ziea. The Axichis won't be able to establish themselves here again. That will be one Elian planet safe from the Axichis. We could even use Ziea as a jumping-off point to retake the system, now that we have these ships that can actually damage Axichis vessels."

"So....what do you want us to do?"

Buca split into a grin. He tried to suppress it, but he couldn't hide the light in his eyes. His whole countenance changed in a flash.

He lowered his voice to a subtle whisper. "You snuck up on the outpost last time. You got closer to it than anyone else could. I want you to do the same thing now. I want you to pull the same trick on them that we pulled by coming here to Nulia. I want you to weaken them from the inside. Neither the battalion nor the Cezians can strike them from the outside without putting the colonists in danger. That's why we need you. We need you to go inside and take out the Axichis without any colonists getting hurt."

LeMaine turned away to pace the room. Infiltrating the Nanov compound had been easy enough last time, but that had been the Hellhounds against just a bunch of civilian colonists. The Axichis would be a whole lot tougher.

LeMaine didn't point out that Buca didn't have the authority to send the Hellhounds on any mission. By rights, LeMaine should be using the Nulia Compound's transmission array to contact Command to receive the Hellhounds' next orders.

LeMaine had only delayed doing that until after the treaty negotiations wrapped up. Everyone insisted that he be present—Heaven only knew why.

Maybe the Maczhi and the Cezians wanted an Elian witness in case anyone contested the treaty later. He couldn't think of any other reason. Now Buca came out with this idea.

"What is it you want me to do, exactly?" LeMaine asked.

"I want you to get inside the outpost and find out what the Axichis are doing to the colonists. The Axichis must be coercing the colonists into sheltering them against attack. Then I want you to eliminate every single Axichis in there down to the last man. Don't leave even one alive."

LeMaine stopped pacing to study him. "You really are the best leader these people could possibly ask for."

"Well?" Buca asked. "Will you do it?"

LeMaine had to laugh. "Yeah. I'll do it."

Buca burst into another grin, and this time, he didn't try to stop himself from beaming in delight. "Wonderful."

"I wish you were coming with us," LeMaine remarked.

"I wish that, too, but I won't be going on any more Hellhound missions. I'm not a part of the squad anymore."

"Have you told the others yet?" LeMaine asked.

Buca locked dead on LeMaine's eyes. "Yes, I have. I apologize for not doing it in front of you. I wanted it to be just between us."

"I understand. I wish...." LeMaine broke off. He couldn't say the rest.

Buca took a step forward. "Thank you, Captain. Thank you for believing in me. You're the one who made this possible for me."

"Not at all," LeMaine insisted. "Do you remember what you said to me that first night? All of this would have happened the same way if you had never left Ziea. You would be in charge of the Maczhi battalion now and you would be negotiating peace with the Cezians. You did this. You did it all."

Buca couldn't hold his gaze, and the next second, they both stepped forward and put their arms around each other.

LeMaine hugged him once, tightly, and then they both stepped back. "I'll go tell the Hellhounds," LeMaine finished. "We'll start formulating a plan and you can tell us the time and day."

Buca nodded. "Thank you, Captain."

LeMaine stepped back, and on pure impulse, he snapped a salute. "Yes, Sir."

Buca returned the salute and LeMaine left the room before either of them had a chance to say anything else. That was the most fitting tribute LeMaine could give this man. LeMaine had rarely met a more competent leader anywhere.

He went back to the common room and walked in to find O'Hara standing on one hand. He balanced himself there as best he could and kept his mouth open while Kellogg, who sat on a chair ten feet away, threw pieces of a ration bar at O'Hara's face and tried to land them in O'Hara's mouth.

The other Hellhounds stood around watching and laughing.

"Throw it a little lower and see if you can get it up his nose," Nunn called.

"Throw it harder and see if you can knock him over," Peterman added.

Kellogg started throwing the pieces lower. He lobbed them in an arc trying to lodge one of them in O'Hara's nostrils. O'Hara started laughing and wobbled dangerously before he corrected his balance.

LeMaine stopped on the threshold, propped his elbow against the door frame, and watched them. They'd been clowning around and playing the fools for years. He'd gotten so used to it that it had just become a normal part of his daily life.

Everything had changed when Buca came into their lives. He had never joined in their play. He always sat off to one side. If they got lucky, he smiled at their foolishness. Other than that, he never gave any sign that he appreciated it or even understood it.

Now he was gone and the whole magic of the squad's irrepressible personality seemed to have dimmed. The Hellhounds didn't act like they knew he was gone and that he was never coming back. They acted as lively and carefree as ever.

The room didn't feel the same without him in it, though. Nothing felt the same. He wouldn't be coming back—not ever.

LeMaine couldn't feel anything but happiness for Buca that he'd finally found his place with his own people. It was himself that LeMaine felt sad for—himself and the Hellhounds. They had lost a good man—one of the best.

The loss stabbed LeMaine in the guts almost as if the squad had lost Buca in combat. LeMaine should have been glad that he didn't lose Buca in combat and he was. He just ached at the thought that Buca wasn't part of the squad anymore.

At last, inevitably, Monk noticed LeMaine standing there. "What's the word, Captain?"

The distraction made O'Hara look over and he fell to the floor, but none of the others saw. "Something's up, isn't it?" Peterman asked. "I recognize that look."

"Yeah," Nunn replied. "That's your we're-going-on-a-mission look."

LeMaine tried to shrug it off, but he could never hide anything from these people. "You're right. We're going back to the Nanov Outpost."

Chapter 16

The Hellhounds stopped under some trees and gathered around LeMaine. None of them wore fatigues or carried any carbines.

They wore the same ragged, torn, hand-patched clothing they'd seen the original colonists wearing when the Hellhounds "liberated" the Nanov array from Nelson Macon's rule the last time.

Each Hellhound carried small, sharp knives concealed in his or her clothes, but that was all. They wouldn't be taking any firearms on this mission.

Lemon got busy pulling her disguise suit over her head, but once she zipped it up, she took the appearance of another ragged colonist.

"My stylist is going to have a fit when he finds out I actually went out in public looking like this," O'Hara quipped.

"Don't worry, Victoria," Heckler growled. "No one will be around to post the pictures on the social network."

"It could still damage my reputation," O'Hara went on in a high-pitched, fake complaining whine. "It might affect my next promotional opportunity."

"You'll just have to slum it with the rest of us," Nunn told him. "Bad luck, babe."

O'Hara shrugged and went back to adjusting his pack. "Oh well. I guess I was always gonna do that anyway."

LeMaine happened to glance up right at that moment and spotted a ration bar in O'Hara's pack. "Hold it right there, Sergeant. What the hell are you doing with this?"

"What do you mean?" O'Hara asked. "I brought it in case I get hungry."

"*In case* you get hungry?" Kellogg countered. "When are you not hungry?"

"Exactly my point," O'Hara gave LeMaine a pleading look. "What was I supposed to do—starve to death?"

"You weren't about to starve to death between the Nulia Compound and here," LeMaine told him. "I told you not to bring anything with Military markings. The wrapper would give you away. Lose the bar, son."

"But...." O'Hara's eyebrows rose in the middle and his lip quivered in a pathetic display of despair. "But....I might get hungry inside the outpost."

"You are such a wuss, O'Hara," Monk rumbled. "Give me that!"

He tried to snatch the bar away, but O'Hara shrieked and clutched the bar to his chest. "No!! You can't!! It's my last remaining tie to sanity!"

The others laughed. "Fine, Sergeant," LeMaine told him. "Just eat it now and stash the wrapper somewhere the Axichis won't find it."

O'Hara instantly relaxed and grinned to himself as happily as ever while he unwrapped the bar and stuffed it into his mouth.

"How long do you think that will shut him up?" Monk asked.

"Probably only as long as it takes for him to finish chewing it," Kellogg replied.

O'Hara only grinned at them and tucked the wrapper under a rock.

"Are you kids finished messing around?" LeMaine asked. "Can we get on with the mission now?"

"Ready when you are, Sir," O'Hara replied.

"Are you sure?" LeMaine asked. "Are you absolutely, positively certain you don't need to freshen up your hair and trim your nails before we go? I wouldn't want the Axichis to get the wrong idea."

Some of the other Hellhounds snickered until Peterman said, "On the other hand, you might *want* them to get the wrong idea. Come on, Sergeant. You can tell us the truth. You've been aching for a little Axichis attention, haven't you?"

The others guffawed in O'Hara's face. "Burn!!" Nunn yelled. "This year's burn award goes to Lieutenant Peterman! Phew! That was a hard one, Lieutenant."

Peterman chuckled. "I'm glad I could entertain you, Corporal. Let's move it out."

LeMaine headed down the hill and the Hellhounds fell in line behind him. They only made it as far as the tree line before they all pulled scarves and hoods over their faces to conceal themselves. LeMaine didn't want any of the real colonists to recognize the Hellhounds—not until after the squad got inside the outpost.

They hiked for another hour across open country. LeMaine sidled up to O'Hara's side. "Can you see sentries on the walls?"

"Oh, yeah!" O'Hara murmured. "And they can see us, too."

"Are they human or Axichis?" LeMaine asked.

"Human.....and are they ever in a tizzy about us coming up on them. This should be interesting."

"Keep cool," LeMaine murmured back.

The squad came within a hundred yards of the main gate and LeMaine lifted his arms to show his hands. All the Hellhounds copied him and the sentries raised their carbines to hold the squad at gunpoint as they crossed the last stretch of grass.

The squad halted thirty yards from the gate. "State your business!" one of the sentries yelled down.

"We're here to trade!" LeMaine pivoted to the side and pointed to his pack. "We brought black market goods from the inner planets."

"Where did you get them?" the same man called down.

"We traded with the Maczhi over the hill over there!" LeMaine told him.

"You're lying! The Maczhi don't trade with anyone."

"I'm not talking about the Maczhi in the camps," LeMaine explained. "There's another group living wild in the mountains......over there."

He turned around and pointed to the mountains where the Maczhi battalion had built their camp.

The sentries frowned at each other and shook their heads. They'd never even heard of the Maczhi battalion.

LeMaine saw his chance. "We have stolen Sozur spices and antibiotics and painkillers—Zanoril, Travofen, and Mycovene—all guaranteed purity from the Elian Military stores."

That definitely caused a response. The sentries held a rapid, whispered conversation and then five of them jumped down to open the gate.

"Approach the gate with your hands up!" the first sentry ordered.

All the Hellhounds raised their hands higher. "We're in," LeMaine murmured.

They stopped at the gate where the same five colonists came out aiming their guns at the Hellhounds. "Take your hoods off," one of them ordered. "Show your faces."

LeMaine made a quick check, but he didn't recognize any of these men. He pulled his hood off and the rest of the squad followed his lead. None of the sentries recognized the Hellhounds, either.

The sentries escorted the squad inside under guard and the gate slammed shut behind LeMaine's back. He started to lower his hands, but one of the colonists jabbed a carbine barrel into his back. "Keep 'em up!"

LeMaine stood still while more colonists surrounded the squad, yanked their packs off, and carried them away. That was all part of the ruse. The Hellhounds didn't need anything in those packs to complete their mission.

LeMaine cast a critical eye around the outpost while he waited for the colonists to make up their minds about what to do with the squad. The colonists had rebuilt the outpost after the Hellhounds destroyed most of it in the last attack.

All the buildings and the outer wall sections that Nunn had blown up had been reconstructed. The place looked quite livable compared to what it had been like when the Hellhounds first arrived on this planet.

Human colonists went about their daily lives from one building to another. LeMaine didn't see a single Axichis anywhere. The whole place bustled with domesticity. Plenty of women hung laundry in the sunshine and children ran and played in the streets.

"Where are they?" Peterman murmured in LeMaine's ear.

"They must be...." LeMaine began, but at that moment, some different armed colonists came over, poked the Hellhounds with their rifles again, and shoved them away. "Get moving," one man growled.

"Don't think you're gonna take our goods without paying for them," LeMaine fired back. "This is robbery. You could get the Elian Military sent out here to dissolve your colony and throw you all in prison."

"Shut up!" the same guy barked and gave LeMaine another shove.

The colonists pushed the squad down a street, around a corner, and into a building. It was just a normal house, but it didn't have any furniture or other comforts. It appeared to be abandoned.

"Stay here and don't make trouble," the guy snapped, pulled the door shut, and locked it from the outside.

"Is that what passes for hospitality around here?" Heckler growled. "I want a refund."

"They're jumpy because the Axichis are threatening them," Peterman explained.

"How do we find the Axichis?" Nunn asked.

"Lemon can find them. Suit up, Sergeant. Find out where the Axichis are, but don't do any....."

LeMaine didn't finish his sentence before three men burst into the room. How they burst into the room without unlocking the door first, LeMaine couldn't figure out.

They shut the door just as fast and the first one rushed LeMaine. "Captain! You're the Special Forces squad who attacked the outpost last time, aren't you?" The guy's eyes darted around the group. "I recognize you."

"I don't recognize you," LeMaine replied. "What can I do for you?"

"You have to help us!" the guy breathed. "The Axichis are holding us all hostage. They say they'll kill everyone in the outpost if we don't cooperate."

LeMaine relaxed. "That's what we're here for. Where are the Axichis hiding?"

"They're hiding in the underground bunker that houses the array. They're using the array to coordinate the rest of the Axichis assault on Elia."

"That's perfect," Lemon muttered. "We can definitely jump them there."

"How many of them are there?" LeMaine asked the colonists.

The guy shrugged. "I don't know. Maybe a hundred or more."

"How can so many of them fit down there?" Kellogg asked. "There was barely enough room in there for us and the array."

The guy shook his head. "There's a whole complex of rooms and tunnels down there. It was designed to protect the government in case of planetary invasion."

Peterman snorted. "Interesting that our enemies would use it for exactly that."

"We can't go against that many Axichis in a confined space—not by ourselves." LeMaine turned back to the colonists. "We're gonna need your help with this."

The guy jumped and cast a terrified glance behind him at his companions. "We can't do anything! We're noncombatants. You guys are the Special Forces operatives here."

"You have armed men out there on the walls and there are only nine of us. Pull all your people back, get them organized, and tell them to get ready to go down into the tunnels."

"But....." the guy protested. "If we pull them off the walls, the outpost will be unprotected."

"The enemy is already inside the walls," Kellogg pointed out. "I think you have bigger problems than someone coming in from outside."

"This is the only way to get rid of the Axichis," LeMaine finished. "Go get your people. Tell them this is their chance to really do something to defend their homes and families. Tell them that, as soon as we get rid of the Axichis, Ziea will be secured and none of you will have to worry about anyone threatening you anymore. Tell them this is what they signed up for when they took up weapons to defend the outpost. Now go on. Come back and tell me when everyone is ready."

The colonists left.

"This should be interesting," Heckler growled.

"How prepared do you think the Axichis will be against an invasion from the colonists?"

"I don't know, but we better be the ones who are prepared in case they're much more prepared than we think. We need to be ready for the Axichis to be waiting down there for us with all their guns pointed at the door."

"So how do we do that?" Nunn asked.

"By sneaking in another way where they won't see us coming." LeMaine squatted down and traced his finger through the dust on the floor. "Do you remember how the array was set up last time? There must be a control somewhere that raises the array through the roof. The Axichis wouldn't be able to use it from underground. They must raise it when they want to transmit to the rest of the Axichis fleet."

"The controls were underground," Polasek replied. "They were in the bunker along with the array."

"Exactly. That's where our good buddy Lemon comes in. Sergeant, you'll suit up and go downstairs to visit our Axichis friends. We'll synchronize our movements so you'll raise the array. Once the array rises out of the bunker, Nunn will drop explosives down inside it. That will make sure the array doesn't get damaged in the firefight."

"The firefight that's bound to start after that," Kellogg pointed out.

Nunn rubbed her hands with glee. "He he he. I love me a good explosion."

"You can lay it on extra thick and give the Axichis a care package they'll never forget," LeMaine told her. "You can blow the whole housing for all I care as long as you don't hit the array."

She kept grinning like a maniac as she squatted down, tore open her pack, and started priming all her Plaostine blocks.

"What about the rest of us, Sir?" Monk asked. "Are we going in through the roof?"

"We'll have the colonists with us, so we'll send half our force through the roof and half through the front door—assuming the colonists don't know another way in. We'll just count on overwhelming the remaining Axichis with numbers. We'll assume they'll be facing the door if they're prepared for an attack at all. The explosion will draw their attention to the roof. They'll be distracted and confused. It will make them perfect targets."

"So we just have to sit around and wait until then?" O'Hara asked. "Why do Nunn and Lemon get all the fun?"

Heckler clapped him on the shoulder. "It's like you said, champ. You should have been a master of disguise. Then you'd be the first man through the door on all our missions."

"You just wouldn't be able to flash the enemy your winning smile," Polasek pointed out. "No one would ever know you were there."

"I couldn't stand that," O'Hara replied. "I'd rather shoot people."

"Stick with what you're good at, Sergeant," LeMaine told him.

Just then, the same three colonists came back. "Everyone's ready," the first guy told LeMaine.

"We need to know if there are any other entrances to the underground complex the Axichis are hiding in," LeMaine told him. "And anything else you can tell us about the complex."

"There are two other entrances, but I don't think the Axichis know about them. The other entrances are in a part of the complex no one has used in years. They're on the other side of the outpost and we couldn't hear the Axichis down there."

"What do you mean you couldn't hear them?" Peterman asked.

"We could hear them through the floor.....in certain parts of the complex—not all of it," a different man chimed in. "It wasn't loud, but you could definitely hear voices."

"It was spooky, the third man added.

"We couldn't hear anything over here, though," the first man finished. "There are families living over there and the floor is thinner there than it is here. We would know if the Axichis were down there."

"The more entrances, the better," Heckler growled.

"Exactly," LeMaine replied. "I want you to divide your forces into four. Get one out on the main courtyard, one to assault the bunker's main entrance, and the other two groups on the other two entrances. You know better than I do where they are."

"How will we know when to go in?" the guy asked.

"Oh, you'll know," Nunn told him. "You'll definitely know."

"Just make sure you don't cave in the tunnels," Kellogg told her.

"You can cave in as much as you want around the array," LeMaine told her. "Just leave the other parts of the complex intact."

"Aw, Sir!" she whined and then laughed at her own joke.

LeMaine pushed the colonists toward the door. "Go get your people in position. Get out of here, Lemon. The whole operation depends on you."

"When you do you want me to raise the array?" she asked.

LeMaine lifted his wrist to check his remote and then remembered that he wasn't wearing it. "We'll just have to estimate it. Give it ten minutes. That should be enough time for you to get through the Axichis and locate the controls."

She nodded, straightened her disguise, and then walked out the door. The colonists didn't bother to keep it locked now. She vanished outside.

"How's it coming, Nunn?" LeMaine asked. "Are you going to be ready in time?"

"I was born ready," she replied.

"All right. Let's go." LeMaine held the door open for the others to leave the house. They slipped through the dusty streets and into the courtyard where all the colonists were getting organized for the assault.

"Polasek and Peterman, you take two groups each to the spare entrances. Kellogg, you can take the main entrance. The rest of you come with me. We'll go through the roof as soon as Nunn blows it."

Chapter 17

LeMaine stopped in the street near where the Nanov array rose from its basement housing. He cast a flinty glance around the outpost and still didn't see any Axichis.

They didn't seem to waste their manpower guarding the colonists to make sure they didn't try something or get the jump on their Axichis intruders.

The Axichis relied on fear and intimidation to keep the Colonists in line. It had been working just fine up until today.

Nunn made some final adjustments to her Plaostine blocks. She wouldn't stop smirking like a kid in a candy store.

LeMaine checked the sun's position. He couldn't tell how much time had passed, but it must be getting close to the time when Lemon would raise the array.

He and the Hellhounds flattened themselves to a wall counting down the seconds. LeMaine really wished he had his remote. He hated waiting.

The other Hellhounds shuffled their feet and fidgeted, too. They were blind and at the mercy of Lemon's success. It might take her longer than expected to get through the Axichis, find the controls, and then raise the array.

The colonists squirmed, too. "What are we waiting for?" one of the men nearest LeMaine asked.

"Just a little longer," he murmured back.

At that moment, a deep boom shook the pavement beneath LeMaine's feet. "Stand by!" he called to the men with him.

The sound got louder and then a tremendous crack split the air. Two sections of concrete slab in the middle of the street split apart and the Nanov array started to rise from its housing.

"Go, Nunn!" LeMaine shoved her forward.

She darted into the street, sprang onto one of the slabs, and dropped her whole backpack down the hole. She had to spring back out of the way as the array rose past her face and loomed higher and higher into the air.

She raced back to the Hellhounds' position and the array rose to its full height including the pedestal on which it sat.

It thumped into place and then a catastrophic ka-boom rocked the whole outpost. Smoke, dust, debris, and fire erupted out of the opening, surrounded the array, and completely cut off visibility for a minute.

"Go!" LeMaine yelled to everyone. "Get down there and kill any Axichis you can find."

The Hellhounds charged forward with the colonists right behind them. Fate threw them a bone and a gust of wind blew through the outpost right at that moment. It cleared enough dust and smoke from around the array that the defenders could see where they were going.

LeMaine scrambled over the broken edge of the bunker. The explosion had completely destroyed the pedestal and the array slumped to one side, but the dish was still intact.

The Hellhounds clambered into the hole, but the colonists got there first. The operation galvanized their spirits and many yelled and cheered as they sprang down into the bunker searching for their enemies.

They found thirty Axichis dead in the room where the array usually rested when no one was using it. The colonists raced away into the tunnels and LeMaine heard gunshots and people yelling down there.

He followed the sound and found the colonists enjoying themselves in a bloodbath of fury killing every Axichis they could lay their hands on. The colonists left not one single Axichis for the Hellhounds to deal with.

"This is a pretty good day's work," O'Hara remarked. "We took the outpost without even getting our hands dirty."

The colonists came back beaming and clapping each other on their backs. The guy LeMaine had been talking to approached the Hellhounds with blood splattered all over his face. "Well, Captain? It's all clear. There aren't any Axichis left."

"Well done," LeMaine replied. "You people deserve to celebrate tonight."

The guy burst into a huge, delighted grin and turned to those nearest him when the sound of engines made LeMaine freeze. He knew that sound. It was the sound of incoming Axichis fighter craft.

He glanced up just as four fighter craft wheeled over the array. Their lasers flickered and danced in the air and then, without warning, they hit the array.

The array exploded in a hellish boom that resounded through the bedrock underneath the outpost. The Hellhounds and the colonists all ducked as the array detonated in a massive shockwave.

Rock, concrete, and rubble smashed through the opening and Lemon hollered from out of sight followed by several screams from the colonists.

LeMaine hunkered for cover under his arms. As soon as the noise died, He straightened up only to hear another shout coming from his right. "The tunnels! Get out of the tunnels! It's caving in!"

"Everybody outside!" LeMaine ordered and herded everyone toward the door. It led to the stairs rising to the surface.

The colonists rushed for the only escape, now that the destroyed array blocked the opening to the courtyard. The stampede barricaded the exit and no one could move for a minute.

More screams echoed from the tunnels and then that same shriek of engine noise split the din. Axichis fighter craft tumbled and somersaulted over each other bombarding the outpost from all sides.

LeMaine kept yelling, "Go! Get out of here!" but half the colonists surged backward trying to stay under cover.

At last, the horde succeeded in forcing those in front out onto the streets just as the Axichis came hurtling in for another pass. Lasers blasted the outpost's outer walls and tore up streets getting closer to the courtyard where all the colonists stood exposed.

LeMaine froze trying to make up his mind. He couldn't push these people out into the open. They would run into the path of those lasers. He couldn't tell them to go back inside, either. They would fall either way.

He didn't even have a rifle to aim at these fighters—as if that would do any good.

One of the colonists whimpered in terrified despair at his side. He had to do something to save these people.

At that moment, another squadron of Axichis fighters dropped out of the sky coming in impossibly fast. They covered the miles in seconds and unleashed a hellish barrage of lasers on the attackers. Two enemy fighter craft exploded.

The others rounded on the incoming craft and a bloody air battle broke out overhead.

LeMaine spun around and accosted the first man he could grab. "Get your people under cover! Hurry! Get everyone off the streets and under whatever cover you can find! Go!"

He pushed people away and hustled through the crowd delivering the same message. The colonists didn't need any encouragement.

They scattered, vanished into houses and buildings, and cleared the outpost in seconds.

LeMaine should have gotten his squad under cover, too, but he couldn't resist the temptation to watch the Maczhi battalion staking their claim on this planet. They'd earned the right to control the skies and the ground.

They flew rings around the Axichis peppering the Axichis with return laser fire. The Axichis tried to fight back and even sent in another fifteen fighters, but the Maczhi only matched them.

Twenty more fighters dropped out of orbit and corkscrewed around the Axichis blowing up one fighter after another. The battle drifted toward the mountains, but the Maczhi battalion ended it soon enough. They overpowered the Axichis with numbers and the Maczhi definitely had ferocity and daring on their side.

LeMaine stayed where he was as the battalion soared past the outpost, turned a few rotations over the surrounding countryside, and then launched back into orbit. No one was coming near this planet without their say-so.

The skies felt lonely without them. He was really started to like these people. He should go inside and deal with the colonists, but he didn't want to tear himself away.

Just then, the same three colonists hustled up to him. The first man glanced at the skies and all around at the wrecked outpost. "What happened? Where are they? Are they coming back?"

"The Axichis won't come back," LeMaine replied. "The Maczhi battalion will protect you."

"The.....what?"

"That was their air force. The Maczhi battalion has secured the planet. They'll make sure the Axichis don't bother you again." LeMaine turned to face him and had to grin when he saw the stunned look on the guy's face. "You should negotiate a pact of friendship with the Maczhi. They're good people and they have the firepower to defend this planet. You'll all be better off working together as neighbors and friends."

"But....the Maczhi are weak. They don't even own guns."

"They do now. Let's go see about....."

LeMaine started to turn away when he heard more Axichis engine noise—louder this time. He and the colonists gazed out at the skies as a giant Axichis warship floated out of the clouds. Fighter craft surrounded it.

"Oh, no!" the guy breathed. "This is terrible!"

"Not so fast," LeMaine told him. "This one belongs to the Maczhi. They wouldn't let it through without attacking it."

The warship set down and a whole crowd of Maczhi disembarked. LeMaine split into another grin when he saw Buca and Zonoth leading them.

LeMaine, the Hellhounds, and several colonists strode out to meet them. Buca smiled back at LeMaine as they came together. "You did it," Buca exclaimed. "I knew you would. Are all the Axichis neutralized?"

"Yeah, they're all gone. We tried to save the array, but the Axichis fighters hit it."

"That's good," Buca replied. "We would have destroyed it if they didn't beat us to it. The Axichis would have tried to come back here and recapture it. They'll ignore Ziea from now on."

"I don't think they'll be able to do that," LeMaine returned and Buca laughed. He looked much happier, now that he'd succeeded in securing Ziea from its enemies.

LeMaine turned to the man at his side. "This is the man we've been dealing with since we got here." LeMaine addressed the colonist who'd first approached him. "Who's in charge of this colony? Do you have a leader since Macon got arrested?"

"We have our council of twelve...." He waved at the men with him. "We make the decisions in consultation with the rest of the population. We don't have any one leader. After Macon....we thought it might work better not to have one man in charge."

"That's fine," Buca replied. "Keep doing what you're doing, but the Maczhi battalion and the Cezian council will want to begin formal diplomatic relations with you as soon as you get this outpost cleaned up."

"You....." The guy blinked at Buca. *"You're* in charge of all this?"

Buca gave him a hard look that definitely made the guy cringe. "I'm in charge of the Maczhi battalion. I hope we won't hear any of that alien scum nonsense we had to deal with when Macon was in charge."

"No...of course not," the guy stammered.

"I've just finalized a mutual assistance pact of friendship with the Cezians and I plan to do the same thing with you," Buca went on. "We're all finished being enemies on this planet. We're neighbors and we're all in the same position when it comes to the Elian community of planets and the Axichis invasion. Any of us working against the others will put us all in danger. I'm sure you agree."

The guy gulped. "Um.....of course."

"Good." Buca cast another sharp look at the wreckage around him. "Get your people to start rebuilding this outpost. As soon as the war ends, we'll contact the Elian Military Command about rebuilding the array. Your colony is a crucial part of Ziea. We want to make you strong—as strong as we are. We want you pulling with us, not against us. Do you understand?"

The guy nodded in stupid amazement and Buca turned back to LeMaine. "Bring your squad on board my warship, Captain. I want you to come back to Nulia with me."

"Yes, Sir," LeMaine replied.

Buca walked away with his entourage of badass Maczhi. The colonist guy crumpled as soon as Buca got out of earshot. "Jesus! Who is that guy?"

"His name is Buca," LeMaine replied. "He's the new leader of the Maczhi battalion and it sure as hell looks like he's taking no prisoners in this war."

The guy laughed nervously. "He's the biggest badass of them all. You better go with him. You don't want to make that guy mad."

LeMaine chuckled. "You're right. I don't. Let's load up, Hellhounds. We're out of here."

Chapter 18

LeMaine stood back and waited while Buca went down the line of Hellhounds hugging each of them and thanking them for all they'd done for him. LeMaine dreaded the moment when Buca got to him.

The rest of Buca's staff from the Maczhi battalion stood around watching. They never left him these days. They'd formed a bodyguard of the most powerful Maczhi in the whole battalion. They surrounded Buca wherever he went and advised him on everything happening all over Ziea.

He'd been working around the clock with the new air force, the Cezians, and now the colonists' ruling council. The three communities coordinated all their resources to make sure the Axichis never came back to Ziea, but Buca remained at the very epicenter of the whole defense operation. Everyone listened to him and they deferred all decisions to his judgment.

The colonists had been more than happy to come under Buca's authority even though no one ever called it that. He strictly maintained the stance that the Maczhi, the Cezians, and the human colonists were all equals. He never tolerated anyone saying anything else.

It didn't work out that way in practice, though. If he said something or made a suggestion, they all went along with it. No one ever questioned his judgment, his dedication, or his commitment to bringing all three species together in one planetary community for their mutual benefit.

The Maczhi battalion had sent delegations back to the camps to recruit more Maczhi into the battalion. Buca had assigned an entire squad of his best fighters just for this purpose.

It didn't take much to convince the young Maczhi to abandon the camps. The Maczhi battalion offered the most astonishing proof of how much better off their lives could be if they only embraced their old traditions.

These new Maczhi still weren't healthy enough to join the battalion's many operations. They had to learn the battalion's ways, regain their strength, and then go through
extensive training, but the battalion kept growing with every passing day. It kept getting
stronger.

Buca had been talking to his men about raiding nearby planets and executing strategic
strikes on the Axichis outside of Ziea. He wanted to steal more spacecraft, weapons, and
other resources to further weaken the Axichis.

His other genius plan was to lure the Axichis into a battle somewhere, not on Ziea but
somewhere else in the outer planets. Buca wanted to engage the Axichis in a front away
from the rest of the war to tie up their resources and distract them from the Elian and
Imoliv fleets.

LeMaine really, really wished he could stick around and watch all of Buca's plans
unfold. The Maczhi were turning into a force to be reckoned with. This battalion might
be the turning point in the whole war. The Maczhi could be the ones who turned the tide
and finally gave Elia a chance to throw the Axichis out of the system.

LeMaine wouldn't be sticking around to see any of that, much as he would have liked
to. The Maczhi battalion's first mission had been a sortie to Zukion. They'd raided an
abandoned Elian position where they retrieved an abandoned Hunter-class vessel to take
the Hellhounds back to the Military.

The ship waited a dozen yards away, all ready to take the Hellhounds away from Ziea.
Once that happened, LeMaine wouldn't find out what happened here. He might never
hear about the Maczhi's exploits until after the war ended.

He hated walking away from good people. He wanted to stay and fight side by side
with them. He wanted to know that they had his back just as he had theirs. That wouldn't
happen now. Life seemed poorer without them.

Buca stopped in front of Peterman and Polasek, hugged them, and talked to them in
low tones. LeMaine couldn't hear what they were saying and he didn't want to. He didn't
want Buca to come toward him. LeMaine didn't want to say goodbye to this man.

LeMaine couldn't forestall the inevitable, though. Buca broke away from Polasek, but
when Buca turned to face LeMaine, Buca stopped again.

They regarded each other for a long moment. LeMaine hardly recognized Buca anymore. He had completely transformed from the quiet, retiring loner he was when he first
met the Hellhounds.

LeMaine didn't know the moment when they both stepped forward at the same time and clasped each other in a deep, quick hug.

They both stepped back at the same instant. Buca's eyes shone in ways LeMaine had never seen before. Buca would keep growing and changing in LeMaine's absence.

Buca had discovered a part of himself here that LeMaine never could have given him. The Hellhounds couldn't have given it to him, but they made it possible for him to discover it within himself.

LeMaine gripped Buca's shoulder one last time. "Let me know if you ever need a job."

Buca laughed. He laughed much more often now, especially when he was with the rest of the battalion. "You'll be the first person I call."

LeMaine tore himself away. "Mount up, Hellhounds."

They went to their new ship. Her name was, *Bombardier*.

The Hellhounds loaded into their cannon placements right away. LeMaine didn't want to get caught with his pants down, not when so many Axichis still buzzed around the solar system. The squad would have to fight their way back to Elia.

Monk and LeMaine went up to the cockpit. Monk fired up the engines and the Hellhounds' voices shot from placement to placement in the back, but LeMaine barely heard them.

Buca, Zonoth, Guza, and the other Maczhi stood on the planes outside the Nulia compound. The Maczhi conducted all their business with the Cezians and the colonists here, so Buca spent a lot of time down here with his closest associates.

The battalion also kept their ships here when they were on the ground. The battalion didn't let anyone come up to their camp in the mountains. They kept that strictly for themselves.

Buca raised his hand and LeMaine waved back as Monk lifted off. LeMaine thanked the stars that someone else was flying the ship. He wouldn't have been able to.

The *Bombardier* soared into the atmosphere. The battalion had enough ships now to divide their air force into rotations. One third of the air force guarded the planet while another third rested and the other remained in readiness in case they were needed.

The battalion didn't need any regular Military intervention or guidance on how to conduct their defense. They took to it naturally. It was in their blood. LeMaine pitied any attacker who messed with Ziea after this.

He also foresaw the day when the regular Elian Military would have to step up and negotiate with the Maczhi battalion about who exactly was going to defend Ziea. If things kept going this way, Ziea might be the only planet in the whole system with its own standing militia.

Ziea would also have more political autonomy than any other Elian planet. LeMaine didn't see any way the Maczhi, the Cezians, and their colonists neighbors would ever give up their self-governance after this. The Elian Assembly would be foolish to even suggest that these people should do anything other than run their planet their own way.

Monk brought LeMaine back to his senses by bumping his elbow. LeMaine glanced over and Monk pointed at the dashboard. "They're hailing us. They're calling us to fall in formation with them."

LeMaine checked the controls. The battalion air force had moved into a protective stance around the *Bombardier*.

A squadron of Axichis hovered near Zukion. The *Bombardier* would have to get past them to make it back to the rest of the Elian line.

"Fall in formation with us, *Bombardier*," a male Maczhi voice came through the communications system. "We'll escort you out."

"Don't leave the planet undefended," LeMaine replied. "This could be a ruse to draw you away from Ziea."

"We'll take you as far as Zukion," the Maczhi pilot agreed. "After that, you're on your own."

LeMaine had to laugh. "You got it. Stand strong, boys."

"Always," the pilot replied and signed off.

LeMaine motioned to Monk. "Fall in. Lock and load, Hellhounds. We're flying into the weeds."

"Bring it," Heckler growled.

"Hey!" Nunn exclaimed. "Buca isn't here anymore. You know what that means."

"The scoreboard is clear," Polasek replied. "You slouches better oil up your trigger fingers and get ready for an ass-whooping."

"You're on, Polasek," O'Hara called back. "How many bogeys do we have, Sir?"

"Only ten of them in view, but more could be hiding in the bushes. Here we go!"

The Maczhi hit their throttles, punched it out of orbit, and Monk slammed his engines into high gear. He had to fly at top speed just to stay in formation with the Maczhi.

The Maczhi raced ahead and engaged with the Axichis right away. Lasers flashed in all directions with the *Bombardier* punching through the middle.

The Maczhi flew rings around the ship and the Hellhounds opened up. The battalion had modified the *Bombardier* so the cannons could pick out the pilot's life signs on any Axichis fighter craft. The battalion had converted their entire fleet to target Axichis pilots and avoid pilots of any other species.

It worked mind-blowingly well. The Hellhounds could target the fighters that were actually being flown by Axichis pilots. The Hellhounds didn't have to worry about hitting anyone from the battalion or getting hit by them.

LeMaine grabbed the cockpit cannon and wheeled to his left hammering the Axichis flying way too close to the *Bombardier*. "We're coming up on Halira! Maczhi battalion—fall back to Ziea! Defend that planet!"

"What about you?" the same pilot asked.

"Holding Ziea is more important. You've done enough for us. We'll take it from here, son."

"Yes, Sir," the pilot replied. "Fly safely."

"You, too, son. You boys are some of the finest pilots I've ever seen. Hit it, Monk!"

Monk slammed the throttle down and sprinted past Halira making for the system's inner ring. The Elian and Imoliv fleets still stood guard around Elia. The planet sure did look a long way off from here.

The Axichis split their formation. Half of them followed the *Bombardier*. The others hounded the Maczhi back toward Ziea, but the Axichis had to break off when the rest of the battalion launched to drive them off.

That left the Axichis free and clear to come after the Hellhounds instead. The Axichis dogged the ship all the way and pounded it with lasers.

The *Bombardier's* cannons didn't do any damage to the Axichis, though. Elian cannons were no good against the Axichis—not like the battalion's lasers. LeMaine didn't hear the Hellhounds racking up even one Axichis fighter kill.

"Keep going!" LeMaine yelled to Monk. "Don't make it pretty. Just go!"

"I'm going!" Monk roared, but the Axichis didn't want to let him go.

They kept dodging in front of him to cut him off. He had to bob and weave. Laser fire hammered the ship, especially from the front. Every strike jostled the ship off course.

"You cocksuckers!" Monk bellowed.

LeMaine did his best to shoot back. His brain didn't want to register that he couldn't kill these bastards.

The tone in the back was just turning murderous when the ship drew level with Zukion, the first planet in from Ziea. "We're almost home!" LeMaine yelled. "Don't stop! We can make it!"

Monk strained his arms pushing the throttle forward, but the ship couldn't fly any faster. He rounded Zukion burning headlong for Elia when, out of nowhere, five warships soared around Evilia, the next planet inward.

"You sons of bitches!" Monk whispered.

"Evade!" LeMaine hollered. "Pull it back! We have to get back to Ziea!"

It was already too late. The *Bombardier* was flying so fast that Monk couldn't adjust the course in time.

He flew straight into a hail of laser fire as all those warships opened up at the same time. The Axichis fighter craft fell back, unloaded on the *Bombardier* from behind, and drove the ship even closer to the warships.

LeMaine flinched as lasers enveloped the cockpit. Something smashed somewhere and yells echoed out of the cannon placements.

LeMaine opened his eyes to see Monk fighting the helm with both beefy arms. He wrestled it first right and then left trying any way and every way to divert the ship's course.

That last assault must have damaged the controls because the ship just kept hurtling forward at top speed.

"Pull out!" LeMaine yelled.

"I can't!" Monk bellowed back. "We got no helm and the throttle is pinned down. We can't stop!"

LeMaine opened his mouth to say something, but no sound came out. What could he say to that?

His stunned eyes darted to the front. The *Bombardier* was flying full blast straight into the side of one of those warships.

Chapter 19

L aser fire smashed into the *Bombardier's* tail and sent the ship spinning out of control. Monk jerked almost out of his seat trying to correct, but the helm didn't respond.

LeMaine slammed his cannon back to the front and pounded the Axichis warship in front of him, but the behemoth never budged. The cannons did no damage and the warship dwarfed the *Bombardier* by miles anyway.

"Get us out of here, Monk!" LeMaine roared over the noise of more shots striking the ship's hull.

"I'm doing everything I can, Sir! All cannons to the front! Target that ship with everything you got!"

The Hellhounds in the *Bombardier's* cannon placements responded instantly, swiveled their cannons to the front, and they all smashed into the warship. The impact jolted the *Bombardier* off its collision course, but not enough to avoid crashing and burning in a fiery ball of wreckage.

LeMaine glanced around and gulped. The *Bombardier* had made it halfway between Zukion and Evilia, two planets in the Elian system's inner ring. The Hellhounds had made it within spitting distance of their home planet, but they would never get there now.

More warships emerged from Evilia's shadow. Where did they all come from so fast?

Their appearance took the Elian Military Command by surprise, too. The fleet had been standing guard over Elia—for all the good it did. The Axichis invasion had reduced the Elian defense to little more than a ragtag handful of crippled ships.

The Imoliv defensive line stood off to one side guarding their border from Axichis invasion, too. The warship's appearance triggered an immediate response from the Imoliv and the two fleets rushed forward to meet the oncoming attack.

The warships remained in orbit over Evilia, but their intention couldn't be clearer. The Axichis wouldn't bring so many warships this close to Elia if the Axichis didn't mean business.

LeMaine scrambled to come up with some way to distract the warships away from Elia. The Axichis didn't need these five that were targeting him right now. They could flatten the *Bombardier* and they would still have plenty of ships left over to destroy Elia and wipe the Military off the map. LeMaine wouldn't be able to stop it—not with one little Hunter-class ship.

At that moment, a devastating smash of lasers struck the *Bombardier* from the starboard. The shot imploded the cockpit right next to LeMaine's shoulder and the ship spun out of control.

LeMaine hollered in pain as the hull buckled. Searing heat burned him through his uniform and then shattered glass and metal fragments stabbed him in the face. A shard went into his eye and he ducked for cover from the blow.

"Captain!!" Monk roared.

LeMaine dragged his head up just as another punishing strike hit the same spot. This one tore him out of his seat and hurled him on the floor between Monk's seat and his own.

"CAPTAIN!!" Monk bellowed.

"What's happening, Monk?!" Polasek's voice came from the back.

"Captain LeMaine is hit! We got a hull breach in the cockpit! We're depressurizing! I'm initiating emergency protocols and locking you all down in your cannon placements!"

"Can we land anywhere?" Polasek asked.

"We got no helm and the throttle is locked at maximum! I don't know how much longer I can...."

LeMaine drifted in and out listening to their voices. He tried everything to get up, but he couldn't even think with this shard in his eye. Everything felt so wrong.

Blistering pain tore his body apart. He felt himself losing consciousness and then a very different voice shattered his awareness.

"We got you covered, brother!" a male voice called. "We're coming for you!"

LeMaine struggled to place that voice. It didn't belong to anyone he knew in the Elian Military.

Then he remembered. It was Sindra, the Imoliv special operative the Hellhounds had met on Kathorpra.

Smashes and crashes slammed the *Bombardier* from one side to another. Monk growled down at LeMaine, "Hang tight, Sir. We're bringing you in."

He rested his hand on LeMaine's shoulder. The pain exploded his mind and he passed out. He couldn't even scream to tell Monk not to touch him.

He drifted back to consciousness still crumpled in the same position between the cockpit seats—or where the cockpit seats would have been if his own seat had still been there.

Kellogg murmured in LeMaine's ear. "Easy, Captain. We're gonna get you out of here."

LeMaine tried to tell Kellogg that he couldn't move to take it easy or do anything else, but his brain wouldn't connect to his voice.

Hands touched him all over and the pain drove him insane, but he couldn't move to do anything about that, either.

They picked him up, moved him out of the cockpit, and the next time he opened his good eye, he looked up at Kellogg, Monk, Polasek, and Sindra all bending over him.

LeMaine couldn't figure out why Sindra was here. Nothing made sense.

LeMaine felt Kellogg working on him. Kellogg's touch hurt like hell, but LeMaine couldn't stop it. He started shaking uncontrollably.

Kellogg put his face directly over LeMaine's and said, "I'm going to electrolyze you. I'm going to knock you out."

LeMaine struggled to get his mouth to work. "Please......do it......"

Kellogg nodded and a lightning bolt hit LeMaine in the head. He passed out for real.

Chapter 20

LeMaine woke up somewhere he didn't recognize. Curved, white walls surrounded him to form some kind of capsule. He lay in a bed covered in soft sheets and he was wearing white pajamas in place of his fatigues.

A thick patch covered his eye with a bandage wrapped around his head. The rest of him felt fine.

He didn't feel any pain from his burns. Kellogg must have healed them....so where was he—both of them—all of them? The Hellhounds weren't here. LeMaine didn't even know where here was.

He picked up his head to look around. It wasn't so easy with one eye.

The bottom end of this capsule opened into some kind of corridor. He couldn't imagine where this might be. He'd never seen any place like this in his life.

He didn't understand what he was seeing until a bunch of Imoliv females strode toward him. He didn't realize until now that the walls of his capsule were partially transparent. The walls outside were so startlingly white that he didn't notice the difference before.

The capsule slid silently back to vanish into the wall behind his head as the Imoliv approached. They stopped by his bed and one of them consulted some kind of device in her hand.

"The medical staff has reviewed your case and found your recovery satisfactory," she clipped in a businesslike tone.

"Where am I?" LeMaine asked.

"Your condition was critical when our fighters intercepted you. Sindra brought you to this destroyer for medical treatment."

"Sindra...." LeMaine strained his brain to put the puzzle pieces together. Sindra had been the one who intercepted the *Bombardier* when she got hit. Sindra had been with Kellogg, Monk, and Polasek when they took LeMaine out of the cockpit.

"Is this destroyer....?" He tried to word his next question as diplomatically as possible. "Where exactly are we....in space?"

"You're on board Sehiri's destroyer," she replied. "We're still airborne inside Elian space....in the defensive line."

LeMaine groaned and started to sit up. "I gotta get out of here."

"You aren't due to be released for another week."

"To hell with that," he growled. "Bring Sergeant Kellogg here to clear me for active duty. Please tell me the Hellhounds are still on board with me."

"They are, but Sehiri says....."

"Please," LeMaine countered. "Just let me see Kellogg. That's not asking too much, is it?"

She glared at him. "Military men make such terrible patients."

She and her companions marched out of the.....whatever this was—hospital or whatever.

He had to smirk as they vanished around one of the white walls. Nurses never changed, no matter which species they belonged to.

Kellogg would get him out of here. LeMaine didn't mind Kellogg making snide remarks about what a terrible patient LeMaine was. He'd been hearing that his entire career.

He stayed sitting up on the edge of the bed and touched the bandage around his head. He had difficulty focusing with only one eye. Other than that, he felt all right. His head didn't hurt.

He pulled up his sleeve. All the burns on his arm had been sealed and replaced with artificial skin. Good old Kellogg.

LeMaine knew Kellogg too well to think the young medic would have left LeMaine's medical treatment to the Imoliv. The Imoliv might be better at everything than the Elians, including medical treatments.

Kellogg would have been three feet up the doctors' asses making sure LeMaine got the best care. Kellogg wouldn't leave LeMaine's treatment to some strangers, even if they were Elia's friends and allies.

LeMaine put his weight on his feet. He didn't have any trouble holding himself up.

He really wanted to get the hell out of here. So the Imoliv defensive line was still inside Elian space. The Imoliv destroyers hadn't withdrawn, not even to evacuate the wounded, which meant the Elian-Imoliv alliance was still in battle against the Axichis. How bad was it?

He stretched and paced up and down. He was just making up his mind to leave his bed and go explore this ward or whatever it was when Kellogg showed up.

He grinned at LeMaine. "I should have known you'd be in here giving the nurses a hard time. How's your head?"

"It's fine except for my eye....and this bandage is a pain in the ass. When can I get out of here?"

"You sound fine. Let me check you out and I'll clear you for duty."

LeMaine cast a glance past Kellogg's shoulder. "Are you sure you don't have to clear it with Her Royal Majesty?"

Kellogg laughed and pulled out his scanner. "You know what nurses are like, especially where military men are concerned. Do you want to sit down or is that asking too much?"

LeMaine snorted and sat down. "Where are the Hellhounds?"

"They're hanging out in their apartments. Sehiri set them up the same way he did us. We've been sitting on our asses getting fat while the rest of the Military fights the Axichis."

"How badly is the battle going?"

"Battle?" Kellogg asked. "We don't call it a battle anymore."

"What do we call it?"

"I'm not sure, but it just keeps going on and on. The Axichis keep sending out more warships. It looks like they used Ziea as a staging point to set up another command center on Evilia. That's how they pulled a fast one on us this time. The alliance is holding for now. The Axichis haven't been able to get any closer to Elia or to Imoliv space. That's about the nicest thing I can say about any of it."

"Are the Maczhi still holding Ziea?" LeMaine asked.

Kellogg cracked a grin. "Now I know you're going to be okay if you asked that. You're clear. You can go back on duty."

"Finally," LeMaine grumbled.

Kellogg laughed. "You've been awake for less than two hours. I think you can exercise a little more patience when it comes to your medical care."

"Yes, Mother," LeMaine growled. "Where are my clothes?"

"They're no good. I'll tell the nurses to bring you some new ones.....or you can just walk around in front of the Imoliv like that. You can come back to the apartment and listen to the squad shoot their mouths off until the Imoliv bring you something else to wear."

LeMaine shot him a look, but Kellogg only beamed at him.

"Fine," LeMaine finally agreed. "I'll wait here. I don't need any more shit from the squad."

Kellogg laughed again. "I'll see you over there. I'm sure the Imoliv will tell you where it is."

He walked out. That left LeMaine with nothing to do but wait for the nurses to indulge him. They would probably delay as long as possible just to keep him in the hospital as long as they could.

He passed the time by pacing around and exploring the ward. It really was a ward. It had several beds just like his own, each with its own capsule. He didn't see them before because they all retracted into the walls when no one was using them.

He examined everything with interest. He must be the first Elian ever to set foot in an Imoliv hospital, not to mention being a patient in one.

The nurses pleasantly surprised him by not taking too long to bring him his clothes. They did make certain to tell him he had to keep the bandage over his eye until Kellogg told him to remove it.

He didn't respond to that. Instead, he got busy getting dressed. He didn't feel right walking around in his pajamas with Elia under attack. The Imoliv better not get any ideas about taking the Hellhounds out of the war over this.

He walked out of the ward and realized he didn't know where to go. He turned one way down the corridor and spotted Sindra heading for him from the other end.

Sindra nodded at LeMaine. "Captain. It's good to have you back."

"Thank you for bailing us out. I owe you big time for that."

"Maybe you can pay me back right now. Come with me. I want to show you something.

"Make it the state of battle and you got a deal. How bad is it out there?"

Sindra gave him a look. LeMaine hadn't realized before now that the Imoliv could give people looks, but this guy sure could. "It's bad."

"What are we going to do about it?" LeMaine asked. "Tell me you and Sehiri have a plan."

Sindra turned off into another room. He and LeMaine entered what looked like an observation deck with windows looking out at space.

LeMaine didn't see anything out there until Sindra crossed to a panel on the wall, tapped it, and the windows changed. A projected image of a deadly battle displayed on the windows. The image superimposed on the stars.

LeMaine's stomach dropped when he saw Elian bombers and Imoliv destroyers in battle against the Axichis. They launched from Evilia, Zukion, and Aora with reinforcements coming in from all over the system. The Axichis even launched more ships from their own system to bolster their reserves.

Laser cannons on all three of those planets blasted into space targeting any ship that came within range. None of the defenders could get near enough to stop them.

The new adjustments to the Imoliv phase cannons did more damage than before, but it wasn't enough. The adjustments weren't as good as the frequencies had been.

"Christ!" LeMaine whispered. "How many ships do they even have?"

"Three hundred and rising. They don't seem to be exhausting their force much. We need to find a way to break their stranglehold on the Elian system. If Elia collapses, Imoliv will be next."

"We don't have the firepower to fight them like this." LeMaine's hand flew to his head. "My God! It's a miracle the Elian fleet is still in the air at all."

"Exactly. Not even Imoliv and Elia working together have the resources to defeat the Axichis. We need a new strategy."

LeMaine whipped around to stare at the young man. "What do you have in mind?"

"That's why I'm showing you this. Sehiri suggested that we do a special operation—me, Galo, Lutov, and Tavon—but I told him it would be more likely to succeed if we worked with the Hellhounds. We can put our heads together, come up with an idea, and execute it together—two teams instead of one. What do you say?"

"I'm game if you are. So what's the mission?"

Sindra turned his gaze back to the windows. "The best way would be to somehow remove their bases on these three inner planets. We need to find a way to stop them from staging from there. Then they would have to withdraw and set up somewhere else or even pull back to their own system. We've tried to hit those bases before, but we can't get anywhere close to them with so many spacecraft in the way. The Axichis craft are even more intent on stopping us from hitting the bases than they are on conquering Elia."

LeMaine followed his gaze. Evilia, Zukion, and Aora hovered in the dark sky beyond the window. They formed a staggered landscape of globes leading to the outer ring of planets.

Ziea didn't look like anything more than a speck from here, but LeMaine couldn't take his eyes off it. Ziea was secure because the Maczhi battalion was there.

Buca's words came back to LeMaine in haunting detail. LeMaine could even see Buca's face in the Nulia command center. *We should have thought of stealing their vessels and using them against the Axichis. We shouldn't have spent so much time buzzing around trying to shoot at them when it didn't do any good.*

"Captain?" Sindra asked. "What's on your mind? Do you have an idea?"

"Yes, I do."

Sindra waited. "Do I get to know what it is?"

"Elian guns and Imoliv phase cannons aren't enough. We need a weapon that's just as effective against them as theirs are against us."

"Where can we find a weapon like that?" Sindra asked. "We don't have anything as strong as theirs."

"We don't have it, so we have to take it from the most obvious available source."

Sindra frowned. "What source is that?"

"From the Axichis themselves. We have to get down on those planets, take control of their cannons, and turn them on the Axichis craft. That's the only way we can defeat them."

Sindra's eyes widened. "You want to take control of the Axichis guns?"

"We just did it on Ziea. That's where we've been for the last couple of weeks. Come on." LeMaine bumped his shoulder. "Bring your guys over to the apartment where the Hellhounds are staying. We can all talk about it there."

Chapter 21

LeMaine strolled into an apartment identical to the one he and Kellogg had stayed in the last time they found themselves on Sehiri's destroyer.

The Hellhounds lounged on the couches, and for once in their lives, they weren't in the middle of some lunatic circus act involving risk to life and limb.

Polasek was reading something on a screen attached to the wall by his couch. Peterman sat at a table that displayed an electronic chart of the Elian system while he jotted notes in his notebook.

Heckler sat on a bench by the window looking out at the stars. Monk was snoring on a different couch while Nunn tried to balance something on the tip of his nose without waking him up.

O'Hara sat on a two-seater across the room polishing his scope. Kellogg stood at the food dispenser and he looked up when LeMaine walked in. "Ahoy there, Long John Silver. Where's your parrot?"

"Watch it or I'll make you take this patch off before you're ready to," LeMaine told him. "Where's Lemon?"

"She's around here somewhere...." Kellogg began.

"I'm right here, Sir." Lemon stepped out of somewhere. LeMaine didn't see where she had been until she materialized out of the wall. She definitely hadn't been there before.

Peterman looked up. "Welcome back, Sir. What's the haps?"

"We're going on a mission."

"It's about time." Nunn tossed whatever she had been trying to balance on Monk's nose into her mouth and then shook him. "Wake up, Monk. We're going on a mission."

His head jerked up. "Huh? Are the Axichis attacking again?"

"They aren't attacking us," LeMaine told him. "We're attacking them."

"What are we doing?" Polasek asked.

"The same thing we did on Ziea, except this time, instead of the Maczhi battalion helping us, Sindra's crew is going with us."

"Whoo!" O'Hara exclaimed and set his scope aside. "Let's go!"

"We need to organize the logistics first. Let us borrow your chart there, Peterman."

Peterman stood up from the table. "Go for it."

LeMaine bent over the chart. "This doesn't show the combatants."

"No, I removed them so I could see the shipping lanes." Peterman did something to the settings on the chart.

It changed and all the combatant spacecraft from all three armies appeared on the table surface. They moved around in real time with the Axichis launching from Evilia, Zukion, and Aora while the Elians and Imoliv tried to stop them from coming near Elia or the Imoliv border.

"How does this help us, Sir?" Nunn asked.

"Our mission is to get down on one of these planets—preferably Evilia," LeMaine replied. "It's the closest and also the best armed. The cannons there are closest to the front line."

"What do we care about the cannons for?" Polasek asked. "We can't steal them the way we stole the Axichis ships on Ziea."

"We're going to steal them," LeMaine replied. "We just aren't going to fly away with them afterward. We're going to turn them against the Axis. We'll be able to hit any Axichis target from there, including their assets on Zukion and Aora."

"Damn it," Nunn grumbled. "I thought you were going to say we were going to blow them up."

"Better luck next time," Heckler growled.

"You can blow things up with the cannons," Kellogg told her and she brightened up instantly.

"The hard part is going to be getting down on the planet," LeMaine pointed out.

"The hard part is going to be getting anywhere near the planet," Lemon countered.

"We can always make it look like we crashed," Peterman suggested. "That worked the last time."

Howls of protest answered him. "I think we'll skip it this time," LeMaine replied. "The Imoliv team will be with us. I wouldn't want to put them in unnecessary danger."

"But you have no problem putting *us* in unnecessary danger?" Polasek asked.

"That's right," LeMaine replied and got a laugh out of the whole squad.

"It would be super helpful if we had a few Axichis fighter craft to sneak us onto the planet," Heckler pointed out. "Maybe we could borrow them from the Maczhi battalion."

"I think we already showed our hand on that one," LeMaine argued. "Besides, we would have to bring the fighters here, which the Axichis would see and would also take defense away from Ziea. If we do anything else, we have to hold Ziea at all costs. We can't give it up, now that we have it."

"So what's the plan, Sir?" Peterman asked.

"Hold up. We're gonna wait until the Imoliv boys get here. Maybe they know something."

Sindra's team showed up just then and gathered around the table. "We were just brainstorming about how to get down onto Evilia," LeMaine told them.

"Evilia is the most heavily fortified," Galo pointed out. "It will be the most difficult to take."

"It will also do us the most good when we do take it," LeMaine countered.

"*If* we take it," Monk pointed out.

"*When* we take it," LeMaine repeated. "We're going. Axichis weapons are all we have that works against the Axichis. We did it on Ziea and we're doing it here. Just imagine what we could do with those cannons. The Axichis wouldn't be able to get inside the inner ring at all. That's something worth risking our necks for. We just need to get through the Axichis front line."

"I think I know a way, Captain. We can take a civilian craft." Sindra changed the chart settings again and brought up the shipping lanes onto and off of Evilia, but he left up the real-time display of battle, too. "Civilian traffic is still going back and forth between all three planets."

"But there's nothing coming in from outside those three planets," Kellogg pointed out. "The Axichis would see another craft trying to break across the line."

"We need to let them see it," LeMaine interjected. "We need to make it obvious that the ship is trying to get through. Trying to hide it will only tip off the Axichis that we're pulling something. We need to make it glaringly obvious, but the ship in question has to have some legitimate excuse to break through—medical or diplomatic or....."

"Or if the ship was out of control," Monk added. "It wouldn't have to crash in a ball of fire, but a civilian craft that got hit in the battle and lost its helm wouldn't be able to stop itself from breaking the line. If it was an unarmed craft coming from.....say......(planet name), the Axichis would have no reason to see it as a threat."

"So how would you suggest we stop the out-of-control ship from crashing in a ball of fire?" Heckler asked. "How do you say we should make it convincing enough to stop the Axichis from gunning us down when we enter orbit?"

"We approach from another direction." Monk pointed at the charts. "These civilian lanes are all well away from the fighting. The ones too near the fighting are all inactive because it's too dangerous. We make it look like our ship is heading for those lanes and then suffers a malfunction."

"I don't know about that," LeMaine countered, "but the idea of the ship malfunctioning could do the trick."

"If we're going to take an unarmed craft, why do we need a malfunction at all?" Lutov asked. "Why not just take an unarmed craft into the shipping lanes? The Axichis won't see it as a threat. We would just need to approach the lane from behind the enemy line."

The Hellhounds exchanged glances. "Good idea," Peterman replied. "Why overcomplicate things with a malfunction?"

"We could still use the malfunction idea," Lemon pointed out. "The Axichis might be monitoring the civilian traffic in and out. If they contact us and ask us to identify ourselves, we could use the malfunction idea to make it look like our communications are down."

"Sweetie!" Monk cried. "You liked my idea!"

"Don't read too much into it," she muttered.

"Getting back to the matter at hand," LeMaine interrupted. "We need a civilian craft and we also need a way to get to (planet) undetected. We're on an Imoliv destroyer. We need a way to get to our craft without the Axichis connecting us to the vessel or the vessel's origin point."

"That's simple, Sir," Polasek told him. "We land on another planet—Elia would be best. We get whatever craft we want and then we take it to three other planets first—(planet names). We make it look like we're conducting business there and then going to Evilia last of all."

"There's just one problem with that," O'Hara cut in.

"Don't even think about shooting down my idea, Sergeant," Polasek teased.

"I was going to point out that we would need a way to conceal Imoliv life signs on board," O'Hara replied. "The Axichis will detect that there are both human and Imoliv life signs on the same ship—a noncombatant ship. That will tip them off quicker than anything."

"I have the solution to that, too," Sindra replied. "We have a way to disguise our life signs."

"You do?" Kellogg asked. "What is it?"

"It's a piece of technology. It connects to the ship's life support system and displays to the enemy whatever life sign readings you program it to display. We can program it to display all human life signs. That won't be a problem."

"So....that's it?" LeMaine cast a glance around the table. "It can't be that easy."

"It won't be," Heckler growled. "We still have to get down on the planet, find the cannons, and take them over."

"One more thing, Captain," Sindra added.

"Oh, just one?" LeMaine teased and the Hellhounds laughed, but Sindra didn't get the joke.

"The Axichis have multiple cannon stations around Evilia's circumference," Sindra told him. "If we take one of them, the Axichis will still be able to use their other cannon stations on the other sides of the planet. We won't be able to stop them and there aren't enough of us to take them all."

"One cannon station would be better than none," Peterman pointed out. "If we took one of their cannon stations, we could deliver one hell of a surprise attack on them. We could hit them before they knew what happened."

"You're right," LeMaine replied. "Let's take one and work on the others after that. We'll need to get Sehiri to deliver us back to Elia."

"I'll handle that," Sindra agreed.

"Perfect. Let's do it."

Chapter 22

"Do we really have to do this?" LeMaine groaned.

"Of course we have to do it," Kellogg replied. "Did you really think I would let you go back into a combat zone with one eye?"

"You cleared me for duty," LeMaine argued. "Why am I going back to the hospital?"

"I cleared you to leave the hospital. No way in hell are you going on this mission with your eye covered."

LeMaine rolled his one good eye to Heaven. "I only need one eye to shoot my carbine."

"Are you seriously standing there telling me that you would have one eye glued to a carbine when you couldn't see anything else that was going on around you? Don't make me laugh."

LeMaine shrugged, but it came out more as a squirm. "Okay. You're right."

"Just get through this. If it works, you'll be ready for action by the time we get back to Elia."

LeMaine hesitated to ask his next question, but he had to do it. He had to get this off his chest before he reentered the hospital. He didn't trust anyone but Kellogg to answer it for him.

"Is it true I might never see out of this eye again?" he asked under his breath.

Kellogg lowered his voice, too. He of all people understood what the Hellhounds meant to LeMaine. If LeMaine lost the use of his eye, Command would retire him from the service—as in forever. He would never go out with the Hellhounds again.

What would his life be then? He had a family back on Elia, but still. His life would never be the same. In fact, it would be over.

He would have to spend years finding out who he was without the Hellhounds. The squad had been his life for decades. These people were his real family.

His wife and children back on Elia had no idea what he'd been doing all these years. He kept it separate from them. He didn't want them to know.

He didn't know how to rebuild after something like that. He didn't know how to put the pieces of himself back together without the Hellhounds. He wouldn't even know where to begin.

"I would say it's quite likely that you won't be able to see out of it," Kellogg told him. "The eye was completely destroyed when you took that shard, but the Imoliv have technology we don't. I talked to some of their doctors about it. They say they have a way to replace your eye with an implant."

"Implant!" LeMaine repeated. "What does that mean? Is it robotic....or organic?"

"I'm not sure. I didn't really understand a lot of the terminology they used. They have a completely different way of doing things.....but I don't see how it could be organic. If they're growing organic eyes in a petri dish to replace damaged ones, those grown eyes would be Imoliv eyes, wouldn't they? Imoliv doctors wouldn't have a stash of human eyes hanging around just in case some injured Elian drops out of the sky onto their operating table."

LeMaine turned away with a groan. "I don't want to talk about this anymore."

Kellogg took him at his word and didn't try to talk to LeMaine all the way to the hospital. LeMaine regretted saying that. He really needed someone to talk to right now. He got progressively more agitated the closer they got to their destination.

He halted outside the door. "You're coming in with me, aren't you? You'll be there for....whatever they do to me, right?"

"Of course," Kellogg replied. "I'm not going anywhere."

"Thanks," LeMaine husked. He'd never been more grateful to anyone in his life.

They walked into the hospital and a bunch of Imoliv doctors and nurses went into a frenzy whizzing around and making a to-do about LeMaine.

They escorted him into a separate room and the nurses parked him sitting on an exam table in front of a large machine. LeMaine had seen this before when the Imoliv doctors used it to test his good eye to make sure there was nothing wrong with it.

The doctor wheeled the machine over and lowered it in front of LeMaine, but the doctor didn't fit it to LeMaine's head—not yet.

The doctor was a very young Imoliv male. He didn't look much older than Lutov, but this guy was taller than all four of the Imoliv operatives that LeMaine knew.

"We'll just take the bandages off first and then we'll see what the situation is," the doctor began.

Kellogg moved over behind the doctor and planted himself right where LeMaine couldn't fail to see him. Kellogg didn't move out of LeMaine's line of sight even for a second.

The nurses started cutting the bandages off. They had to cut some of LeMaine's hair where the bandage stuck to it.

Then came the nerve-wracking moment when they peeled the patch away from his eye socket. They took it away with a sickening sticky pull, but nothing changed. LeMaine tried everything to see out of his injured eye, but there was nothing there.

"I'll just cover up your good eye and you can tell me if you see anything," the doctor told him. He spoke in a hushed undertone. Everyone in the room already knew the truth.

He covered up LeMaine's good eye and the whole bright, stark-white hospital room went dark. "Anything?" the doctor asked.

LeMaine shook his head trying to swallow down the lump in his throat.

The doctor took his hand down just in time for Kellogg to step around the doctor's chair to LeMaine's side. Kellogg clamped his hand on LeMaine's shoulder, squeezed, and gave him a very gentle shake.

"What were you saying about giving him an implant to replace the eye?" Kellogg asked.

"Yes, of course," the doctor replied. "That won't be a problem. We just need to remove the old eye first....."

"Wait a minute," LeMaine choked. "This implant.....what is it?"

"It's a synthetic eye that interfaces with your cerebral cortex...."

"I mean is it mechanical or is it some kind of modified organics?"

"It's mechanical. It's robotic with nano-fiber optics that merge with your optic nerve...."

"So.....I'll have a robotic eye.....like a machine?" LeMaine's voice cracked on the last words.

He wasn't so worried about what anyone in the Military thought of him having a robotic eye. He could just imagine the shit the Hellhounds would come up with when they found out.

It was his wife he worried about. He wouldn't like to face her looking like some kind of half-robotic monster. How would she ever look at him again?

"The implant is constructed with a synthetic iris on the other surface for cosmetic purposes," the doctor was saying. "It looks like any regular organic eye from the outside. The robotic parts are all concealed inside the eye socket itself....although we do construct them to look like Imoliv eyes. We can make some modifications to make the implant appear more human if you prefer."

"Of course he prefers," Kellogg interrupted. "He wants the eye to look as human as possible."

"I understand." The doctor stood up. "We'll need you to lie down while we remove your old eye and install the implant."

"What are you going to do?" LeMaine asked. He heard how shaky his voice sounded, but he sounded a lot steadier than he felt.

He would rather get shot up with carbine fire, nearly lose his life, and get patched up by Kellogg in the middle of a war zone than go through this, but what choice did he have? He had to have an eye or he would be out of the service.

"Don't worry," the doctor chirped. "It's a superficial procedure. You'll be conscious through the whole process and I assure you that it's completely painless."

"How would you know?" LeMaine growled. "Have you ever had it done?"

The doctor only smiled at him. "As a matter of fact, my infant son had it done. He was born with a birth defect. His left eye was misshapen and blind at birth. I held him in my arms while the doctors removed his eye and replaced it with an implant. I can assure you that the procedure is completely painless and the implant is absolutely indistinguishable from a normal organic eye."

LeMaine couldn't look at him. LeMaine really didn't want to go through with this.

Kellogg didn't give him a chance to back out. Kellogg squeezed LeMaine's shoulder and said, "Lie down," in that way that LeMaine had come to understand as a direct order. Kellogg's authority exceeded even LeMaine's when it came to anything medical.

LeMaine stretched out on the table and the nurses lowered the machine over his head. LeMaine stared up at the ceiling. He couldn't stop himself from shaking. He dreaded the moment the procedure started.

He didn't believe for an instant that it would be painless. The very thought of a bunch of alien medical experts drilling into his head, removing his eye, and replacing it with a robotic one made him sick to his stomach.

Kellogg kept his hand clamped to LeMaine's shoulder the entire time. Kellogg's grip grounded LeMaine, but it also gave him a continuous subtle order to cooperate and not to move until the doctor finished the procedure.

LeMaine had gotten so used to obeying Kellogg all these years that nothing could move him as long as Kellogg kept his hand there. Obeying Kellogg had become wired into LeMaine's cells.

The machine started to whir and a brush of air touched LeMaine's cheek and forehead. Then he felt a very faint vibration going through his head. That was it. It didn't hurt at all.

This went on for only a few minutes before they removed the machine. "The eye has been removed," the doctor told him. "Stay where you are while we modify the implant and then we'll insert it."

LeMaine blinked up at the ceiling again and his good eye darted over to Kellogg. "How does it look?"

"Scary," Kellogg replied and bit back a grin. "It's too bad you can't go back to the squad like this. You would scare the ever-loving shit out of them."

LeMaine found himself laughing. His nerves wouldn't calm down, but he felt better already. He was going to be okay.

The doctor came back, but he didn't fit the machine over LeMaine's head again. The doctor wheeled his stool over to LeMaine's head. Kellogg had to move out of the way, so he shifted around to the other side.

This time, he just rested his hand on LeMaine's shoulder in a very medically comforting way. He didn't have to order LeMaine to lie still anymore.

"I've adjusted the colors and shades of the implant to match your good eye," the doctor announced. "It looks much more human than an Imoliv eye. Take a look and tell me what you think."

The doctor held up the implant in front of LeMaine's face where he could see it. The back part of the ball and all the wires and strings hanging off the back made it look as gruesome and demonic as LeMaine could have feared.

The cosmetic blue iris on the front looked so much like a normal human eye that LeMaine froze. He really did feel like he was staring back into his own disembodied eye.

Kellogg gasped. "That's amazing! It looks just like it!"

"Do you really think so?" the doctor asked. "Well, I was rather pleased with the result, but since we don't get many Elian patients, I wasn't sure if it would fit the bill. Are you ready for me to insert it, Captain?"

LeMaine nodded, too stunned to speak.

The doctor bent over LeMaine's head, did something to his eye socket, and then pushed what felt like a golf ball into the hole where his eye should have been.

This felt incredibly weird, but it didn't hurt, either. LeMaine couldn't be certain, but it actually felt like the implant squished and molded to the eye socket, firstly so it could fit past the surrounding bones, but also so it adjusted its shape to fit his skull.

All at once, something connected in his brain and his vision cleared. He could see with both eyes. He stared up at the doctor in amazement.

"How is it?" the doctor asked.

"It's....it's incredible!" LeMaine breathed. "I can see better than before."

"The implant is designed for enhanced visual acuity and reaction time. You may notice an improvement in processing as well. Information travels faster through the implant to the brain than through an organic eye."

Kellogg leaned over LeMaine. "It looks exactly like the other one. I never would have known the difference."

"Sit up, Captain," the doctor ordered. "We'll run some routine tests just to make sure the implant is interfacing correctly and then you'll be free to go."

LeMaine sat up and the doctors and nurses went through the same routine with their machines that they'd been using on his left eye. They checked the implant's acuity scale and its processing speed.

The doctor covered up LeMaine's left eye and LeMaine had to admit that his right eye worked better than the original. It picked up more detail with no delay between when he saw something and when his brain reacted to what he was seeing.

Kellogg stayed where LeMaine could see him, but LeMaine didn't mind the procedure now. He was just fine. He had his eye back.

When the doctor finished, he handed LeMaine a mirror so he could see his new eye. Kellogg was right. It looked exactly like his left eye. No one ever had to know unless he told them.

A bunch of new scars surrounded his eye socket and covered the right side of his face. They gave him a barbaric, cutthroat appearance that he didn't have before, but his eye looked the same. He could definitely face his wife like this.

The doctors finished and released him. He and Kellogg left the hospital on their way back to the hospital.

"Do you want me to keep this quiet from the other Hellhounds?" Kellogg asked on their way back to the apartment.

LeMaine pretended to raise his eyebrows. "Do I have a choice about that?"

"Of course you do. This is confidential medical information. If you don't want your subordinates to know you have an artificial eye, I won't tell them."

"I guess I don't care if they find out," LeMaine replied.

"Are you sure you don't want them calling you One-Eyed Jack from now on—or One-Eyed Owen?"

LeMaine burst out laughing in pure relief. Leave it to Kellogg to think of something like that. "It doesn't quite have the same ring, does it?"

Kellogg joined in the joke. "No, it doesn't. We would have to come up with another name for you."

LeMaine beamed at him. LeMaine couldn't think of anyone he'd rather have with him for something like this. "I'll leave it up to you whether to tell them."

"They were all as anxious as you were to find out if you were going to be able to stay in the service," Kellogg went on.

"Did you talk about it behind my back?" LeMaine asked. "I should have known."

"We didn't talk about it. None of us ever mentioned it, but we were all worried about it. You know how they all get real quiet when something is bothering them. It's been like that for days. No one wants to lose you."

LeMaine couldn't answer. It meant a lot that the Hellhounds cared as much about him as he did about them. He already knew that, but it sure was nice to hear it every now and then.

They returned to the apartment and strolled right in. LeMaine went to the food dispenser. He'd been too nervous to eat or drink anything before the procedure. Now he needed to make up for lost time.

"Looking good, Captain," Nunn called from across the apartment.

"Thanks, Corporal. You, too."

The others exploded in laughter and O'Hara elbowed Nunn.

LeMaine joined in their laughter, got his food, and flopped on the couch next to Polasek.

"You got the old pirate captain look going on," Heckler remarked.

"Show that face to the Axichis," O'Hara teased. "That will send them running for the hills."

"Just don't make the captain mad," Monk added. "He can kill you with one wrong look."

He cocked one eyebrow, narrowed his other eye, and gave the rest of his squad mates the side eye. His expression made them all laugh.

LeMaine stole a glance at Kellogg, but Kellogg didn't say anything about LeMaine having a mechanical eye. That would definitely trigger jokes about him being able to kill with a look.

The squad might start to wonder and worry if LeMaine's implant really did have superhuman powers. That might be the end of their comfortable relationship with him.

One minute, one hour followed another and Kellogg still didn't tell. After the second hour, LeMaine finally got it through his head that Kellogg would never tell the others about the implant. He would never tell anyone.

The squad was still on an Imoliv destroyer. Maybe no one in the whole Elian Military Command would find out that Captain Owen LeMaine had a fake eye installed by the Imoliv medical staff.

Chapter 23

LeMaine stepped into the main room of his apartment on Sehiri's destroyer. LeMaine hadn't seen Sehiri once on this trip, but that hardly mattered.

Sindra liaised between his father and the Hellhounds. Sehiri left Sindra to handle all the Imoliv team's dealings with the Hellhounds.

LeMaine stopped in the middle of the room to adjust his disguise. He wore a plain black suit, and instead of a backpack, he carried a businessman's attaché case.

It didn't contain any business devices or documentation. It carried his first aid kit, emergency rations, a few tools, and no weapons. The Hellhounds' disguise depended on Axichis seeing the squad's civilian craft as totally unarmed.

LeMaine had been hearing nonstop grumbling for days from the whole squad about how stupid it was to go into a war zone behind enemy lines without a weapon. LeMaine couldn't disagree with them, but this was the plan they had come up with.

Lemon came out of her room disguised as a Vularean male with a beard and eyebrows down to his knees. She carried all her supplies under the Vularean's shaggy fur.

The other Hellhounds emerged from their rooms, each one dressed in the traditional attire of some Elian culture. None of them looked the same as anyone else.

Peterman came out dressed as a bounty hunter from Diliv. He wore a broad-brimmed hat, leather pants, leather boots, and a leather vest over his beaten brown cotton shirt. He wasn't carrying any weapons, either, but other than that, he looked perfect.

LeMaine threw his hands in the air. "Don't shoot!"

Peterman laughed. "I won't if you don't rob my bank account."

"Are you ready to go?" LeMaine asked.

Peterman nodded. "Ready when you are."

"The rest of you Hellhounds wait here until I give you the signal. Then you can come on over to the vessel."

LeMaine and Peterman headed for the door only to meet Sindra and his team coming to meet them. Galo ran his eyes up and down LeMaine's clothes. "What are you supposed to be?"

"Don't you start shooting off your mouth to me, too. This is normal attire for an Elian businessman."

Galo chuckled. "You'll never be that, Captain."

"Let's hope not. Stay here. I'll signal you when to come over."

LeMaine and Peterman left the destroyer. Sehiri had landed the squad at Elian Military Command. Now LeMaine had to face the devastation of the capital.

He and Peterman took a high-speed railcar to the other side of town where they negotiated passage on a civilian freighter bound for Coruta.

From there, they would get a different vessel to Diliv, and finally, a third vessel to Faega, and the last leg to Evilia. If that didn't throw the Axichis off the squad's trail, nothing would.

LeMaine and Peterman boarded the craft, went to their assigned quarters, and used the ship's communications system to send a signal to Sehiri's destroyer. It was a wordless signal that no one eavesdropping on the system would be able to decode.

Several minutes later, the Hellhounds arrived on board with Sindra's men. LeMaine had disguised Sindra, Galo, Lutov, and Tavon in the full-body coverings of devout female Idaevis pilgrims. Their heavy robes covered them from head to foot and left only a small grille of holes around the eyes so they could see out. No one would know they were Imoliv in disguise.

They entered the cabin LeMaine had arranged for them and Sindra fixed a small device to the wall. He activated it. "Now no one will be able to read Imoliv life signs on board."

"I sure hope that thing works," LeMaine remarked.

"So do I," Tavon replied.

LeMaine turned away. "You boys try to relax. We have a long way to go. I'll bring you some food later."

He went down the corridor checking each room. The Hellhounds were staying three to a room with LeMaine, Polasek, and Peterman in the last cabin.

He flopped down on his bunk. "Now there's nothing to do but wait."

"And keep our fingers crossed," Peterman added.

"And pray," Polasek finished and the other two laughed.

What followed was the most boring passage of LeMaine's life. He had to restrain himself not to go up to the bridge every few minutes to check the ship's progress.

He paced his cabin a lot, but nothing worked to settle his nerves. He paced the corridors, too, until he discovered Monk out there.

They met in the corridor outside the Hellhounds' cabins and the two men eyed each other. It wouldn't do for anyone to realize that two of them were out here pacing to keep their nerves down.

LeMaine went back to his own cabin only to find Polasek and Peterman playing a nice rousing game of twenty questions. They'd decided to use exotic Elian life forms as their subject.

Listening to them racked LeMaine's nerves even more. He had to leave, so he went to the bridge anyway.

The ship was on its approach to Coruta, thank God. LeMaine couldn't stand much more of this and he still had two more passages to make.

He delivered the same message to the rest of the squad, including the Imoliv team, to stay on board until he came back and told them which ship they would be transferring to.

LeMaine considered the four Imoliv part of his squad now. They acted the same as the Hellhounds and LeMaine trusted these four just as much as if they were Hellhounds. Them being Imoliv didn't seem to make any difference anymore.

He went back to his cabin and broke up the game between Polasek and Peterman. LeMaine wouldn't have to listen to their constant back-and-forth about animals and creatures, some of which LeMaine had never even heard of.

Unfortunately for his sanity, in the hours between then and when the ship actually docked and gave the passengers permission to disembark, he had to listen to the two of them discussing the animals and creatures from the game.

LeMaine didn't understand half of what Peterman and Polasek were talking about and he cared even less. He really needed to get the hell off this ship, but he had to face many more hours of the same before the squad arrived at its destination.

He decided to go visit the Imoliv team instead, so he got some food from the galley and took it to their cabin. He didn't realize until he actually got inside it that he'd made another giant mistake.

The four of them sat on the floor in a square playing some game in their own language. LeMaine didn't understand them any better than he understood Polasek and Peterman, but this was definitely NOT twenty questions.

The four men made hand gestures to each other, shouted key words at strategic times, and then roared with laughter and shouts of triumph when they won. Then they exchanged money based on the outcome.

LeMaine was just making up his mind to remind these guys that they were supposed to be quiet, retiring female pilgrims. Any other passengers would be able to hear these men bellowing, laughing, thumping the floor, and throwing money at each other.

He opened his mouth to do just that when the ship slammed into the dock and the captain gave the word to disembark.

LeMaine raced back to his cabin, grabbed Peterman, and they went into the dockyards to secure their next transport. The process went way too smoothly. LeMaine had no choice but to return to their original ship, give the word to the rest of the squad, and then transfer everyone to their second vessel.

By the time they all made it to Faega, LeMaine's nerves were at the breaking point and the Hellhounds weren't doing much better. The Imoliv team seemed fresh, rested, and perfectly at ease. They showed no indication that they even knew they were undertaking such a dangerous mission.

The squad disembarked at different times and everyone went their separate ways. LeMaine strolled through the market looking for somewhere he could buy some weapons.

He stiffened when he saw Axichis walking through the streets. They always traveled in pairs and they all carried laser rifles. More Axichis stood guard on rooftops and balconies to keep the city under constant watch.

LeMaine didn't see the laser cannons firing from here nor did he see any Axichis craft in the air. The Axichis kept all of that far away from the civilian trade centers.

LeMaine headed off to the rendezvous point where the squad changed out of their disguises—all except the Imoliv. They couldn't let anyone see them on this planet or the game would be up.

The Hellhounds changed into the outfits of male Idaevis pilgrims. These covered the whole body but left the face free. Nunn and Lemon used the same full-body coverings as the Imoliv. Now the squad all looked like they belonged together.

LeMaine related what he'd seen at the market. "I was going to suggest that Peterman and I go into town to buy weapons, but it's too dangerous. We can't risk the Axichis seeing us and asking questions."

"The cannons are well guarded and the Axichis have patrols searching the grounds around the cannon stations," Sindra chimed in. "We can get some weapons from them."

"Good idea," LeMaine went on.

The group went back into town. Now they could walk right in front of the Axichis without getting caught.

The Hellhounds caught a fast-moving ground transport that took them far out of the city. LeMaine relaxed slightly when the craft left the Axichis behind, but that only meant the squad was moving closer to their destination—and trouble.

Chapter 24

LeMaine and the Hellhounds stepped down from their transport craft in the middle of nowhere. Rolling countryside surrounded them on all sides with no houses, towns, or any other mark of civilization.

"Well, this is the shit-end of nowhere if I've ever seen it," Heckler growled.

"Not quite," Peterman replied just as a massive laser cannon erupted across the landscape from the Hellhounds' position.

The cannon belched into the atmosphere and then another ten shots went off in rapid succession. Deep thumping booms reverberated through the ground into LeMaine's feet every time the gun went off.

"Holy mother-loving hell," Lemon muttered. "We're taking *those?*"

"You better believe it," Peterman replied. "Just imagine the damage we'll be able to do to the Axichis with those."

"We need to figure out how to take the rest of the stations, too," Sindra insisted.

"One thing at a time," LeMaine interrupted. "Let's get over there and see what's waiting for us."

"Keep an eye out for Axichis patrols," Galo reminded him.

"The sooner we see one of them, the sooner we can start killing those bastards," Kellogg added and the squad started forward.

They followed the road on which the transport had dropped them off and then the squad cut overland. No one in their right mind would believe Idaevis pilgrims would be hiking overland on their way to an Axichis cannon station, but no one saw. The countryside couldn't be more deserted.

The squad jumped several fences and snuck up on the station. The cannons thundered at a deafening pitch here. Their lasers crackled in the air and every shot hurled the cannons back against their moorings.

A single gunner sat in each gun's control capsule. The gunners reclined in their seats, completely insulated from both the noise and the shock.

The Hellhounds crouched outside a high wire fence that surrounded the station and LeMaine observed the surroundings.

"What do you think, Captain?" Sindra murmured in his ear.

"I think we would need those cannons just to get on the station."

Galo chuckled. "That would defeat the purpose, wouldn't it?"

"What about using deception again? Lutov asked.

"How do you figure?" LeMaine asked.

"We're disguised as pilgrims in a part of the country where no pilgrims should be. We could blunder upon the station begging for help to get back to the city. The Axichis don't know anything about the Idaevis or their pilgrimage."

"What could possibly go wrong?" Heckler growled and the others laughed.

Lutov frowned at them. He didn't understand that expression. "The worst that could go wrong is that they take us into custody and take us inside the station, which is what we want. They won't leave us walking around outside it."

"No, chump," Lemon fired back. "The worst that could go wrong is that they shoot us on sight."

"That's why we'd pretend to be helpless and stupid," Lutov told her.

"I think it's a good idea, but we would have to go with you," LeMaine cut in. "If you went alone, they would rip off your head coverings, see that you were Imoliv, and then they really would shoot you."

"What do we do once we're inside?" Sindra asked.

"That depends on what they do with us," Peterman replied. "If they lock us up, which they're bound to do, then we have a whole new problem."

"I don't care if they lock us up as long as they lock us up in the same place," LeMaine told him. "If they lock us up together, we can break out and then we'll be on the station ready to take some cannons."

"Wait a minute, Captain," Tavon interrupted. "There's a problem with that."

"What problem?"

"There are thirteen of us. If we take those cannons, the Axichis will be on top of us in seconds the minute we start shooting at Axichis targets. We need to neutralize every Axichis on that station before we take control of the cannons."

LeMaine turned back to the station. His new eye implant turned out to be a lot sharper than he ever realized. Tavon was right. The station would be crawling with Axichis.

"Okay, here's what we're going to do," LeMaine finally announced. "We're going to use Lutov's idea of pretending to be helpless and stupid. We beg for help and they take us inside. We make a huge fuss and a big noise—the biggest we possibly can. Lemon, you slip away just in case something goes wrong. Once they decide what to do with us, we get free and go on a run through the countryside."

All the Hellhounds nodded and started preparing their disguises.

Galo frowned at LeMaine. "How will you go on a run through the countryside?"

"It's an expression," Polasek explained. "It means you run wild killing as many Axichis you can as quickly and as quietly as you can so the remaining Axichis don't realize anything is wrong. You sneak up on them, shank them, and move on."

"Shank?" Galo furrowed his brow even more. "I don't know that word."

"It means kill them," Lemon snapped. "It means snap their necks, slit their throats, smash their heads against walls—anything you want to do and can do without getting caught and without alerting the other Axichis what you're doing."

Galo's expression cleared. "Ah! I understand now."

"Thank the stars!" she muttered.

"Can you do that, son?" LeMaine asked.

"Of course," Galo replied. "I can do it very well."

"All right. Let's roll, Hellhounds."

The Hellhounds got to their feet, pulled their disguises into place, and set off to the east. They skirted the fence and approached the station's main gate.

LeMaine saw a problem with this plan right away. It could turn into an advantage or a disadvantage. There was no way to anticipate how it would work.

The noise from the cannons grew to such a pitch that he couldn't hear himself think. He wouldn't be able to hear anyone else's voice nor would the Axichis be able to hear him.

There was no turning back now, though. Armed Axichis inside the fence spotted the squad coming and held the lost pilgrims at gunpoint as they neared the gate. LeMaine raised his hands and the rest of the squad did the same.

Fortunately, the four Imoliv had adjusted their robes to conceal their hands. They wore gloves so no one could see that their hands were Imoliv hands.

The guards traced their rifles to follow the approaching Hellhounds. LeMaine started calling out long before he got to the gate.

He moaned loudly about how lost and hungry and pathetic he and his fellow pilgrims were, but his voice vanished in a sea of noise. He couldn't even hear himself.

He halted at a safe distance from the gate and stood there sobbing, gesticulating behind him toward the road, and carrying on at length about how the transport had dropped him off at the wrong spot, how he and his companions didn't have any money or food, and begging the Axichis to help him.

He happened to catch a glimpse of the other Hellhounds out of the corner of his eye. All of them held out their hands in beseeching agony to the Axichis. The men's faces that LeMaine could see contorted in sobs and desperate pleas, too. They really played up the act to the limit.

The Axichis stayed inside their fence with their guns raised. They couldn't hear a word the Hellhounds said, but at least the Axichis didn't shoot.

After a while, one of them strode off and entered a gatehouse near the front fence. He did something inside and the cannon fire cut out.

Throbbing silence fell over the landscape. LeMaine found it difficult to comprehend that silence after the bone-crushing noise of the cannons a second before.

The so-called pilgrims fell silent, too. That silence seemed to threaten anyone who dared to break it. The gate rolled back and a bunch of armed Axichis stormed out still holding the squad at gunpoint.

Something about the Axichis set LeMaine off again and he broke into the same pathetic sobbing, begging tirade demanding that the Axichis help him and his poor, pathetic, confused, lost companions.

The others started up, too, and they took their distraction strategy to the limit. They made almost as much noise as the cannons.

The Axichis yelled back at them, but LeMaine couldn't hear them over the Hellhounds' combined yells. LeMaine took a chance, staggered several paces toward the nearest Axichis, and held out his arms like he wanted to grab the guy.

The Axichis guard backstepped rapidly to keep some distance between himself and LeMaine. The Axichis kept bellowing for LeMaine to back away and for the whole squad to be quiet, but the Axichis didn't shoot.

That one guard moving back toward the gate gave LeMaine the opening he needed. He kept going and the guy kept backing away. LeMaine burst into a fresh bout of sobs. He was almost inside.

The other Axichis guards kept whipping their guns from LeMaine to the squad and back to LeMaine. None of the Axichis could figure out what to do. Their superiors never expected a situation like this.

At the last second before his target reached the gate, LeMaine lunged, grabbed the guy, and then collapsed on his knees. The guard still had his gun raised until LeMaine knocked it out of the way with his own body.

His weight pulled the gun down and LeMaine pinned it between his own body and the guard's body. LeMaine didn't have to worry about the guy shooting him now.

LeMaine laid it on even thicker begging and pleading for help. The guard roared in his face to get back and shut up.

The tension escalated to the breaking point, and without warning, one of the other Axichis charged LeMaine from behind and clubbed him across the back of the skull.

His implant short-circuited, but only for a second. He buckled to the ground in front of that one guard, but that moment broke the tension.

The other guards laid hold of the Hellhounds and dragged them through the gate. More guards helped haul LeMaine inside and they dumped him at his companions' feet.

The Hellhounds pulled him upright, but that blow did something to his implant. It kicked into high gear and he started seeing things even more clearly. Maybe the acuity setting got knocked to a higher level than it had been.

The implant skittered this way and that picking out details LeMaine hadn't noticed before. Every twitch of the Axichis' facial expressions, every hazy outline of another guard crossing the cannon station at a distance, and even the sparks of power on the fence showed up as clear as day.

He shook his head trying to clear his mind. His Hellhounds patted him down, but his attention snapped back to the guards in front of him. One of them returned to the gatehouse, no doubt to communicate with someone higher up the chain of command.

The others stood guard around the squad, but the Axichis didn't raise their guns to hold the squad at gunpoint. The ruse worked. The Axichis didn't see the squad as a threat since none of the Hellhounds were armed.

LeMaine's implant picked up the subtle relaxation of the guards' fingers on their triggers. They let their vigilance slacken. They spent more time looking around and watching their comrade in the gatehouse than they did watching the Hellhounds.

Without warning, before LeMaine even realized what was happening, Galo spun around the nearest Axichis, grabbed the man's head, and snapped his neck. The body collapsed right there in the dirt and the other Imoliv struck just as fast.

Each one grabbed a guard and another three went down. The Hellhounds reacted on instinct. Lemon, Heckler, Monk, and Kellogg all attacked different guards.

Kellogg snatched a gun from one of them, cracked the butt stock into the guard's face, and drove the guy to the ground. Kellogg slammed his foot onto the guy's jaw so hard that his neck snapped, too.

Lemon sprang on top of another Axichis, grabbed his head, locked his neck under her arm, and gave it a violent upward jerk to end the bastard.

Heckler punched the nearest guard so hard in the chest that the guy buckled on the spot. Heckler dropped the guard on his face and punched again into the back of his victim's head to shatter the skull.

Monk attacked his victim with a hail of punches, pounded him into the dirt, and just kept on pounding until he pulverized the guard's head to a pulp.

LeMaine grabbed Monk's arm. "That's enough. He's dead." LeMaine rounded on Galo. "Are you insane? This isn't what we agreed on."

"You said....." Galo began, but just then, the guard came out of the gatehouse.

Sindra rushed him, tore the gun out of the man's hand, and turned it on him. Sindra fired a laser into the man's chest and swiped it sideways to cut him in half.

LeMaine stared at the Axichis bodies all over the ground. They were all dead and no one else on the station knew it yet. How long would that take?

"You said to take a run through the countryside," Galo finished. "You said to shank them."

"Yeah, but.....not now!" LeMaine exclaimed. "Not just like that with no warning."

"Would you have preferred to let them lock us up first?" Lutov asked.

LeMaine searched the station. His implant kept picking up more details. No more Axichis were coming this way, but they would eventually.

"All right. You four help me hide these bodies."

"Where?" Galo asked.

"In the gatehouse. Hurry. You Hellhounds cover up the bloodstains and then go on and make your run....and for Jesus's sake, keep it quiet."

The Hellhounds relieved all the dead guards of their weapons and LeMaine, Heckler, Monk, and Sindra dragged the bodies into the gatehouse.

Monk had to heave the last ones in by himself to throw them on top of the stack. Then LeMaine shut the door. No sign remained of the scuffle....and no sign remained of the other Hellhounds.

"Go!" LeMaine urged the other three. "Get it done—fast.

They ran off in four different directions, but LeMaine's implant kept acting up—or at least, it kept feeding him information it shouldn't have. It didn't function like a normal human eye. Was this how the Imoliv saw all the time?

He raced through the station spotting Axichis footprints leading everywhere. He occasionally spotted human ones following them, so he ran off in different directions.

The cannons started pounding again. LeMaine stopped to listen, but he couldn't hear anything over the constant booming thump. The sound only helped to cover up what the Hellhounds were doing.

He came to a corner and looked beyond it. A pair of Axichis guards crossed near the fence, came to one of the buildings, and Nunn and O'Hara jumped out of hiding to attack the guards.

The two Hellhounds brought the guards down easily, but Nunn and O'Hara didn't see another squad of four Axichis moving in from behind them.

LeMaine took off running to intercept the Axichis soldiers. He might have been more cautious about attacking four Axichis on his own, but for some reason, his implant made him more confident.

He skirted a different building. The four Axichis didn't see him. They raised their guns to shoot Nunn and O'Hara. If the Axichis succeeded, Nunn and O'Hara wouldn't know what hit them.

LeMaine exploded out of hiding behind the four guards and cracked two of their heads together. The other two whirled around to aim their guns at him.

His implant fed him information so fast he didn't have time to think about it. He judged the soldiers' movements without thought.

He sprang for the nearest guard, shoved the gun out of the way, punched the guy in the face, and then spun backward to clamp the gun under his arm. The guard fired and LeMaine steered the laser to slice down the other three.

They fell while LeMaine held the fourth man immobile. LeMaine cracked his elbow back into the guard's face and then shoved the guy backward into the fence. The energy LeMaine had seen pulsing through the wires jolted the man's body and flung LeMaine off.

LeMaine sprawled across the ground, but the guard remained stuck there jerking, writhing, and firing his weapon into the ground.

Eventually, the current shorted out and the body collapsed next to LeMaine. He picked himself up slowly. Now he had three laser rifles and no one to shoot them at.

He picked them up and turned around to find Nunn and O'Hara watching him from fifty yards away. They stared at him in amazement. He didn't think he'd done anything out of the ordinary, but this implant gave him a strange feeling.

He went over to them, but he didn't know what to say and no one would have been able to hear each other anyway, so they all walked off together. They snuck up on another squad of four guards. This time, LeMaine signaled the others to hide behind a different building and shoot the guards at a distance. They dropped without seeing who attacked them.

The Hellhounds swept through the station and met back up at the gatehouse. The cannons kept pounding into the air. The gunners had no clue what was going on.

The noise made conversation impossible, and since the gunners didn't see the intruders, LeMaine decided to play it safe. He pointed at the Hellhounds and assigned them to each cannon. Then LeMaine made a quick study of the guns.

Thick power conduits ran from each cannon back to the gatehouse. The guards at the gatehouse had been able to call the gunners to stop firing when the Hellhounds showed up. There must be a way to control the cannons from there.

He went back and got Monk to help him drag all the bodies out of the gatehouse. Finding the cannons' power supply cutoff wasn't hard. The Axichis were still using Elian technology with the instructions all in English.

He threw the lever and the noise stopped again. He returned to the cannons to find all the Hellhounds standing over all the dead gunners.

"So....that's it?" Lemon complained. "That was way too easy."

"We aren't done yet," LeMaine told her. "It's time to take back our solar system and show these Axichis who's boss."

Chapter 25

LeMaine climbed into the nearest cannon capsule and a communications system connected with the other cannons. The Axichis had definitely modified these guns. He'd never seen anything like the firing and targeting mechanisms.

A 360º-scanner display showed him everything happening off the planet. The controls automatically delayed every shot and led every target so the lasers struck with pinpoint accuracy.

The gunner's seat wheeled in all directions, but only one small slice of the sky concerned LeMaine. The battle going on between the Elian-Imoliv alliance and the Axichis covered all the space between Evilia and Elia. The Hellhounds couldn't miss.

"This is what I'm talking about!" O'Hara crowed. "When the war is over, let's get us a ship with a few of these on board. Hell yeah! Who wants to be the first to put some numbers on the board?"

"This is just like shooting fish in a barrel," Heckler growled. "Come on, little fishies. You know you want some."

"These are great," Peterman exclaimed. "So smooth...."

"Here they come!" Nunn yelled as a fleet of Axichis warships soared into view coming from Zukion. They soared past Evilia, totally oblivious to how quickly their fortunes were about to change.

Cheers broke out down the line of gunners and the Hellhounds opened fire. Lasers erupted all over the station, but these capsules insulated the squad from the noise. LeMaine hardly heard anything.

His capsule spun effortlessly following the warships on their casual glide past Evilia.

The Hellhounds unloaded on them and a sheet of lasers rocketed into space. Those lasers popped and boomed on the warships' sides, but that sound remained far removed from LeMaine's reality.

"This is way too easy!" Kellogg gloated. "Kellogg: three."

"Polasek: four."

"O'Hara: six."

"Why are you counting?" Sindra asked.

"We keep score," Kellogg told him. "Whoever gets the most enemy kills, wins."

"What do you win?" Galo asked.

"Bragging rights," Polasek replied.

"A big head," Heckler rumbled. "Just ask O'Hara."

"Not to mention endless shit from the rest of the squad," Nunn added. "Here we go! Incoming!"

Laughter broke out among the gunners, but at that moment, another much larger fleet of warships zoomed around Evilia. They were coming from Zukion, too.

The other Hellhounds were all too busy shooting at the ships in front of them. They didn't see this new Axichis contingent.

LeMaine's implant kicked into high gear and he wheeled his capsule around. He didn't realize he was firing until he'd already hit seven of them.

He hammered them with lasers one after another. He'd barely finished landing several shots before his implant snapped to a different warship. The implant connected up different parts of his brain that he thought were already working at their best.

He didn't make the decision to change targets. Something beyond him made him move faster than thought. His eyes darted rapidly over the battlefield and all his reflexes reacted just as fast.

His cannon stuttered in his hands as countless lasers erupted from the gun. Some of the warships turned around to see who was firing at them only to take his barrage right in their own forward cannons. They never got a shot off before they all exploded.

The debris field started to drift apart right there at Evilia's farthest western horizon. The warships didn't make it any farther than that. They never even made it into the center of the other gunners' field of view.

"Holy shit!" Nunn breathed. "Did you see that?"

"How many was that?" O'Hara asked in the same hushed undertone.

"I didn't have time to count them," Kellogg replied.

"My controls are reading thirty enemy kills," Peterman chimed in.

"Thirty!" Nunn whispered.

No one said anything for a second, and then another grouping of Axichis fighter craft streaked out of the eastern sky. "They're coming from Aora!" Monk called. "Now's our chance to catch up! The system is reading sixty of them."

All the gunners rotated their cannons that way. The sight of more enemy targets triggered LeMaine's attack response again and he joined in.

"Hey!" Lemon yelled. "LeMaine is horning in on our patch!"

"Go fight your own battles, Sir!" Nunn yelled.

"Okay," LeMaine replied and chuckled as another bunch of warships loomed into view.

These came from the main battle closer to Elia. They broke away from the fight against the Elian Military and the Imoliv defensive line.

The Axichis pulled back to target Evilia "It looks like someone upstairs finally noticed that things were rotten in the state of Denmark," Peterman remarked.

"What's Denmark?" Lutov asked and the Hellhounds laughed at him.

"It means there's trouble in the kitchen," Monk replied.

"I don't understand," Galo told him.

The others laughed even louder, but they didn't have time to target these warships. LeMaine turned his cannons on them and the same thing happened. His implant switched gears and all his reactions became supercharged and automatically much, much faster.

He fired without thinking and pounded the warships to smithereens.

"I don't even want to know how many points he has now," Heckler muttered.

"He's out of the game," Kellogg announced. "His numbers don't count."

"You mean he has too many for you to count," Polasek fired back. "We're eating his dust."

"You stay over there in your corner and shoot your warships, Sir," Monk told him. "We'll be over here playing around with our fighter craft. We'll see you at suppertime later."

LeMaine joined in with their laughter, but this implant made him feel strange. He didn't feel like himself at all. He would almost have preferred to glue his one good eye to his carbine without being able to see anything else around him.

That was never going to happen now. He was stuck with this implant, for better or for worse.

He didn't see anything bad about it. It picked out targets with incredible accuracy. The connection between his eyes and his hands got so fast that he watched from somewhere outside himself.

More warships split away from the main battle to threaten Evilia, only to wind up smashed to space dust by the ground cannons.

The Axichis sent more vessels from other planets farther out in the system. The cannons' scanners couldn't pick them up with Evilia in the way, but pretty soon, the Axichis stopped sending any more craft to come near these cannons.

The battle cooled without so many warships there. The Axichis stood off for a while and the gunners stopped firing. They didn't have any more targets.

The Axichis flew away and made sure to take a wide detour away from Evilia so they wouldn't come within the cannons' range. Then they vacated the battlefield entirely.

Cruel laughter broke out among the Hellhounds. "We kicked their asses!" O'Hara sang. "We kicked their asses!"

"Who do we get to shoot next, Sir?" Monk asked. "Please say we can stay here and keep these cannons."

"You Hellhounds better unload," LeMaine replied. "It will be dark soon. We need to set up a watch to make sure the Axichis don't get the jump on us when the planet turns toward the outer ring."

"How are we going to stop them?" O'Hara asked.

"First, we gotta figure out how to send a message to Command. We need them to send some other gunners down here to man these things so we can pull out. We have two other stations to hit and not much time to do it before they turn toward Elia."

"How will you communicate with Command from here?" Polasek asked. "The station will only have Axichis channels."

LeMaine made up his mind in a split second. "We'll contact the Maczhi battalion through their fighter craft. They can relay the message to command through the Nulia array."

LeMaine left the Hellhounds to guard the station while he and Polasek went to find the Axichis communications system. It didn't take long to relay the message between the Maczhi battalion and the Elian Military Command.

LeMaine got Colonel Nicholson on the horn. "I'm sending you four bombers with gunners and troops to hold the station," he told LeMaine. "They'll relieve you and the Hellhounds so you can go after the other stations."

"Copy that, Sir. We don't know if the Axichis found out our ploy to get inside this one, so we'll have to come up with some other dirty trick."

Colonel Nicholson laughed. He hadn't sounded this happy since the invasion started. "I'm sure you will, Owen. You and the Hellhounds better deploy back to the city using your covers. I'd offer to send one of the bombers to deliver you, but that would only alert the Axichis that you're coming."

"Yes, Sir," LeMaine replied. "We'll handle it on our own."

"Good man, Owen. Congratulations. This is the first big break we've had. If we can take Evilia, we'll be on our way to driving these cocksuckers back."

"Yes, Sir. That's the plan."

They hung up and LeMaine started to turn away from the system, but Polasek stopped him. "Look at that."

He pointed to a different signal. It came through the Axichis communications system like all the others. It showed up all the Axichis outposts, bases, and operations centers the Axichis had set up inside Elia since they first invaded.

The two cannon stations the Hellhounds wanted to capture showed up as plain as day, but Polasek indicated something else. It wasn't a cannon station and it wasn't a base. In fact, it had no infrastructure at all—not on the surface where anyone could see it.

The system read more than five hundred Axichis warships hidden in an underground bunker.

"It's at the very center of the far northern continent above the frost line," Polasek pointed out. "No Elians live up there. It's uninhabited for thousands of miles in any direction. That explains why no one has noticed the Axichis moving in hundreds of ships without anyone noticing."

"They couldn't have brought in that many," LeMaine countered. "Evilia is too close to the inner ring. Command would have monitored that many ships coming so close to the home planet. Command would have watched them to see where they were going."

"How do you explain no one finding out about this?"

LeMaine shrugged. "Maybe they moved them disassembled. Maybe they had a way to transport the parts up there, put the ships together underground, and arm them to be ready to deploy if the war ever turned against them—or, more likely, they're keeping this force to use against the Imoliv. Evilia is too close to the Imoliv border. Come on. We gotta inform Sindra's team about this. We might need to change our strategy."

Chapter 26

The Hellhounds stuck around the cannon station just until the Elian bombers showed up to relieve the squad. Then LeMaine called a transport to take them back to the city.

They arrived after dark, which was perfect for LeMaine's plans. He didn't see any Axichis patrolling the streets at this time of night.

LeMaine also detected another reason the Axichis may not have been keeping too close an eye on the inhabitants. The cannon station getting captured and the Axichis fleet getting sent packing by their own guns must have made the Axichis sit up and take notice. They were probably scrambling to rearrange their resources to deal with this reversal.

LeMaine halted on a deserted street corner and called another transport to take the squad across the planet to the next station on their list.

They disembarked in the middle of another broad, empty landscape without a soul in sight. This one wasn't as green and easy, though. Rubble fields surrounded the station for hundreds of miles. Not a tree grew anywhere.

"Not your best choice of nightlife location, Sir," Nunn quipped. "I'm putting in for a transfer."

"Just wait until after the mission," he told her. "Then you can go to the spa and get your nails done."

"Hey! What about my nails?" O'Hara called out.

"You need a few more nails in your coffin," Lemon replied and everyone laughed.

LeMaine squatted down on the bare rubble and pulled open the pack of supplies he'd taken from the bombers. "We'll build a fire to keep warm. We need something to help us think up a way to get inside this station."

He pulled an emergency torch out of his pack and set it alight with some dry scrub from the rubble field. This landscape wasn't as nice as having a cave to hide in, but at least this one didn't have any wind.

The fire's heat stayed close to it and the squad gathered around to get warm. The Hellhounds pulled out their ration bars and started talking.

"How are we going to hit this hangar you told us about, Captain?" Monk asked.

"Please say we'll be using lots of Plaostine," Nunn added.

"You aren't allowed Plaostine anymore, darling'," Heckler countered. "You might break a nail and then where we would be?"

"Up shit's creek," Lemon chimed in.

Sindra turned to LeMaine. "How do you think we should hit the hangar? You always have good ideas."

LeMaine stared into the fire and didn't look up. "I'll let you know if I think of something."

"At least we don't have to worry about these ships getting airborne," Polasek interjected. "There were no Axichis life signs around the hangar. It was deserted."

"Are you saying the Axichis aren't even guarding it?" Galo asked. "How could they be so stupid?"

"Before we took that cannon station, they had no reason to guard the hangar," Kellogg pointed out. "No one on our side could get anywhere near the planet with the cannons there. The Axichis probably thought they didn't need to guard it. With three cannon stations covering every side of the planet, they probably thought they had Evilia in the bag."

"Which they did," Heckler added. "They had it in the bag and we took it back."

"Just like we're going to take the other two back," Sindra replied. "We'll take out the stations and then hit the hangar."

"I think we should do it the other way around," LeMaine told him. "I think we should do the hangar first and then the stations."

Sindra frowned at him. "Why? The hangar is undefended."

"It might be boobytrapped."

"I didn't think of that," Sindra replied and he turned to stare into the fire, too.

The others started making rude remarks about the Axichis the squad had hit during the battle and then O'Hara said, "What are we going to do to pay Captain LeMaine back for beating us so badly?"

All eyes turned to LeMaine, but he didn't look up. He didn't want to think about that battle, but he couldn't stop it from playing before his eyes. He still couldn't explain to himself what his implant did to him.

He needed to think about this. He needed to figure out if it was even good or bad. It certainly made his shooting better, but he liked it better the old way. He liked having control over what he was shooting instead of having some piece of machinery in his head doing it for him.

Would he ever get used to this? He didn't want to.

The Hellhounds kept talking, but he barely heard them. They laughed at their own jokes, but he didn't hear them, either.

They eventually pulled their blankets out of their packs, curled up, and went to sleep one after another. The four Imoliv did the same thing. They did everything the squad did now. They were as much a part of this as anybody.

"What's on your mind?" someone asked. The voice seemed to come from outer space.

He looked up to find Kellogg sitting at his side. Kellogg had been sitting across the fire from LeMaine. LeMaine didn't see him move.

LeMaine cast a glance around the ring of sleeping bodies. No one stirred. No one would hear him say the words, but he still hesitated to say them. He didn't want to admit even to himself that there was something wrong with him.

"My implant....." he muttered. "It did something weird during the battle."

"What did it do?" Kellogg asked. "You seemed to be shooting just fine."

"That's the problem. It worked too well. It went into some kind of hyper battle mode. It started moving incredibly fast—too fast for a human eye—but it somehow connected with my other eye so they were both working together. It also connected to my mind so my reactions.....the implant took them over. It made all my reactions ultra-fast and automatic. I never could have fired that fast or that accurately on my own."

Kellogg frowned. "That's strange. The doctors didn't say anything about that."

"It was spooky. It was almost like my mind just switched off and the implant did everything for me. It was.....scary."

"Weird." Kellogg pulled his scanner out of his pack and pointed it at LeMaine's head.

He hated Kellogg treating him like a patient, but there was no way to get his old eye back. That's why he had this implant—because his old eye had been destroyed.

"Your brainwaves are all reading as normal. I can't read the implant. The scanner doesn't understand the technology. Maybe we could ask Sindra....."

"No!" LeMaine fought his voice down. "Don't tell them anything."

"Then you just have to learn to live with it." Kellogg put his scanner away. "It hasn't caused you any ill effects, has it? It wasn't bothering you before—no pain or blurred vision or confusion?"

LeMaine shook his head. He had to keep his head down. He didn't want to see Kellogg or for Kellogg to see him.

"Maybe this is how the Imoliv see all the time," Kellogg suggested. "They were moving pretty fast back at the station."

"That's what I thought, but then I watched them shooting during the battle. They were shooting normally. You saw. They didn't rack up any more points than the rest of you."

"That's true." Kellogg turned in his seat to stare into the fire. "We don't understand this technology, so I can't explain it to you. When we finish this mission, you can talk to the Imoliv doctors and find out. Maybe the implant has some kind of combat settings and you could tell the doctor that you need the settings turned on."

"I don't like it," LeMaine grumbled.

"I think you probably just need to get used to it. It won't function the same as your old eye and it's still new. You'll get used to it in time. It beats the hell out of retirement, right?"

LeMaine nodded, but he didn't answer. Would he have taken the implant at all if he'd known it was going to take him over like this? He wasn't sure and now it was too late.

"Can I ask you something?" he blurted out.

"Sure," Kellogg replied.

"How do you know you're human?" LeMaine stumbled over the words. He didn't even realize he was asking himself this question before it just slipped out. "I mean, at what point do I cease to be human? If this implant starts making decisions for me....."

"It isn't making decisions for you, is it?" Kellogg interrupted. "You were the one who decided to shoot at those warships.....weren't you?"

"Of course, but the implant decided *how* to shoot at them. I might have done it differently if I only had time to think about it."

"You don't know that," Kellogg replied. "The brain has many dimensions of thought and decision-making, some of which aren't conscious. We can be influenced by things and make decisions without even realizing it. We make decisions about other people by seeing their facial expressions and body language. We make those decisions in a split second without even thinking about them. I'd say it's more likely that the implant tapped into a subconscious part of your brain. Maybe it intercepted messages from your decision-making faculties and translated them into action without giving you a chance to think twice about them."

"Well, maybe I need to think twice about them," LeMaine countered. "Maybe I wouldn't be doing my job if I didn't think twice about them. My job is more than shooting first and asking questions later."

"I know it is," Kellogg murmured.

LeMaine sighed and his shoulders slumped under the weight of his concerns. "Maybe I'm just getting old. Maybe I should have been retired with one eye. Maybe that's what this is all about. Maybe I'm too old to do the job if I need my body parts replaced by machines."

"You know that isn't true," Kellogg countered. "That laser could have hit the *Bombardier* on the port side and then Monk would be the one walking around with an artificial eye. This has nothing to do with you being too old to do the job."

"How would I know, though?" LeMaine asked. "How would I actually know if I'm too old to do the job?"

Kellogg hesitated for a second and then said, "Do you honestly think there is anyone who is better qualified to do your job than you are? Can you think of one person—even one—in the whole Elian Military—who could even do your job, much less do it better than you could? Why the hell do you think they keep you on? You're the best there is. Look at Polasek and Peterman. If you retired, one of them would get promoted to take your place. Can you honestly, in all seriousness, look me in the eye and tell me that they would do a better job than you would?"

LeMaine stared into the fire and didn't answer. He didn't like to say anything against Polasek or Peterman, but Kellogg was right. Neither of them would be better at commanding the Hellhounds than LeMaine was. That was just objective fact. Polasek and Peterman would probably be the first to admit it.

They *would* be the first to admit it. They both thought the sun rose and set on LeMaine. Neither of them wanted to take his job. No one *could* take his job. Everybody said so because it was the truth.

"It's my job as the medical officer on this squad to monitor your fitness to command," Kellogg went on. "If there was anything about you, either physically or mentally, that made you unfit to command this squad, it would be my responsibility to pull you from active duty. You know me. You know I wouldn't leave you in command for a single second if I had any doubts about your fitness. I would never put my squad mates in jeopardy like that."

"Yeah," LeMaine murmured. "I know."

"There is nothing wrong with you," Kellogg insisted. "Not physically—not mentally—not your age. You're healthy. You're smart. You're strong and you always make good decisions. You made good decisions during that battle and there's no doubt in my mind that you'll keep making good decisions with this implant. Like I said, you might just need to get used to it. You've had it for such a short time. It may be extra fast because it hasn't calibrated to your brainwaves yet or it might just seem extra fast because you aren't used to it. Give it time. Either way, you have to wait until we get back to the Elian line before you can consult one of the Imoliv doctors. You might as well give the implant a chance to work before you decide it's a bad thing."

"I don't think it's a bad thing. I don't know if it's a good thing or not."

"It's a good thing because it allowed you to stay in command. It's a good thing because it means that you didn't have to retire and the best man stayed in the job. Right?"

"Yeah. I guess so."

"Then it's a good thing. It's a good thing until it stops being a good thing."

"How will I know when that is?" LeMaine asked.

Kellogg shot him a grin. His cheeks and teeth glowed in the firelight. "I trust you to tell me when it stops being a good thing. I know you well enough to know that you wouldn't hesitate to tell me if that was the case. That's why we're having this conversation. If you honestly believed someone else was better qualified to command this squad, you would remove yourself. You wouldn't stay. You care about this squad too much."

"Of course I do."

"It's the same with the implant. You'll tell me if it isn't working right or if it's interfering with your judgment. You'll tell me when it's time. You'll tell Colonel Nicholson and you'll retire. That isn't now—not by a long way. I'm certain of it. Your fitness to command is one of the very few things I do believe in."

LeMaine let his gaze fall even farther toward the ground. "Thank you, Mason."

"You bet." Kellogg squeezed LeMaine's shoulder. "That's what I'm here for."

Chapter 27

Lemon pulled her disguise suit over her head and she vanished completely. "How do I look, Sir?"

"You look like the most beautiful woman in the world," he teased.

"Spoken like a man who hasn't seen his wife in three years," Heckler called from the back of the squad.

LeMaine only grinned at him. "Keep telling yourself that, Corporal."

"You don't even have a wife, Heckler," Nunn countered. "How long has it been since you even had a girl?"

"That's enough of that," LeMaine interrupted. "Do you know what to do, Lemon?"

"Yes, Sir. I'll see you soon."

"Good luck, Sergeant."

The rubble around Lemon's feet moved aside as she took a step and then even that disappeared. All sight and sound of her evaporated into the desolate landscape.

"How long do we have to wait for her to let us in?" O'Hara asked.

"As long as it takes." LeMaine stretched out on his stomach and crawled a few yards away.

A slow rise gave just enough space for the squad to hide behind. The other Hellhounds crawled up next to him and they all looked down the other side to the cannon station in the distance.

It sprawled in the middle of the vast rubble fields, completely alone. The same thunderous eruptions of lasers spouted from the cannons. They shook the ground even from here.

O'Hara watched for a while and then flipped over onto his back. "Wake me up when something happens."

"I can't watch this, either." Heckler inched backward, returned to their original spot, squatted down, and started messing with his pack.

The squad had brought plenty of laser rifles stolen from the first station they had captured. These rifles worked better than carbines—or it seemed that way where the Axichis were concerned.

LeMaine had found himself starting to think that only Axichis weaponry would work against the Axichis. The same attitude had infected the whole squad.

The four Imoliv gathered around Heckler, talked in an undertone, and after a long wait, Monk and Nunn went back there, too.

Polasek and Peterman stayed in position with LeMaine, but the two lieutenants didn't pay as close attention to the station as LeMaine did. That was his job, not theirs. They didn't have to pay attention until he told them to.

Maybe that was what Kellogg had been trying to tell LeMaine last night. He was the one who was always in command simply because he was the one who was always in command.

If he hadn't been here, whoever took his place would have to be the one to pay attention while the others snoozed. Peterman or Polasek would rise to the occasion, but today was not that day.

LeMaine raised his binoculars to his eyes and searched the station again for anything out of the ordinary. Sindra's voice cut in on his thoughts. "Do you see anything?"

"Naw," LeMaine murmured back. "We won't see anything until we *do* see something."

"What will we see?"

"I don't know. It just depends on how Lemon decides to play it. She'll have to use her judgment and figure out the best way for us to get in. I'm sure she'll figure it out."

"You leave a great deal to your subordinates," Sindra remarked.

"Yes, I do," LeMaine remarked without taking his binoculars down. "They have their skills and strengths. It's my job to make the best use of them. I don't know the situation inside the station. She'll know better than I do how to get us in."

"You said last night that you thought we should go to the hangar first. Why did you change your mind to come here first?"

"Call it a hunch," LeMaine replied.

"I don't understand you."

LeMaine took his binoculars down to meet the young man's gaze for the first time, but LeMaine didn't feel like explaining about the Maczhi battalion right now.

He went back to looking through his glasses at the station in the distance. He still didn't see anything.

His implant didn't seem to be doing anything out of the ordinary. Then again, he wasn't in a stressed or combat situation. Maybe it only kicked in when he put himself in danger.

"Can I ask you a question, Captain?" Sindra asked.

"Yes," LeMaine replied.

"That other Hellhound you had on your squad—the one that wasn't human—Buca was his name if I recall."

LeMaine stiffened. "What about him?"

"Is he the first non-human you've ever had on your squad?"

LeMaine took his glasses down fast. "Why do you ask that?"

"I'm just curious. Have you only ever had humans before him?"

"Yes. He was the first. Now tell me why you want to know."

"I'm just curious." Sindra's eyes darted toward the station and back to LeMaine. "Would you consider taking another non-human?"

"Of course. I don't care what species a person is. It's what's inside a person that makes them a Hellhound."

Sindra turned away completely and squinted across the landscape. "Are *we* Hellhounds?"

LeMaine gaped at the side of the young man's head. LeMaine was too stunned to make a sound, not even to tell Sindra that he and his team were Hellhounds. What was Sindra really asking?

LeMaine swallowed hard and put his glasses back to his eyes, but he couldn't stop his brain from spinning in a million directions.

He almost gave up and put his binoculars down when he saw it. "There it is! We're on!" LeMaine kicked O'Hara. "Wake up, Sergeant! Everybody get over here now! We're going in."

LeMaine stayed glued to the ground with his binoculars plastered to his eyes as the Hellhounds gathered their gear and assembled behind him. Far in the distance, something was moving inside the station.

He didn't see it at first. Then one lower section of the outer fence peeled back by itself. Nothing seemed to be moving it. It rolled out of the way and left a two-foot open gap between the fence and the ground.

Another ripple of something unseen disturbed the fabric of reality and Lemon peeled off her suit down to the waist. Her lower body remained invisible. She waved one arm over her head to call the squad in. Then she pulled her suit over her head and vanished.

"Let's move!" LeMaine hopped to his feet, threw on his backpack, stuffed his binoculars into the outer pocket, and took off at a fast stride across the rubble field.

The Hellhounds fell in behind him and they all got busy pulling their laser rifles forward and preparing themselves for battle.

All of them cast glances around, behind, in front of, and above them, but the whole area remained clear and undisturbed.

LeMaine focused on the fence directly ahead. He counted down the seconds before the sentries showed up and discovered the breach that Lemon had created. Did she remove the sentries, too?

He could only hope. He stopped outside the fence, pulled up the lowest stretch of wire, and waved everyone underneath. He stood guard with his rifle in his other hand. That was when his implant kicked into high gear.

One glance around the station brought up all the detail he remembered from the last battle. The smallest indentation in the dirt showed him exactly where the Axichis sentries had passed this point on their usual rounds. He also saw Lemon's footprints heading in the opposite direction.

He ducked under the wire and pushed the others away. "Go!" None of the Hellhounds could hear him over the cannon's pounding thump, so he pushed them away. "Go!"

They separated and LeMaine's implant took over all his senses and reactions. He followed those tracks and hunted down a pair of Axichis sentries.

He attacked them much faster than he should have been able to, snapped their necks, and dragged the bodies into a corner where no one would find them.

He crouched there listening for any sound in between the cannons' deafening pound. Did the implant take over his hearing, too, or did he just imagine it?

He peeked out searching for his next target and spotted the gatehouse. He could shut down the cannons from there.

One Axichis soldier sat inside. LeMaine really wished he had Lemon's disguise right now, but he would just have to use the next best thing.

He crept behind several buildings until he got into the most favorable position, picked up a pebble, and threw it at the gatehouse. The pebble hit the walls and made a soft clunk. The guard looked up and through the windows at the station around him.

The guard shrugged and went back to whatever he was working on in front of him. LeMaine threw another pebble and the guard scowled through the windows. He didn't go back to what he was doing this time.

LeMaine did the same thing twice more and the guard got to his feet. He paced inside his little house, and when he turned his back and LeMaine threw another pebble, the guard came out.

LeMaine snuck a little closer....and a little closer......He came up right behind the gatehouse and tossed a pebble right in front of the guard. It landed in more gravel and the guard took a few more steps to examine the spot.

LeMaine attacked in silent fury, punched the guy to the ground, and then turned the guard's laser rifle on him. LeMaine dragged the body back inside the gatehouse and got busy on the controls.

He shut down the cannons and then went through the same process of relaying a message through the Maczhi battalion.

"You're really starting to scare me, Owen," Colonel Nicholson told him when LeMaine explained that the Hellhounds had secured the second cannon station.

LeMaine laughed nervously. "I'm really starting to scare myself, too, but we have another problem we need to worry about. I have an idea to take the third station. It will go much quicker than the Hellhounds it."

"Just don't let it include our bombers getting blown away by the cannons."

"No, not at all. That would defeat the purpose of the operation, but you can overrun the station with ground troops. The cannons won't be able to shoot at them from the ground and these stations aren't guarded by that many Axichis. They haven't been able to move in reinforcements."

"I'm willing to give it a shot, but how will we get ground troops near the station? The cannons would be able to target any bomber that came near them."

"Land the ground troops with attack cruisers then.....and send an attack cruiser here for me and the Hellhounds. We have another mission we need to run before the Axichis get wind of this."

"All right, Owen. We're on our way."

They hung up and LeMaine used the controls to shut down the cannons. The system in front of him gave him a scanner view of the Hellhounds working their way through the station one sentry at a time.

The cannon gunners stayed in their capsules for a few minutes and then got out, milled around, and headed for the gatehouse to find out what was wrong with their guns. They would be here any second.

Out of nowhere, two blinding streaks of Imoliv life signs rushed up behind the gunners. The Imoliv raced down the line snuffing out Axichis life signs in a whirlwind. The gunners' life signs vanished off the display one after another.

LeMaine marveled at the Imoliv's speed. They seemed to go into that blind state of instantaneous reaction time the same way LeMaine did. Maybe his implant was just doing what was normal for the Imoliv. Maybe it didn't make him a freak after all.

He stayed at the gatehouse while the Hellhounds eliminated all the Axichis from the station. Then he and the Hellhounds took over the guns and cleared the air of all Axichis craft the way they did yesterday.

The process didn't take as long this time. The Axichis were starting to wake up to the fact that some Elian force was taking the ground cannons on Evilia. The Axichis retreated much more quickly and they didn't send fleets of warships to try to retake the position.

"Chickenshits!" Monk yelled at them as the Axichis force cleared away from the front line around Elia.

"It only means they're regrouping somewhere else," LeMaine told him. "Pull out, Hellhounds. We gotta move."

The Hellhounds stood guard only long enough for the Elian Military to reinforce the station with its own gunners. Then the Hellhounds resupplied from one of the bombers and loaded into the ship that Colonel Nicholson sent for them.

LeMaine had asked for an attack cruiser, but instead, Colonel Nicholson sent another Hunter-class named the *Sea Dragon*. Colonel Nicholson really knew what the Hellhounds liked.

LeMaine sat up in the cockpit with Monk. LeMaine secretly thanked the stars that he always let Monk do the flying. LeMaine didn't trust his implant behind the wheel of any spacecraft. He wasn't ready to take this whole implant thing that far.

Monk powered up and the *Sea Dragon* rocketed away across the landscape. Monk shot into the atmosphere and took up a holding pattern within scanner range of the bunker.

"What are we waiting for, Sir?" he asked.

"Just keep knit, Monk," LeMaine told him. "We're in no hurry here."

Monk frowned at the scanners. "There's nothing down there."

"Let's hope not."

Monk turned to scowl at him. "What do you mean?"

LeMaine pointed out a spot. "Land over there."

Monk shuddered. "It's freezing down there."

"Aw, Monk!" Nunn sang from the back. "Are you worried about chilling your little tootsies off?"

"I'll make you my tootsie if you don't shut up," Monk fired back and the others laughed, including LeMaine.

Monk set the *Sea Dragon* down at a safe distance and set the controls to lift the ship back into orbit while the Hellhounds ventured out on their own.

LeMaine went into the back to find all the Hellhounds wrapping themselves in heavy winter gear to go out onto the frozen ice sheet.

Strong winds blasted the ship's sides and rocked the vessel on its landing gear. Monk shook himself again. "I never did like the cold."

"It's nice!" O'Hara chirped. "I think I might take my next vacation leave here."

Heckler smacked the back of his head. "That's 'cuz you have no brains. You wouldn't take your vacation leave anywhere without an audience to fall all over your lousy jokes."

"And girls," Kellogg added. "You wouldn't take your vacation leave anywhere without girls."

"You're right, but that's what I have my best girl Lemon for, right?" O'Hara hooked his elbow around Lemon's neck and tried to pull her into a rough hug.

She responded by punching him in the stomach and then giving him a vicious upper-cut to the lower jaw.

His head snapped back and he collapsed on his knees with an agonized groan. LeMaine was just about to intervene and tell the Hellhounds to stop fighting amongst themselves when O'Hara staggered a few stumbling inches on his knees. He raised his arms to Nunn and choked out, "Nunn....help me....you be my best girl instead....."

They all laughed and O'Hara got to his feet grinning, rubbing his jaw, and smirking at Lemon in delight. She glared at him and then turned her back on him.

Chapter 28

LeMaine popped the *Sea Dragon's* hatch and bitter, stinging wind blasted into the rear compartment. All the Hellhounds pulled their hoods and masks over their faces, positioned their snow goggles over their eyes, and stepped out onto the ice sheet.

LeMaine couldn't see a thing. He steered Polasek to the front and Polasek followed his scanner array into the ice storm. The *Sea Dragon* lifted off behind them and vanished into the clouds.

The Hellhounds struggled over almost a mile of treacherous terrain before Polasek steered them into a hollow that blocked the wind. They still had to yell to make themselves heard.

"The bunker is two hundred yards ahead, Sir!" Polasek hollered. "There's still no sign of Axichis life signs."

"Patch into the *Sea Dragon's* scanners and let's see the battle."

Polasek adjusted his controls and pulled up a wider view of the area of space around Evilia. There was no battle raging anymore between Axichis and everybody else.

The Elian Military had secured the second cannon station. That left one. Hundreds of Elian attack cruisers were already skimming into position at a safe distance from the third station where the cannons couldn't hit them.

The Axichis definitely knew what was up now. The cannons swiveled downward and fired across the landscape, but they couldn't target this close to the ground. The attack cruisers avoided them easily, streaked into position, landed hundreds of ground troops, and then whizzed away out of danger.

Once the ground troops unloaded, the cannons at the station couldn't do a thing to stop their advance. The sentries' activity got more frantic and confused as the ground troops closed in from all sides, but the Axichis had lost their advantage. They took their victories too much for granted. Now the stations stood exposed with far too few Axichis to guard them.

The attack cruisers kept darting, landing their troops, and sprinting away until a ring of thousands surrounded the station. The troops stood off and waited until the planet turned to face Elia. The Axichis no longer had enough ships in place to stop the assault.

At some unseen signal, all those troops rushed inward in a tidal wave of bodies. The sentries at the station must have been on the phone to their superiors screaming about this because the Axichis sent in warships trying to bombard the ground troops from the air.

The Elians and the Imoliv attacked at the same instant, but the cannons couldn't decide who to shoot at. They pivoted downward trying to drive the ground troops off and that left the alliance vessels to occupy the warships.

"NOW!!" LeMaine ordered.

The Hellhounds sprang out of their hiding place and they took off for the bunker, but it still appeared totally deserted.

Polasek kept checking his array. LeMaine had to keep an eye on the terrain ahead. The ice storm made visibility nearly impossible and his implant didn't give him any clues.

Even knowing he was going into danger couldn't make up for the lack of visual input. The world disappeared behind a white curtain of ice floating in front of his face.

Polasek halted in the middle of the blizzard. "The slabs are twenty yards ahead!"

"What slabs?" Heckler roared.

"The concrete slabs that slide back to let the fighters out," Polasek explained. "They're right over there."

He extended his gloved hand and pointed into the void. A plain white landscape stretched away into nothing. LeMaine didn't see anything over there—not that he didn't trust Polasek.

"There must be another entrance," LeMaine told him. "See if you can find a way for us to get down into the......"

He broke off as a deep boom shook the ice sheet under his feet. "I don't like the sound of that!" Peterman yelled.

LeMaine glanced down at his remote, but it still didn't tell him anything. The bunker looked perfectly quiet.

"What's happening?!" Polasek cried.

"You tell us!" LeMaine countered. "You're the only one with a scanner!"

Polasek started to lift his scanner to take a look at it when the ice beneath the squad's feet cracked. It split under their feet and the crack widened as it ran away toward where Polasek said the slabs were.

The Hellhounds staggered trying to catch their balance and then a gut-wrenching crack exploded from directly over the slabs. Ice shards erupted into the air and two sections of the ice sheet slid back.

Dozens upon dozens of Axichis fighter craft launched into the sky, wheeled overhead, and then turned their sights downward to where the squad stood out in the open for all the world to see.

"RUN!!" LeMaine roared and spun away, but it was already too late.

The squad took off racing for....nowhere. They had nowhere to go.

The fighters unleashed lasers onto the ice sheet and it shattered under the Hellhounds' feet. LeMaine aimed his laser rifle behind him and returned fire over his shoulder.

That seemed to work well enough to at least make them back off. He wouldn't have been able to do that with a carbine.

"Get back to the hollow!" LeMaine bellowed. "Polasek—get the *Sea Dragon* down here NOW!!"

Polasek fumbled with his array while he tried to run and shoot at the same time. The other Hellhounds fired behind them, too.

Their combined lasers held the fighter craft off just long enough for them all to spring down into the hollow, but this position didn't give them any better protection. The fighter craft just flew around behind them and targeted them anyway.

"Hurry up, Polasek!!" LeMaine thundered. "Get us the hell out of here!"

"I'm trying, Sir!" Polasek yelled back. "There are too many fighters in the air. She can't get through!"

"She better and she better do it fast!"

LeMaine turned back to the business of shooting, sealed his cheek to his rifle, and targeted all the fighter craft buzzing around, but that was the least of his worries.

Axichis ground troops poured from the same breach these fighter craft came from. How did the Axichis man these ships when there had been no Axichis life signs anywhere nearby just a few seconds before?

The Axichis had been using masking technology since the war began. They must have found a way to house all these troops on the same site and to hide their existence from everyone.

Now the bunker disgorged a fighting force unlike any LeMaine had seen yet. The assault on the third cannon station must have triggered the Axichis to launch their doomsday force.

It poured across the landscape in an unbroken wave of troops and spacecraft. Warships launched into the atmosphere with flocks of fighters surrounding them—all except the group coming after the Hellhounds right now.

LeMaine's implant switched on. He jerked his rifle this way and that shooting fighters out of the sky, but he couldn't hit them all. More and more of them kept on coming.

A laser ruptured from somewhere behind LeMaine and Polasek screamed as his array exploded in his face. LeMaine didn't even have time to check on Polasek. The *Sea Dragon* wasn't coming to get them. The squad was stranded here.

The *Sea Dragon* would never be able to get through this mess. LeMaine couldn't see the end of the Axichis horde. A dozen fighters replaced every one he shot down.

His eyes snapped in all directions faster than he ever thought possible, but they only showed him how hopeless this situation was. His implant couldn't save him or his squad from this.

Another laser smashed into something to LeMaine's left and he heard Kellogg yelling. LeMaine didn't have time to turn around and see what was happening until Kellogg grabbed LeMaine's sleeve.

"The *Sea Dragon* is coming in!!" Kellogg bellowed in his ear. "We have to pull back!"

LeMaine hunkered down and turned around to face the rest of the squad. That's when he noticed Polasek, Lemon, Galo, and Heckler all lying on the bottom of the hollow in a pool of blood.

LeMaine didn't see the *Sea Dragon* anywhere. He saw only the Axichis.

"Take them!" he yelled to Kellogg. "I'll cover you as best I can."

"I'll help you." Lutov stepped forward to LeMaine's side and then Tavon did the same thing.

LeMaine nodded and the three men turned their backs to each other. LeMaine felt the other two move and his senses exploded.

The three of them sprang out of hiding and fired their laser rifles at the same time. LeMaine felt the two Imoliv fighters' muscles moving through his own back. They jerked one way and then another at lightning speed.

The three men worked as a seamless unit to carve a hole in the Axichis assault. They held the fighter craft at bay just long enough for Kellogg, Nunn, and Monk to drag the wounded out onto the ice sheet.

The whole process too way way too long. LeMaine went into a mindless state of just shooting. He couldn't think and he didn't want to think. He let go of all effort to control his implant. He had to keep shooting and he had to shoot fast.

He fired again and again—a thousand times. Fighter craft exploded in front of him and all around him.

Kellogg dragged Heckler out of the hollow while Nunn pulled Polasek. They left slick bloody trails across the ice. Monk sprang out carrying Lemon on one shoulder and Galo on the other.

The other Hellhounds surrounded them in guns and the whole party took off across the ice, but LeMaine and his two comrades had to move slowly to keep up with the wounded.

LeMaine didn't take his eyes off his targets. He didn't believe for an instant that the *Sea Dragon* was coming to get them. This was all an exercise in hopelessness.

He had to go down shooting. Nothing else mattered. He would just keep shooting until he couldn't anymore. Then he would fall and he could stop thinking entirely.

A laser sliced through his arm and hit Peterman. He went down and LeMaine sprang out of position to straddle Peterman's body. LeMaine shot another fighter and then had to spin the other way just as fast to stop more fighters from flanking him. He didn't see the rest of the squad.

Peterman flopped onto his stomach and crawled across the ice trying to reach the rest of the squad. LeMaine backed away keeping up with him, but so many fighters surrounded them that LeMaine wasn't sure anymore where the squad was.

Kellogg charged him out of the confusion. "Get back! Get to the *Sea Dragon*—NOW!!"

LeMaine got so consumed with shooting that he had to force himself to pause and see what Kellogg meant. That was when LeMaine noticed four Imoliv destroyers hovering directly over the ice sheet.

They hammered the Axichis with phase cannons and stood guard over the *Sea Dragon* parked directly under the destroyer's enormous sides. The *Sea Dragon's* rear hatch stood open waiting for the squad to get on board.

Monk was already inside putting Lemon and Galo on the floor. Heckler lay sprawled not far from the hatch and Nunn was still hauling Polasek on a trail of blood.

Kellogg seized Peterman, tried to lift him, and Peterman's knees buckled. Peterman had passed out. Kellogg rolled him onto his back, grabbed Peterman's jacket, and started sliding him backward across the ice.

Phase cannon fire boomed over LeMaine's head, but it still couldn't wipe out this horde. The Axichis shot past the squad and surrounded the lone destroyer. They traded fire and then more warships rocketed out of the underground bunker to come after the destroyer, too.

LeMaine backed up a few more steps and then Kellogg screamed as a laser hit him in the leg. He collapsed next to Peterman.

LeMaine went down on his knee next to Kellogg. "Come on! I'll get you inside!"

"To hell with that!" Kellogg bellowed. "Help me get Peterman!"

Kellogg fumbled trying to get his backpack off. LeMaine tried to keep shooting and help Kellogg at the same time, but it didn't work.

"Give me that!" Kellogg tore the rifle out of LeMaine's hands and started shooting the Axichis fighters instead. Nunn got as far as the ramp and Monk ran out to get Polasek. The rest of the squad had almost made it to the ship.

LeMaine pounced on Kellogg's pack, tore out a sealing plaster bandage, and slapped it onto the wound in Kellogg's thigh. He roared in pain. LeMaine didn't give himself a single second to check how bad the wound was.

He jumped up, grabbed Kellogg from behind, wrapped his arms around Kellogg's chest, and dragged him at a fast backward run to the *Sea Dragon*.

Kellogg kept bellowing and shooting LeMaine's rifle all the way. LeMaine muscled Kellogg into the back just as the others raced inside.

Kellogg shot his arm out toward the ice storm and the air battle winding up to another catastrophe outside. "My pack!"

LeMaine didn't hesitate. He didn't have a weapon anymore. He just had to make up for it with speed.

He bolted out of the ship and bent his head to run the last dozen yards to where Kellogg had gone down. None of those people on board the *Sea Dragon* would survive without Kellogg's pack.

LeMaine raced to it, grabbed it, and turned to run back when a powerful blow struck him from behind. It wasn't a laser. Maybe one of the fighters exploded and the shockwave knocked him down.

He sprawled on his face and looked up at the *Sea Dragon* in front of him. She hovered off the ground with all her engines burning and her landing gear retracted. She was just waiting for him to get on board before she flew away under the Imoliv's covering fire.

Nunn struggled to get out of the hatch to come and help LeMaine, but both O'Hara and Sindra held her back. Lutov hung out of the hatch waving to LeMaine to come on. They would all die if they stayed here a minute longer.

He forced himself to his feet and summoned the last remaining ounce of his strength to race on board before the ship took off.

Chapter 29

LeMaine struggled across the *Sea Dragon's* blood-smeared floor to where Kellogg sat. He kept his legs straight out in front of him while he yanked tools out of his pack to work on Lemon.

"Check on Galo," Kellogg snapped. "No, belay that. Lutov—you check your brother. We don't know enough about Imoliv medicine. Take this, Captain."

Kellogg shoved things into LeMaine's hands and barked orders at everyone.

"Nunn—stop the bleeding on Heckler's leg. Find out where Peterman is hit, Monk."

Nunn and Monk scrambled to help him. LeMaine had his hands full with Lemon's side, which had been blown open.

They all worked at top speed to save the wounded, but when Kellogg tried to get his scalpel out of his pack, the *Sea Dragon* lurched wildly out of control.

Everyone yelled. LeMaine braced himself against the wall and held Lemon in position to stop her from sliding on the wet floor.

"Hang on!" O'Hara called from the cockpit. "We got us a shit parade coming in!"

LeMaine glanced toward the cockpit. Tavon sat in the pilot's seat maneuvering the *Sea Dragon* through a tornado of ships—Axichis, Imoliv, and Elian. LeMaine couldn't see them all from here.

O'Hara manned the cockpit cannon bombarding the enemy as fast as he could shoot, but the Imoliv destroyers were the ones who really turned the tide. The *Sea Dragon* wouldn't have made it off the ground without the Imoliv guarding it.

Tavon ripped the ship upward at wicked speed. Lasers and even friendly fire drummed the outer hull as the ship climbed into the atmosphere. The cannon roared and slammed in all directions as O'Hara changed angles.

LeMaine turned back to Lemon when a deafening smash rocked the ship, hurled everyone out of position, turned a somersault in midair, and then slammed down hard.

LeMaine landed sprawled across Lemon and peeled himself out of the slick of blood. Thick trees blocked the cockpit window, so the *Sea Dragon* wasn't on the ice shelf anymore.

"Is everyone okay?" he asked.

The other Hellhounds picked themselves up and looked around. The ship was on the ground somewhere and LeMaine saw trees through the shattered cockpit window.

Kellogg rolled over a few feet away and then scrambled to sit up and drag himself back to Lemon. "Hold this, Captain," he ordered.

LeMaine concentrated on doing what he was told, but more blood kept bubbling out of Lemon's side. Blood saturated her fatigues, LeMaine's fatigues, Kellogg's fatigues, and everything else.

"How's Galo?" Kellogg called over his shoulder.

"He has blood coming out of his nose and he keeps slipping in and out of consciousness," Lutov replied. "I don't think he recognizes me."

"Take my scanner and scan his head." Kellogg glanced down at his pack, but he didn't take his hands off Lemon.

Nunn gave the scanner to Lutov, who pointed it at Galo's head and then frowned at it. "I don't know what this means."

"Show it to me," Kellogg ordered.

Lutov held it in front of Kellogg's face, but he shook his head. "I can't understand these readings. I'm sorry, Lutov, but I can't do anything for him. I just don't have the tools or the knowledge."

Sindra stepped in. "Let me take a look." He studied the scanner readings. "His brainwaves are erratic, but only slightly. His skull is fractured, but he doesn't have any internal bleeding."

"Electrolyze the fracture," Kellogg ordered. "Monk, electrolyze Galo's head."

"Me?!" Monk hollered. "I can't electrolyze anybody! I don't know how."

"Pull your pants up, Monk!" Kellogg snapped. "We're in a combat zone. You could be saving this man's life and we need every man fit for duty."

"I'll do it." Nunn stepped forward and took the electrolyzer out of Kellogg's pack. "You'll just have to tell me what to do."

"Show her where the fracture is, Sindra. Fix the electrolyzer over it and zero it in on the fracture."

"I'm ready," Nunn replied.

"Fire," Kellogg ordered.

She fired and Galo jolted before he crashed down hard on the floor. "You've killed him!" Lutov yelled. "You killed my brother!"

"He isn't dead," Nunn replied. "He's just unconscious."

"Give him the antidote and rescan," Kellogg ordered.

Nunn obeyed him and Galo revived. His bleary eyes drifted over to Lutov. "Lutov...." he husked. "Are you all right?"

"He knows me!" Lutov exclaimed and his lip quivered.

"Check on Heckler and Peterman," Kellogg ordered.

Nunn used the scanner on both of them. "Heckler has a laser shot to the chest. He has multiple broken ribs and a shattered sternum."

"What's his blood oxygen concentration?" Kellogg asked.

"94%," Nunn replied. "And he has a concussion."

"Leave him until later, but keep an eye on his stats. What about Peterman?"

Nunn bent over him. "He has a full in-and-out laser shot through his upper chest and another one through his thigh, but both are fully cauterized. He isn't bleeding out and his blood pressure is holding."

Kellogg wilted. "Thank God for that."

Silence fell over the ship except for the howl of wind and the scour of ice on the outer hull. It sure sounded cold out there.

Just then, O'Hara struggled out of the cockpit lugging Tavon's unconscious body. Blood trickled from Tavon's scalp.

"He hit the window," O'Hara panted. "Damn it, he's heavy—oh, and the controls are all dead We're stranded here."

"What's the situation outside?" LeMaine asked.

"The air battle is moving off. The Imoliv are taking it on the chin to lead the Axichis force away from us, but we're grounded until someone comes to get us."

"Monk," LeMaine ordered, "you and Sindra go out to that forest and bring back some wood for a fire. Keep the hatch closed unless you're going in or out."

Monk muttered, "Yes, Sir," and started pulling his hood over his head.

"Put Tavon over there with the others," Kellogg told O'Hara. "Scan him, Nunn."

She did. "He has a concussion, too, and a broken nose. That's it."

"Leave him. What's Polasek's status?"

LeMaine let Kellogg take over. He kept snapping orders at everyone, including Lutov.

Galo got progressively more lucid as the minutes turned to hours. The sky went dark outside. LeMaine checked his remote a few times, but no fighter craft came back from either army. Wherever the combatants were, they were outside the remote's range.

Monk and Sindra returned and built a small fire in the center of the *Sea Dragon's* rear compartment where it wouldn't put any of the wounded in danger. The heat did everybody good and calmed Kellogg down as he got closer to stabilizing Lemon.

He finally told LeMaine to leave and go work on the others while Kellogg finished patching her up. LeMaine spent another hour electrolyzing fractures, sealing wounds, and checking everyone's brainwave patterns.

He had just finished and positioned all the patients near the fire when Kellogg stood up and wiped his bloody hands on his shirt. "You next, Captain."

"Huh?" LeMaine asked. "What do you mean?"

"Your arm. You're bleeding—or you were."

"I am?" LeMaine glanced down and saw blood saturating his sleeve. He didn't feel the pain until now. He had assumed that blood was Lemon's.

He took off his shirt long enough for Kellogg to seal the wound and then Kellogg staggered over to the fire, collapsed next to it, and stretched out his legs. "Now I gotta deal with this piece of shit."

LeMaine stared at him as Kellogg tore open the leg of his own fatigues. The sealing plaster still stuck to the laser wound that Kellogg took getting everyone on board the ship.

LeMaine kicked himself for forgetting that Kellogg was injured, too. Kellogg had been working for hours with that untreated injury.

"Aarrgh!" he bellowed when he took the plaster off. "I need some painkillers." He held out his hand to LeMaine. "Could you pull my pack over here, please?"

LeMaine slid it over. He would have liked to be the one to take care of Kellogg, but Kellogg was already injecting himself with painkillers and sealing the wound.

He collapsed back, shut his eyes, and sighed heavily. "I'm hungry."

"Here!" LeMaine pounced on Kellogg's pack, pulled out two ration bars, and un-wrapped them for Kellogg.

No one said a word while Kellogg chewed his bars, but LeMaine definitely caught the other Hellhounds watching Kellogg, especially the four Imoliv.

"How did you come to join the Hellhounds, Kellogg?" Sindra finally asked.

Kellogg looked up and raised his eyebrows. "Why do you want to know that?"

"I'm just curious."

Kellogg shrugged and stuffed the rest of his ration bar in his mouth. "I always wanted to be a doctor, but when I got older and found out what it was really like, I decided to become a medic instead. I didn't want to sit behind a desk interviewing patients all day and listening to old ladies complain."

"So he decided to come out here so he could listen to us complain instead," O'Hara interrupted.

The others laughed and so did Kellogg. "I joined the Military, but even being regular Military wasn't enough. I guess you could say I'm too much of an adrenaline junky. I wanted to see action, so I signed up for the Special Forces training instead."

"What about you, son?" LeMaine asked Sindra. "How did the son of a bigshot like Sehiri wind up in a Special Forces team?"

"My father didn't want me to become a soldier," Sindra replied. "He wanted me to become a politician like him. He still does."

"Is he a politician?" Nunn asked. "He's a military commander."

"Our defense force works differently than yours," Sindra replied. "He's part of the government. He would never be a soldier. He thinks he's made for better things. He thinks the same thing about me."

"How did he react when you joined the Special Forces?" Kellogg asked.

"He was very disappointed and angry. It took years for him to get over it. Sometimes I think he still isn't over it."

"How did you reconcile?" LeMaine asked.

"'Reconcile' isn't the word I'd use for it. I went into the Special Forces and didn't see him for years. When I came back, he decided he could tolerate talking to me again, so we started talking—not about that—about anything but that. After a while, it became okay for me to talk to him about my work—the part of it I was allowed to talk about with my family. Things improved after that."

"That sucks," Monk rumbled. "I couldn't stand it if my dad didn't want me to become a soldier."

Sindra cocked his head. "Did he?"

"Of course. He was so proud the day I joined up...." Monk trailed off and stared into the fire.

"I'm jealous," Sindra murmured. "I know Sehiri is proud of me—he is now—but I wish he'd say so."

No one said anything for a while until O'Hara turned to Lutov. "How did you join the military?"

"I only ever wanted to be like Galo," Lutov replied. "He joined first, so the only thing I wanted to do was join."

Galo grabbed him by the back of the neck and shook him. "I'm proud of you."

LeMaine glanced over at Tavon. He had his eyes open, though he still stayed lying down on the floor. "What about you, son? What's your story?"

"My father and grandfather, all my brothers and cousins, and all our relatives—they're all military people," Tavon replied. "There was never any question about what I would do."

"What about you, Captain?" Sindra asked. "How did you come to command the Hellhounds?"

LeMaine shrugged. "It's so long ago that I can hardly remember."

"Shut up!" Nunn countered. "You aren't that old."

"I'm a lot older than you think," LeMaine replied. "I'll be turning into a mummy soon."

Laughter and jeering answered him and LeMaine had to join in.

"Really, Captain," Sindra urged. "How did you end up in this job?"

"I'm telling the truth—in part at least. I don't remember when I decided to become a soldier. I never really wanted to be anything else and then I started learning about what kind of missions the Special Forces went on. I decided when I was a teenager that I wanted to join the Special Forces, and after that, I got promoted to being in command of my own squad. It wasn't the Hellhounds then. It became that after several years."

"How do we stack up against your former squads?" O'Hara asked. "Are we as good as the other squads you've had?"

LeMaine turned around to stare at him. None of the Hellhounds had ever asked LeMaine that and he had to check himself when he saw that O'Hara was perfectly serious. He wasn't joking around. He really wanted to know.

"I'll tell you this much, Sergeant. This is definitely the squad with the biggest attitude."

That made O'Hara laugh. Nunn and Kellogg joined in. "I can live with that," O'Hara replied. "Don't say anything else."

LeMaine wasn't finished. "I've had squads that were more skilled than you and I've had squads that were more experienced than you. I've never had a squad that I felt more comfortable with. I've never had a squad that I felt more at home with....and I've never had a squad that I've been prouder of. You Hellhounds are something special. I wish it could have been like this the whole time. I just had to wait for all of you to come together to make this squad as good as it could be."

Silence fell over the ship and no one spoke for a while. They listened to the fire crackling and then Lemon started to come around.

Kellogg shifted over to sit next to her as her eyes drifted open. She groaned and then her eyes darted around the group. Her expression changed and her gaze snapped to Kellogg. "Kellogg....." Her voice broke. "Am I....am I gonna be okay?"

"You're gonna be fine, sweetie." He grabbed her hand. "You lost a lot of blood, but you've had two transfusions. You're gonna be spectacular. I promise."

She gulped, pinched her lips, shut her eyes, and nodded. He squeezed her hand, stroked her cheek, and then turned back to the fire just as Heckler sat up. "I think I need to change hobbies," he growled.

"Welcome back, Corporal," LeMaine told him.

Heckler frowned at the surroundings. "Where the holy hell are we?"

"We're stranded somewhere on the Evilia ice sheet," Kellogg told him. "This is where O'Hara decided to take his vacation leave, so if you don't like it, take it up with him."

"I didn't mean *this!*" O'Hara yelled back. "I meant in a nice, warm, luxury hotel with room service, hot tubs...."

"Girls," Nunn added.

"Yes! Girls!" O'Hara snapped his fingers and pointed at her. "I'll take three."

The others laughed and the Imoliv joined in this time.

"Any idea how we get out of here, Captain?" Monk asked.

"Nope," LeMaine replied. "The Imoliv know where we are. Maybe when they aren't too busy fighting the Axichis, they'll send someone down to get us."

"That could be months," Nunn pointed out.

"Things could be worse," Kellogg countered. "At least we're on an Elian planet. We aren't on a moon without a ship to get off of it."

"We're thousands of miles from civilization," Heckler growled. "How the crap would we get a ship to get out of here—walk? We might as well be on a moon." He rubbed his arms. "It was warmer on the moon."

"You're cold?" Kellogg grabbed his scanner and pointed it at Heckler. "Do you need another blood transfusion?"

"No," Heckler grumbled. "And I don't need you holding my hand, either."

Kellogg put his scanner away and didn't say anything. The other wounded came around one after another and Monk went outside to get some more firewood. Snow and wind blew in every time anyone opened the hatch. The ship took a long time to warm up after that.

Monk kept going in and out until he gathered a supply for the whole night the way they did on the moon. LeMaine wasn't looking forward to a night of this—or several nights of this—so he started planning their escape early.

When the others stretched out and went to sleep, he lay down on the cold metal floor. His blankets didn't protect him from the cold.

In that silence, he heard the shriek of Axichis fighter craft engines zooming overhead. The *Sea Dragon* hadn't made it that far away from the bunker. The Axichis must be running flights from there.

Did they know the *Sea Dragon* was here? They must not believe a crashed ship was much of a threat.

His thoughts kept going back to the Maczhi battalion. Turning Axichis weaponry against them was the best defense against their technology. The squad needed a ship to get out of here, but the Hellhounds were within traveling distance of one of the greatest sources of Axichis weaponry anywhere.

The Maczhi battalion had been able to pull down Axichis fighters and rob them of weapons and supplies. The Hellhounds could do the same thing.

The Hellhounds had one distinct advantage they'd never had before. They had laser rifles stolen from the Axichis themselves. These rifles were much more effective than carbines. Laser rifles even worked against fighter craft. That was saying something.

He just had to figure out how to shoot down a fighter without damaging it. Then the squad would be able to fly anywhere they wanted to.....except that everyone would think the Hellhounds were Axichis.

He fell asleep thinking about it and listening to those engines. They blended into the sound of the wind and ice, but that sound soothed him and lulled him to sleep. He knew what he had to do now.

Chapter 30

Heckler peered through the open hatch at the icy white landscape stretching away to the horizon. A vast, snowbound forest stood to one side of the spot where the *Sea Dragon* had crashed.

Evilia's northern ice sheet ran away in the other direction. It didn't stop all the way to the pole.

Heckler groaned. "This is hopeless!"

"No, it isn't," LeMaine countered. "Not at all. It's going to be fine."

"Since when are you so chipper?" Heckler growled.

LeMaine laughed at him and realized a second too late that he probably shouldn't have been. Heckler glared at him.

Heckler had been surly ever since his injury. Kellogg kept telling Heckler to eat something, drink some water, and to take another blood transfusion, but Heckler refused to do any of those things, not even to improve his mood.

O'Hara came to the hatch and squinted at the sky. An iron-grey dome of cloud covered everything. It completely blocked the sun. "What are we doing?"

"We're walking north to the bunker," LeMaine replied. "Then we're going to stake out the place, shoot down one of their ships, and use it to fly away."

"Well, why didn't you say so in the first place?" Heckler fired back. "I thought we were just going to sit around here and wait for the Second Coming."

"We don't have time for that." LeMaine went inside the *Sea Dragon* where Lemon, Polasek, Peterman, and Tavon still lay on the floor. "Are you going to be okay here on your own?" LeMaine asked Kellogg.

"Of course. They're just recovering. We'll be fine."

"Are you really going to shoot down an Axichis fighter?" Lemon groaned and turned her face to the wall. "I can't believe I got hurt! This is so not fair."

"You can help us shoot down the next one, Sergeant. Do what Kellogg says and rest up. We'll be back in a little while."

He left them there, shut the hatch, and turned away for the long hike north. Nearly everyone in his party had gotten injured in the last disaster. They would need to be careful this time.

He stepped away from the *Sea Dragon* when that all-too-familiar whine of engines startled everyone to high alert, but this time, it sounded way too close.

LeMaine's head snapped up as seven fighter craft pivoted over the trees above the *Sea Dragon's* position.

"Take cover!" he yelled and dove behind the ship just as the fighters opened fire.

Their lasers hissed in the snow and pounded the *Sea Dragon's* hull. LeMaine crawled to the edge of the ship, yanked his rifle to his shoulder, and took aim.

He barely remembered in time that he was supposed to be shooting them down, not destroying them. "Disable them!" he yelled to the squad. "Don't destroy them! We can use these fighters to get away!"

Lasers erupted on both sides as the squad returned fire. A spray of lasers fired from the *Sea Dragon's* other side and smashed one of the fighters to smithereens. "Sorry!!" Nunn yelled from out of sight.

"How the hell can we get out of here with you blowing up all the ships, you trigger-happy nutjob?!" Heckler roared.

Nunn laughed and the Hellhounds fired again.

This time, LeMaine targeted the same ship as they did. Both beams hit it, one on its lower edge and one on its upper corner.

The fighter twirled and slammed into a tree. "NOW!!" LeMaine yelled and sprang out from behind the *Sea Dragon*.

The other Hellhounds stormed into view and LeMaine sprang between them and the rest of the Axichis craft. He trained his weapon on them and his implant took over.

He fired fast and true, downed two more, and made the others back off while the Hellhounds ran for the stricken ship. It tried to get airborne again, but Heckler wasn't taking no for an answer.

He fired into the hatch release on the ship's backside. The engines ignited and the ship started to take off.

O'Hara didn't get to the ship in time. He didn't have to. He dropped on one knee in the snow, took aim, and fired a laser through the outer hull. It pierced the ship's skin and the vessel slammed down in the snow. The engines died and Heckler, Monk, Nunn, and the three Imoliv stormed inside.

LeMaine didn't see them. He was too busy holding the other fighters at bay. He kept shooting at blinding speed until someone grabbed his arm. "Captain—we're in! We're loading on our wounded."

LeMaine glanced behind him to find O'Hara at his side. The three Imoliv were busy pulling dead Axichis out of the fighter while Monk and Kellogg helped or carried the wounded on board.

Another laser from the airborne Axichis hit a tree near the downed fighter, but just as fast, the captured fighter opened up its own cannons and blasted two more enemy craft out of the sky.

Debris rained around LeMaine's head and he let O'Hara pull him away. They sprang on board just as Monk lifted off.

LeMaine couldn't get near the cockpit with all the wounded in the way. They had to cram in side by side just to fit everyone into the tiny craft. Polasek sat up front with Monk, but LeMaine didn't care. Everyone was on board. They were getting out of here.

The fighter vaulted into the atmosphere heading toward Elia, but as soon as Monk flew the ship around the planet, the cannons opened up from the stations the Elians had taken.

A brutal concussion slammed the ship off course. "We have to contact them!" Monk hollered to Polasek. "Patch a message through the Maczhi battalion!"

"We don't have time for that!" Polasek yelled back. "Get away from the planet! Head for the front line!"

"Are you nuts?!!" Monk roared. "The Imoliv will blow us out of the sky!"

Sindra elbowed his way closer to the cockpit. "Hail the Imoliv destroyers! Let me talk to them!"

Monk peeled the fighter away from Evilia and gunned it into the atmosphere trying to outrun continuous cannon fire on his tail. Polasek scrambled to hail the Imoliv as the fighter neared the front line, but he couldn't get through.

Thirty destroyers rotated out of position to confront the Hellhounds. "I don't think they're too happy to see us!" Polasek yelled over his shoulder.

Sindra shouldered into the cockpit and motioned Polasek out of the seat. Polasek had to lean against the bulkhead to support himself.

Sindra sat down, adjusted the communications system, and started talking into it in his own language. Monk kept the fighter streaking toward the Imoliv at a dead sprint. "This better work!" he yelled.

At those words, a massive Axichis force launched from the bunker. Warships and fighter craft that had been returning all night erupted from the planet and closed on the rogue fighter. Lasers flickered all around the fugitive ship.

"Hurry!" Monk yelled at Sindra. "Can't you get them to understand?"

Lasers smashed into the ship from behind. Heat seared through the hull right behind LeMaine, who stood all the way in the back.

Sindra kept yelling into the communications system as Axichis craft surrounded the fleeing ship. Crashes and explosions bombarded the ship all over.

Peterman squatted down and then his energy failed. He crumpled onto the floor and Tanov did the same thing.

LeMaine did his best to remain standing as the bombardment escalated. The Axichis hit the fighter's starboard engine and it detonated right against the hull.

The impact flung the ship sideways and everyone fell over each other again. Kellogg tried to check everyone, but more pounding blows wouldn't let him get near them or even stay upright.

Another shattering crash dropped everyone into a confused pile and then a deafening boom blasted everyone off the floor. They landed together in a tight wad near the front bulkhead.

LeMaine landed on top of everyone else and scrambled to get off them. He looked up....and found himself staring at the blank back wall of an Imoliv cargo hold. The Imoliv had rescued the crew after all.

He pushed himself up and all the able-bodied helped the wounded untangle themselves. LeMaine opened the hatch and then got to work helping Kellogg get everyone out of the fighter.

The hold in which they found themselves was closed and they were all alone. Were they back on Sehiri's ship? LeMaine should have known Sehiri would come for his precious son. He would never let anything happen to Sindra.

Sindra didn't rush off to go see his father. Sindra worked with the rest of the Hellhounds to lay the wounded on the floor and then he told Kellogg, "I'll go get the medical staff. We'll take these people to the hospital."

LeMaine did a head count on all the squad members. Everyone was here....except for Polasek.

LeMaine went back inside the fighter and found Polasek in the cockpit. He hadn't been the healthiest of the patients when the squad left to capture this fighter.

Polasek sat slumped in the seat where he'd been sitting next to Monk—the seat Polasek gave up so Sindra could call on the Imoliv defensive line for aid.

Polasek's shoulders slumped and he looked pale. "Polasek?" LeMaine asked. "Are you okay?"

Polasek raised his eyes to meet LeMaine's. LeMaine froze when he saw tears in those eyes and then the most magnificent smile spread across Polasek's face. "I found them!" he whispered. "You won't believe it, Sir! I found them!"

"What?" LeMaine murmured back. "What did you find?"

"The frequencies! They're right here!" Polasek's slender fingers danced over the fighter's controls. "I got the frequencies and I also hacked the scrambler code they're using that changes the frequencies from one set to another. We got 'em, Sir! This is it! We can defeat the Axichis! They'll never be able to change the frequencies on us again! This is it! We're gonna win!"

LeMaine's throat constricted. He wanted to cry, too, but he couldn't do that. "What do you need to do, Lieutenant? What do you need to do to deploy these frequencies to the whole fleet?"

"I...." Polasek's smile faded and he looked back down at the controls. "I'm not sure, but it's all here. We just need to figure out how to use them."

LeMaine let his hand fall on Polasek's shoulder. "You did real good, son, but you need to go to the hospital right now. Come on. I'll help you if you can't walk. Then I'll tell Sehiri what you found and we'll get these out to the whole fleet."

Chapter 31

LeMaine sprawled on the couch in the same apartment on board Sehiri's destroyer. All the Hellhounds sprawled around him. It seemed like they'd never left it.

Peterman and Polasek had both been released from the hospital. Lemon was still in there, but Heckler was in a much better mood since the doctors had given him the electrolyte boost and additional blood transfusion he needed. No one mentioned that Kellogg had been trying to do just that and Kellogg didn't' mention it, either.

The squad was preparing to play a drinking game the Imoliv team was planning to teach them. The Imoliv members of the squad used the food dispenser to cook up some deadly brew they said was intoxicating to Imoliv.

No one knew what effect it would have on Elians. "I guess we're about to find out," Tavon told LeMaine.

"I should use my command authority to forbid this game," LeMaine remarked. "We could wind up dead for real."

"You be the test subject, Sir," Nunn volunteered. "If you die, we'll know."

LeMaine laughed. "Thanks a lot, Corporal."

"No, Captain LeMaine is too valuable," Monk interrupted. "I'll test it out."

"You don't count," O'Hara told him. "You're too big. It might be fatal to us, but the dosage for you would be too high."

Monk shoved him out of the way. "Stand aside, pipsqueak. This is all mine."

"Why don't you let Heckler test it out?" Kellogg asked. "He's closer to our size."

"Are you seriously telling me a lethal dose of this stuff for Heckler will be the same as a lethal dose for Nunn?" Polasek asked. "That's hogwash."

Monk pushed everyone out of the way and approached the table where Sindra and Galo were busy pouring the liquor into small shot-sized glasses.

"Be careful, Monk," Heckler warned. "You might burn your eyebrows off."

"You might burn your whole face off," Peterman added.

"I'm taking one for the squad." Monk slapped his chest, planted one fist on the table, and took a glass. His massive fist dwarfed it.

He took a few deep breaths and everyone fell silent to watch except that Nunn kept giggling.

Monk straightened up, put the glass to his lips, and pounded it. It vanished down his throat and he cocked his head looking at the ceiling.

"Well?" LeMaine asked. "Are you still alive?"

Laughter answered him. After too long a wait, Monk shrugged and put the glass down. "It tastes like strawberries."

"Did it give you a buzz?" O'Hara asked. "That's all we care about."

Monk had to think about it again. "I don't feel anything."

"Take another one," Lutov told him.

"Not so fast," Heckler rumbled. "I'm next."

He approached the table and tossed back one of the shots. "Monk is right. I don't think this stuff has any effect on Elians."

"We need a smaller lab rat," Kellogg decided and pushed Nunn forward.

She protested. "Hey! Don't sign me up for this! Lieutenant Peterman is smaller than I am!"

"You're right," Kellogg agreed. "Come on, Lieutenant. Take one for the squad."

Peterman grinned and took his place at the table. "Do you know I've never drunk anything alcoholic before?"

The whole squad howled with glee that they were going to deflower Lieutenant Peterman with something that might actually kill him.

Peterman took his shot, put his glass down, and turned away without saying anything. "Stuart?" LeMaine asked. "Are you all right?"

"Monk is right. It's delicious."

"Is that it?" O'Hara grumbled. "This is boring. I quit."

"Okay, okay!" Sindra interrupted. "We've determined that it isn't detrimental to Elian health....."

"Not necessarily," Kellogg countered. "We haven't done any long-range studies....."

No one listened. Everyone started talking at once and the Imoliv squad members took the drinks over to the living room. The Hellhounds sat down while they set up on the living room table and started explaining the rules of the game.

"Every person has to reveal something about the person to his or her right that no one else knows," Sindra announced. "If you can't think of anything or you just don't know, you have to take a shot. If you get it wrong and reveal something that isn't true, you take two shots...."

Excited talk and laughter broke out. "Oh-ho!" O'Hara gloated. "Wait, wait! I need to change places so I'm to the right of Nunn."

"Go right ahead," she countered. "You don't know shit about me."

"If you don't want the person to reveal the information, you can buy their silence by taking three shots," Sindra finished. "Do you all understand the rules?"

LeMaine glanced around. Kellogg sat on his left. If Kellogg wanted to, he could tell the squad about LeMaine's implant.

LeMaine didn't move, though. Kellogg wouldn't tell—not for anything. Not even getting shit-faced drunk on some alien brew would loosen Kellogg's tongue when it came to confidential medical information.

LeMaine glanced to his right. He was sitting next to Heckler.

"Whoa! Hold the phone!" Heckler growled. "We got a problem with this game." He waved to Lutov, who sat to Heckler's right. "How are we supposed to come up with something about you guys? We don't know anything about you guys."

"Then you'll be the first to pass out, big guy," O'Hara told him.

"No way! This is not fair," Heckler protested. "You four should reveal information about each other." He swiped his finger around the group. "The next human along from me is Nunn. I'll reveal all you want to know about her and Sindra can reveal information about Lutov, the next Imoliv down from him."

"I guess that makes sense," Polasek replied.

"Are you ready to get started?" Galo asked. His eyes sparkled with mischief as he scanned the circle.

A few people snickered, but no one protested.

"I'll go first," Galo went on and pointed to Tavon, who sat at his right. "Tavon had a girlfriend at the training academy and he would let her....."

"Quiet!!" Tavon exploded off the couch, attacked Galo, and slapped his hand over Galo's hand before he could say any more.

Everyone burst out laughing. "Three shots, Tavon!" Nunn yelled.

Tavon squared his shoulders and downed three shots. They didn't affect him that much—not right away.

After he finished, he turned to Sindra. "Sindra had a medical condition when he was a child and couldn't use his right leg. He was crippled until he reached the age of fourteen. He had his leg replaced and had to relearn how to walk. He has an artificial leg."

No one laughed. All eyes turned to Sindra. The Hellhounds stared at him and then down at his leg. It looked as normal as LeMaine's eye implant and it sure as hell didn't slow him down. LeMaine never would have known if Tavon hadn't told them.

Sindra smiled at them all. "It's true."

"Wow, man," O'Hara remarked. "You really are a badass."

Sindra blushed and changed the subject by pointing at Lutov across the circle. "Lutov won the Academy Medal for Marksmanship. He even beat his brother."

The whole squad cheered and Heckler thumped Lutov on the back. "That's my boy!"

Lutov turned bright red and looked down at the floor. "Hold up, hold up! My turn!" O'Hara called and turned his beady little eyes on Nunn.

She glared at him. "You better watch it, asshole. I know where you live."

He blushed and then said, "Nunn got a special commendation from her training sergeant. She won an outstanding decoration for merit in the Special Forces training program."

"Isn't anyone gonna miss?" Polasek chimed in. "None of us is getting any drinking done here."

"It always works out this way," Lutov told him. "People go around telling the things they know. Pretty soon, they run out of things to tell. That's when the drinking starts."

Nunn turned to Peterman, who sat next to her, and a wicked gleam came into her eye. She smirked at Peterman, and when he saw her looking at him, he blanched. "No. You wouldn't."

She waved at the table. "You can buy my silence by taking three shots."

"Oh, hell no!" Heckler bellowed. "You HAVE to tell us now, Nunn!"

The others laughed. Peterman turned a deeper shade of grey and leaned forward to pick up a glass.

"What does she have on you, Lieutenant?" O'Hara asked.

Peterman didn't answer. He took his second shot and then his third.

"Another rule of the game," Sindra explained, "is that you can only buy silence on one piece of information at a time. You can't threaten someone with the same piece of information more than once."

"Thank Heaven," Peterman muttered and everyone laughed.

Peterman gulped down his drinks and turned to Polasek. Peterman rallied and said, "Polasek went to law school before he joined the military. He was going to go into politics."

"I was not going to go into politics!" Polasek shouted back. "You made that up."

"You told me once you wanted to become a diplomat. That's politics."

LeMaine glanced across the circle at the Imoliv. "We need an impartial judge."

"I'm going have to rule in favor of Peterman on this one," Sindra replied. "He was telling the truth on both counts, even if they disagree on whether diplomacy is politics."

"You dodged a bullet on that one, Peterman," Heckler added.

Polasek turned to Kellogg. "Kellogg won the Elian Assembly Medal of Honor for heroism during the Miania Disaster."

A gasp went through the group and jaws dropped as everyone turned to stare at Kellogg. "No way!" Nunn breathed.

Kellogg looked down at the floor. "I was just doing my job."

"He saved more than five hundred people," Polasek went on. "He was treating the wounded in a mobile hospital and he was the first to notice an incoming swarm of enemy fighter craft. He raised the alarm and helped evacuate the hospital in time."

"That's enough," Kellogg interrupted. "Captain LeMaine won the Elian Assembly Medal of Honor, too."

"We all know that," Peterman replied. "He won it during the Soclitese Campaign. We were all there."

"No, before that," Kellogg explained. "He won it twice, once then, but the first time he won during the Miania Disaster. He was there with his unit at the time. He took his men around the battle lines, executed a surgical strike on the enemy command post, and wiped them out. He turned the tide in our favor. We would never have won if not for him."

All eyes turned to LeMaine. "Is that true, Captain?" Galo asked.

"Yeah, it's true," LeMaine murmured.

"So.....tell us something we don't know about Heckler."

LeMaine glanced at Heckler and Heckler scowled at him. LeMaine burst into a grin. "Heckler failed the Special Forces selection his first time through."

All the Hellhounds went nuts yelling and howling. Heckler sat there in silence through it all.

"Did you really fail?" O'Hara chortled as soon as the noise died down.

"Yes, I did," Heckler boomed.

"Whoo! This is great!" Monk gloated. "Why did you fail? Tell us. Were you a weak little scarecrow back then?"

Heckler didn't say anything for a long time. He waited for the jeers and laughter to die down. Then he turned to LeMaine. "Go on. Tell them why."

"Heckler entered selection with his best friend. They trained together for five years getting ready to pass the entrance test. They made it right up until the last week and then his friend fell and broke his ankle on one of the long-distance rucks. It was a freak accident. Heckler carried his friend the last ten miles and came in last. He got bumped out of the selection, but both he and his friend received letters inviting them back for the next one. They both passed."

No one had to ask if it was true. Heckler's sharp eyes darted around the circle challenging anyone to call him weak or spindly or to laugh at him again. No one did.

Polasek broke the silence. "Your turn, Lutov. Tell us something about your brother that no one else knows."

Lutov opened his mouth to speak when a bell went off by the apartment door. It was the signal that someone was standing outside asking to come in.

LeMaine went over there and answered it to find Sehiri standing outside.

Chapter 32

Sehiri raised his eyebrows when he looked in and saw all the glasses standing on the living room table. "Am I interrupting anything, Captain?"

"No, not at all. Would you like to come in and join us?"

Muffled giggles broke out behind LeMaine's back, but Sehiri didn't react. "As a matter of fact, I'd like a word with you, Captain. I'm sure your squad can spare you for a few minutes."

"Is Lemon all right?" Monk called out. "Is anything wrong with her?"

"She's fine as far as I know, Corporal." Sehiri turned back to LeMaine. "Captain?"

"Uh....okay." LeMaine stepped out of the apartment and the door closed behind him. He expected Sehiri to walk off and take LeMaine away, but he didn't.

"What's going on?" LeMaine asked.

"My crew has extracted the frequencies and the code from the Axichis fighter. Your Lieutenant Polasek really is an exceptional specimen."

"Yes, he is," LeMaine replied. "Does that mean.....?"

"We're ready to deploy the frequencies to the rest of the Elian fleet, to the Imoliv defense line, and to the Maczhi battalion. We're in communication with the Elian Military Command as we speak. We're organizing another coordinated assault using all three of our forces, this time with the right frequencies. Our objective is to drive the Axichis out of Elian space for good."

"So....what do you want me to do?"

"Your Command is requesting that the Hellhounds return to the Elian Military immediately. Colonel Nicholson is on his way here now to collect you."

"Oh." LeMaine blinked trying to put all that together. He and the Hellhounds had just gotten here. Now they would be leaving again.

"We won't transfer you until Sergeant Lemon is healthy enough to leave the hospital, but that shouldn't be more than twenty-four hours," Sehiri's eyes skipped sideways toward the apartment. "I understand if you and your squad want to take some time to say goodbye. I don't foresee our forces working this closely again."

"I see. Thank you for telling me." LeMaine turned back to the apartment and Sehiri headed down the hall.

At the last minute, LeMaine turned back. "You know....."

Sehiri paused and turned around.

"Your son....." LeMaine went on. "He's an outstanding soldier and an outstanding man. You should be very proud of him."

"I am proud of him, Captain," Sehiri replied. "I'm very proud of him."

"You might think about telling him that sometime. That's the kind of thing sons need to hear from their fathers, especially when it's been so hard to win."

LeMaine strode into the apartment without waiting to hear Sehiri's response. The door shut behind LeMaine's back.

The Hellhounds still sat around talking and now they were definitely drinking. The drink didn't make them shit-faced blotto, though. It just made them very relaxed, warm, and happy.

Monk looked up. "What was that about, Sir?"

LeMaine hesitated to tell them. He didn't want to spoil this moment, but he had to. "They're sending us back to the Elian Military. You four are staying here with your people. We're going home."

A chill fell over the group as they all looked around at each other. No one had to tell these people what this meant.

LeMaine didn't want to let these four men go any more than he'd wanted to let Buca go. All these wonderful, talented, brave, selfless people kept coming into his life and leaving way too soon. He couldn't stand it.

"I'm gonna go see Lemon," he announced. "We have twenty-four hours before the Military comes and gets us. Then we'll be fighting on separate flanks from now on."

LeMaine walked off to the hospital on board Sehiri's destroyer. When he got there, he interrupted a meeting between three doctors and five nurses. They all bunched together in the middle of the room. LeMaine saw in a heartbeat that something was wrong.

"Where's Lemon?" he asked the doctor who'd replaced his eye. "Is she all right?"

"I'm afraid not, Captain. She's....well.....none of us knows how to help her."

LeMaine's stomach dropped. "What's wrong with her?"

"You better go see." The doctor waved to one of the capsules farther down the ward. "We can't do anything more to help her."

LeMaine turned away feeling sick. What would he find when he went to see Lemon? Was she dying? Was she already so far gone that he could only stand aside and watch her die?

Sehiri said she was due to be released from the hospital in twenty-four hours. Why would he say that....unless she was going back to Elia to die?

LeMaine approached the capsule, but he didn't want to go in there. He dreaded what he would find.

He stepped into it, stared down at the bed, and everything made sense. Lemon lay on her side with her back to him. Her whole body shook with sobs.

"I told you to get the hell away from me!!" she roared without turning around. "Just keep away from me, you freaks! Don't ever come near me again! Can't you understand that much?" Then she went back to sobbing her eyes out.

LeMaine stood still for a minute watching her. She'd always been so tough. She was one of the toughest Hellhounds he'd ever had the privilege to command. What could make her break down like this?

"Sergeant...." he murmured. "It's me."

She burst into such an agonized flood of tears that he couldn't stand it. She didn't turn around at those words, but she definitely recognized his voice.

She twisted her face into the pillow and howled in anguish. She buried her mouth in the pillow to muffle the sound, but he couldn't fail to hear her pouring out all her heartbreak in loud, roaring sobs.

He took a grip on himself, crossed to the bed, and sat down behind her. He didn't touch her. She wouldn't appreciate that.

He didn't say anything. He had no idea what was wrong with her. No wonder the Imoliv doctors didn't know what to do. Maybe their species didn't express grief and rage and heartbreak like this. They might have thought she really was dying. She sure sounded like it.

She finally put her head down straight on the pillow and blurted out in a full-throated bellow cracked with sobs, "It's all over! They ruined everything! They took it all! It's all over!"

LeMaine could hardly make his voice heard. "What's over?"

"They.....they replaced some of my organs. Kellogg sealed the tears, but that last crash tore my organs loose. I was going to bleed to death and the Imoliv doctors replaced them with mechanical implants. They replaced my liver and my gallbladder. They had to!"

She broke down again like saving her life was the worst thing they could possibly do.

"I don't understand, Sergeant," LeMaine replied. "What's over?"

"Don't you see?!" she wailed. "The suit! The suit is designed to mask organic matter. It doesn't work on mechanical devices. I won't be able to do my job anymore! The Military will retire me! I'm out of the Hellhounds!"

She crumbled in wretched, pathetic sobs. The pain coming through her back was more than LeMaine could stand. She cried with such sadness now. He'd almost rather hear her roaring in fury than this.

Of course it would come down to the job. What else could getting out of the hospital mean?

He couldn't think of anything to say to make her feel better. There was no worse fate for the Hellhounds than getting retired to civilian life. None of them could think of anything worse than that.

There was nothing he could say to her....except the truth.

He stared down at his hands. Aching cold gripped his insides and he shivered. He didn't want to say the words out loud, but he had to.

He smashed his hands between his knees and braced himself. "When that shard pierced my eye.....it ruined my eye. The Imoliv doctors replaced it with an implant......"

She whipped around fast and stared up at him through her tears. "They did? You never told us."

"I didn't want any of you to know. I thought it was some kind of crutch to keep me out of retirement. It was weird at first. Do you remember when we took the first cannon station and I shot all those warships? The implant....it did something.....all my reactions changed. I started to question everything and ask myself if it might not have been better if Command put me out to pasture and...."

"NO!!" she screamed. "You can't.....!"

He tried to shrug it off. "I just thought, if I can't be the way I was before, maybe it's better if I'm not out here at all. I didn't want to be different, even if it was better. Hell, I don't even know if it *is* better. I only know it isn't me....and yet it is, somehow."

She relaxed considerably. She stared at him for a minute and then her eyes drifted up to the ceiling, but she didn't turn her back on him and she didn't start crying again.

"You don't have to leave the Hellhounds," he told her. "You're still a Hellhound even if you can't use the suit."

"But....if I don't use the suit....then they'll all find out....." Her face twisted in misery and she wrestled to control her lips.

"There might be a way," he told her. "There might be a way to modify the suit to mask your implants. We could talk to Polasek about it....."

She rolled away. "Then he would know."

"Would that be worse than retiring?" he asked. "We've all taken our share of hits, Sergeant."

She didn't answer. She kept her back to him.

"Krista.... look at me," he told her.

She rolled over. Her eyes glistened with emotion, but it was mostly confusion—and fear.

"There's nothing wrong with you," he told her. "You're one of the best Hellhounds I've ever known. You can't leave over this. We need you. We're on the verge of driving the Axichis out of the system. Don't give up. There has to be a way. If it comes down to it, I'll tell them about my eye and you can tell them about this. We'll do it together. You don't have to go through it alone. You know what the Hellhounds are like. They'll accept it."

"Yeah. I know."

"Do you want to know something I just found out? Sindra has an artificial leg. He was born crippled and had his leg replaced when he was fourteen. He had to learn how to walk all over again....and now look at him."

She didn't answer.

"Don't give up, Sergeant. We can work this out. There has to be a way."

Chapter 33

The Hellhounds got all mixed up with Sindra, Galo, Lutov, and Tavon. They all hugged each other and promised to keep in touch and fight together again one day.

Sehiri and his staff stood off to one side watching. Colonel Nicholson, Commander Lodge, and Captain Hurst stood on the other side while they waited to take the Hellhounds back on board the *Lucidity.*

LeMaine hugged Sindra. "Keep up the good work, son. It's been an honor to have you on my squad."

"Maybe we can do it again sometime," Sindra suggested.

"I'd be delighted. Just...." LeMaine waved behind him. "Get your father's permission first. Don't run away from home."

Sindra laughed and the four men stepped away to their own side of the destroyer's hold. The Hellhounds walked backward toward the *Lucidity* while everyone waved goodbye.

Colonel Nicholson, Commander Lodge, Captain Hurst, and the rest of the Elian military personnel didn't say anything until they all boarded the *Lucidity* and Captain Hurst went back to the bridge.

"You and your squad have quarters assigned to you on board, Owen," Colonel Nicholson told him. "We'll debrief in four hours and discuss our next move. You and your squad can go off duty until then."

"Yes, Sir," LeMaine replied.

He and the Hellhounds went off to their quarters, but LeMaine felt strange staying in a tiny cabin by himself. He'd been staying in the apartment with the Hellhounds for so long. He didn't like being separated from them.

He left the cabin and wandered the decks for a while until he found the *Lucidity's* crew lounge. He spotted Lemon standing outside it, but she didn't go in. She stared in at the *Lucidity* crew sitting around eating and talking.

He went over to her and followed her gaze inside. This couldn't continue. She couldn't continue to feel outside of everything, especially not with the upcoming campaign looming over all their heads.

He nodded to her and she accompanied him back down the hall in the direction LeMaine had first come. He stopped outside Polasek's cabin and rang the bell.

Polasek called from inside, "Come in!"

LeMaine and Lemon entered. Polasek looked up in surprise. "Captain! Is anything wrong?"

"That's what we're hoping you can tell us, Lieutenant. It's like this. Lemon suffered some severe injuries on Evilia...."

"I know, but didn't Kellogg save her......?" Polasek glanced at Lemon. "You?"

"Yes, he did," LeMaine went on, "but when we crashed into the Imoliv destroyer's hold, Kellogg's seals tore out and Lemon suffered irreparable organ damage."

Polasek frowned at her. "She looks fine to me."

"She looks fine because she is fine," LeMaine replied. "The Imoliv have the technology to replace damaged organs with synthetic implants. They replaced some of her organs with mechanical ones and now she's worried she won't be able to use her disguise suit. It's designed to mask organic matter. She's worried the enemy will be able to detect her implants and she won't be able to do her job."

Lemon stood right inside the door through his whole speech. She didn't make a move to enter Polasek's cabin.

He jumped up as soon as LeMaine finished. "Oh! Is that all? I can fix that."

"Are you sure?" LeMaine asked.

"Of course. The suit contains a microfiber computer relay system that deflects electromagnetic energy....."

Polasek went over to a desk and started messing around with the controls on it. All at once, he looked up. "I'll need the suit. Then I can reprogram the system."

"Just like that?" LeMaine asked. "Are you sure you can do it?"

"Absolutely. It's been done before. There was a disguise operative in the Special Forces about ten years ago who lost a leg in combat. They gave him a prosthetic and they had to reprogram his suit to hide the leg. There are at least five other examples I've heard of." He glanced over at Lemon. "Do you want to go get it?"

She raced out of the room and vanished.

"Thank you for this," LeMaine murmured to Polasek after she left. "She's been really broken up about this."

"I don't see why," Polasek asked. "She should have told me sooner. It's no big deal."

"It's a big deal to her. She doesn't want any of the other Hellhounds to know."

"Why?!" Polasek cried. "We've been saying for years that getting injured in the line of duty is the most honorable thing there is. How could she even consider that we would ever think less of her because of this?"

"She just does. Don't tell anyone, okay, Polasek?"

"All right. I won't if she doesn't want me to." He went back to tapping on his controls. He treated this as the most casual thing in the world.

Lemon came back and shoved her crumpled suit at Polasek. He muttered to himself, spread it out on his desk, and went back to messing around with his controls. "I'm just accessing the settings now....."

Lemon and LeMaine waited in silence. LeMaine sensed the discomfort radiating off her while Polasek worked on the suit. She shrank back toward the door like she wanted to be anywhere but here. Maybe LeMaine should have come alone.

Polasek worked on the suit for ten minutes. He turned it over a few times, put sections of it nearer to the controls, and kept muttering to himself.

He finally looked up. "It's all finished."

"Are you sure?" LeMaine asked again. "How do you know it will work?"

"You can test it out if you want to." He waved Lemon toward the next room, which was the bathroom attached to his cabin. "You can go in there and put the suit on. I'll turn on my scanners and you can try to sneak out of the room without me detecting you. Will that satisfy you?"

She changed colors a few times, tucked her chin, and strode off to the bathroom. She snatched the suit off Polasek's desk on her way past. She didn't look at him once.

She disappeared into the bathroom, shut the door, and Polasek adjusted something on his controls. "There. I've set an alarm to sound if the relay picks her up anything moving through this cabin besides you and me."

LeMaine collapsed on the couch. "Thanks."

"No problem." Polasek returned to the same seat where he'd been working when Lemon and LeMaine entered. "What do you think they'll send us out to do next?"

"Your guess is as good as mine. Colonel Nicholson said he wants to debrief me before he reveals his master plan."

Polasek chuckled. "I'm glad someone has one."

"You're a hero, Polasek," LeMaine told him. "You'll probably get the Assembly Medal of Honor for finding those frequencies."

Polasek blushed. "Naw. I wouldn't have been able to find them if you hadn't thought to capture that Axichis fighter."

LeMaine didn't insist. He nodded at the device on Polasek's lap. "What are you working on?"

Polasek turned pink again. "Just a little side project I've been tinkering with for a while."

"What is it?" LeMaine asked. "Is it a classified military secret?"

Polasek laughed. "Nothing I do is a classified military secret. You should know that." He held up the device. "It's an Imoliv phase cannon. I asked one of the Imoliv technicians to give it to me so I could study how it works. I was wondering if there's a way to fit them to Elian bombers. Then we would get the same advantage the Imoliv have."

"So how does it work?" LeMaine asked.

"I have no idea. I can't figure it out."

They both laughed and LeMaine relaxed back on the couch. "How long do you think it will take Lemon to make it out of this cabin?"

"She's probably out of it already," Polasek replied. "We'll never know."

"Well, she hasn't come out of the bathroom and she hasn't tripped the alarm. I suppose I could go see if she's in her own cabin or something."

Polasek grinned at him. "You could do that. Let me know how it worked out."

"I'm sure you'll know the next time she uses her disguise."

"I'll know if you don't come and tell me there's something wrong with the suit," Polasek replied and went back to what he was working on.

LeMaine stood up and squeezed Polasek's shoulder once. "Thanks."

"Sure," Polasek replied and LeMaine walked out.

He went back to his own cabin and changed to get ready for the meeting with Colonel Nicholson. He was on his way there when he passed the crew lounge he'd seen before. Lemon was in there hanging out with some other Elian personnel. She had her back to the door and didn't see LeMaine.

He hurried away so she wouldn't know he was there. So that was it. The suit worked and she was still in the squad as much as ever.

LeMaine headed for Colonel Nicholson's office, walked in, and saluted him and Commander Lodge. "At ease, Owen," Colonel Nicholson told him. "We don't really need to debrief you. Sehiri has been telling us all about what you and the Imoliv team have been up to."

"I hope he hasn't been telling you *all* we've been up to, Sir," LeMaine replied.

Both officers laughed. "I don't want to know. The point is that we need to take you and the Hellhounds off of Special Operations for a while. We're launching a system-wide campaign against the Axichis using Polasek's new frequencies. We need every available pilot, and since we don't have any Special Operations right now, we're reassigning you to the flight squadrons."

"Yes, Sir," LeMaine replied. "That will make a nice change."

"We also understand that you and Sergeant Lemon received medical treatment from the Imoliv. We'd like our own medical staff to examine you both and study these implants the Imoliv gave you."

LeMaine stiffened. "Is that strictly necessary, Sir?"

"Of course it's necessary," Commander Lodge interjected. "If we learned how to copy their technology, we could improve reaction time and firing speed in the entire flight corps."

"By replacing all the pilots' eyes with implants?" LeMaine countered. "I don't think so."

"Your duty to the Elian people compels you to let us at least study this technology," Colonel Nicholson urged.

"My duty to the Elian people does NOT compel me to make myself the subject of scientific experiments," LeMaine growled. "Lemon and I received these implants under drastic circumstances. The Imoliv only gave her the implants to save her life and I accepted this implant so I could continue to do my job of commanding the Hellhounds in Elia's defense. Neither of us asked for this. You aren't going to turn either of us into test subjects in whatever human engineering project you have in mind for the pilot corps."

"We have no intention of turning you into a test subject," Colonel Nicholson replied. "We only want to study the Imoliv technology. If we could use these implants to save lives in the future, wouldn't it be worth studying them for that reason alone?"

LeMaine pulled himself together with an effort. "I'll consent to you taking one scan of my eye—that's all—one scan. Nothing more—no examinations—no testing—nothing. You get one scan. Your doctors and researchers can study that and get any information from that. That's all. If you really want to know how it works, why don't you ask the Imoliv? They'll tell you."

Colonel Nicholson shuffled his feet and averted his gaze. "We already did. Sehiri said they can't share any details with us. They have a policy of not sharing their technology with any other outside species. He said the Imoliv only gave you and Lemon these implants in appreciation for your efforts against the Axichis."

"Then I don't see why I should share it with you, either. You can take one scan. That's all. Take it or leave it."

Colonel Nicholson and Commander Lodge exchanged a glance. They both knew LeMaine well enough to know he wouldn't change his mind about this. He didn't budge once he dug his heels in.

"Very well, Owen. I suppose we have no choice but to honor your wishes...."

"You got that right," LeMaine snapped a lot more harshly than he intended.

"You're dismissed, then. You and your Hellhounds report to the pilots' corps by the end of watch today."

LeMaine saluted them both, but he didn't trust himself to say anything else. He stalked out of the office, but he had to take a few laps around the *Lucidity's* many decks before he cooled down enough to go find Lemon.

She scowled when he told her what the two officers had suggested. "Those bastards! How dare they try to exploit this?! Don't they know what these implants cost us?"

"Apparently not," LeMaine replied. "They think the implants are a godsend....and I'm not saying they aren't. Maybe they could save a few lives. I don't know. I consented to give them one scan of my eye—no examinations and no tests—just one scan. You don't have to consent even to that if you don't want to. I just figured, if the scientists want to study something, they can study that."

"How do we know they won't do more the next time one of us goes in for surgery?" she asked. "We'd never know the difference."

"I don't think that will happen. Kellogg is the only person who ever operates on either of us and he won't do anything."

"Are you sure?" she asked.

"Yes. I'm sure. He's known about my eye from the beginning and he's been solid. He's had my back all the way and I'm sure he'll have yours. You know Kellogg. He's our man. He'd never sell us out."

She looked away. "Yeah. You're right."

"As long as we stay in the field, we'll never have any kind of surgery where they would be able to study our implants. Anyway, I guess we just have to let it ride and see where the chips fall. God knows we get enough flack in our line of work. Who knows when the next mission might be our last?"

"You're right. I guess this whole implant thing just brings up so many questions I never asked before."

"Yeah, I know. It's the same for me."

She raised her eyes to meet his. "Thanks, Captain. I couldn't go through this without you."

"I won't say I'm glad this happened to you, but I am glad I'm not the only one. I was really starting to feel like maybe I wasn't even human anymore. Talking to you about it helps a lot. I won't tell Kellogg about your implants, but I really think you should. He needs to know in case he ever operates on you again—or I should say *when* he operates on you again. He's a decent guy. He won't tell anyone, but he does need to know."

She gulped and nodded. "I see that."

"You can trust your squad mates, Sergeant. We all want what's best for you and we all want to have your back if you let us."

"What about you?" she asked. "You haven't told them."

He couldn't look at her. "You're right. It's hard. Sometimes I wish not even Kellogg knew. Then again, sometimes I wish I'd left the service instead of getting this damn implant in the first place."

"Don't say that," she insisted. "We couldn't do this without you. *I* couldn't do it without you."

"I feel the same way about you, so don't think about pulling out. We're gonna get through this."

She nodded again, but she didn't look happy. "Yes, Sir."

He jutted his chin down the hall. "Go see Kellogg now. We're transferring to the pilots' corps by the end of the watch. He needs to know before then. You won't get a better chance than now while we're all off duty."

Chapter 34

LeMaine stood in the ranks of Elian pilots as the Pilots' Corps lieutenant strode down the line giving orders to each squadron in turn. LeMaine couldn't hear him very well from here.

The Hellhounds clustered in a group, all of them wearing Elian pilots' uniforms. It felt strange not to be wearing fatigues, but Elia needed the squad in the air for this campaign.

LeMaine didn't allow himself to look right or left at the pilots gathered in the hangar. He was by far the oldest man here. Most of the pilots were younger than the Hellhounds.

LeMaine let his mind drift to the larger battle. Every Elian bomber, cruiser, and every other vessel with any kind of weapons had been fitted to deploy the frequencies and the scrambler code that Polasek had discovered.

The Military had tested it out a few times already and it worked. The Axichis had even changed their frequencies a few times and the scrambler compensated for that, too.

LeMaine snapped out of his trance when the lieutenant halted in front of the Hellhounds. The man scowled at his clipboard. "Squadron 3874......Special Forces...." He looked up and frowned at LeMaine. "Aren't you a little senior to be down here, Captain?"

LeMaine dipped his chin and kept his eyes trained straight ahead. "Whatever it takes to prosecute the enemy, Lieutenant."

The man frowned at his clipboard and his eyes darted amongst the Hellhounds. "Lieutenant Peterman......Lieutenant Polasek......Shouldn't you be assigned to commanding your own squadrons?"

"I don't think so, Lieutenant," LeMaine replied. "I'm pretty sure Colonel Nicholson gave orders that our squad should be kept together."

"My orders are to assign you to a Hunter-class," the lieutenant went on. "This is highly out of order."

"I realize it's unusual," LeMaine replied, "but since we aren't a normal part of the pilots' corps, the brass figured it would be better to do it this way."

The lieutenant frowned at each of the Hellhounds in turn and then shrugged his eyebrows. "Whatever works. You can take the *Belligerent*. She's at the far end of the tarmac beyond the cruisers."

"Thank you, Lieutenant."

"You're assigned to Quadrant 48 during the assault," the lieutenant went on. "You'll be on the far end of the Elian line closest to Axichis space. Your orders are to penetrate the enemy swarm as deeply as possible, coordinate with the Maczhi battalion coming in from Ziea, and pull a rear attack on the enemy, either to drive them into our guns or to harass them from behind and weaken their force."

LeMaine's heart leapt, but he forced himself to remain impassive. "Thank you, Lieutenant. We can definitely do that."

"This is one of the most dangerous maneuvers in the whole battle plan," the lieutenant went on. "But I suppose you folks are used to that."

"Yes, we are, Lieutenant. I'm sure we'll be just fine."

"And you understand that the Maczhi battalion will be flying stolen Axichis fighter craft. You'll need to work fast to modify the *Belligerent's* scanners to pick up which fighters are flying Maczhi pilots instead of Axichis pilots."

"That won't be a problem, either," LeMaine replied. "Lieutenant Polasek can get onto that as soon as we board the ship."

The lieutenant nodded, but he didn't stop frowning at both his clipboard and the Hellhounds. Someone forgot to send him the memo that the Hellhounds would be coming today.

He moved on and LeMaine went back to zoning out for the rest of the briefing. He wanted to get off the ground and into the battle. He wanted to fight the enemy, now that the frequencies would finally give the Elian Military a fighting chance at winning.

The briefing took way too long, so he let his thoughts range beyond Elia to the battle ahead. At least the Hellhounds wouldn't be stuck with the regular Military. The squad would be flying deep into Axichis territory, rendezvousing with the Maczhi battalion, and doing some real damage. Good.

The briefing finally broke up and the Hellhounds went outside to find their new craft. *"Belligerent*. She sounds perfect," Monk breathed.

"Any Hunter would be perfect for you," Kellogg told him.

"What can I say?" Monk countered. "I'm a man who likes what he likes."

"There she is," LeMaine pointed out. "Let's get the hell off this rock."

The Hellhounds got down to business loading into their cannon placements. Monk went up to the cockpit, but LeMaine stayed out of it so Polasek could work on the scanners. He had a lot to do to reprogram all the cannon placements as well as the cockpit cannon.

LeMaine stuck his head in after twenty minutes. "Are you ready to fly, Corporal?"

"Ready when you are, Sir," Monk replied.

"Good. Take us out and get into position in Quadrant 48. Polasek can do this on the way. I'm buckling in back here until you're done, Polasek, or just in case you want to try on the captain's chair, you can stay up here and man the cockpit cannon."

Polasek smirked up at him. "Are you getting ready to retire?"

"You wish."

LeMaine swatted his arm and made Polasek laugh. Then LeMaine went into the back and climbed into Polasek's cannon placement.

"Hey, you Hellhounds!" Heckler crowed. "Captain LeMaine is in the house! He's riding with us lowlifes today."

"You better rack up the numbers, son," LeMaine replied. "I'll be right on your ass through the whole battle."

"Is Polasek riding up front?" Nunn asked.

"It sure looks like it." Lemon swung her cannon around so LeMaine saw her from the front. "I'm gonna beat the captain today. I feel it. Today's my lucky day."

LeMaine laughed. "Bring it on, Sergeant."

"Hey!" O'Hara yelled. "My targeting system just shut down!"

"Cool your jets, son," Polasek replied. "I'm reprogramming your placement so you don't kill any Maczhi pilots while you're blowing the rest of the sector to hell."

"Oh, right," O'Hara muttered.

"Is Buca coming out for this?" Kellogg asked.

"I haven't heard," LeMaine replied, "but I'd be surprised if he did."

"No, he's the big cheese now," Heckler muttered. "He doesn't come out with alien scum like us."

"Someone has to stay in charge," Peterman replied. "He's too important to fly in a battle like this."

"Someone has to keep the Cezians and the colonists in line," Nunn added.

"Holy shit!" Polasek whispered.

"What's wrong?" LeMaine asked.

"There are Cezian life signs in the Maczhi battalion. Cezian pilots have joined their ranks. Now I gotta reprogram this thing all over again."

"Do what the Maczhi did," Peterman told him. "Program it to only target Axichis. Program it to leave any other pilot, no matter what species it is."

"I should have thought of that first," Polasek agreed.

"Here we go, folks!" Monk announced. "Buckle your seat belts."

He lifted the *Belligerent* off the tarmac. She was the first Elian ship to launch. The other pilots were still on their way to their cruisers.

Monk picked up speed, and when he got into the atmosphere, LeMaine's placement cut out. He freaked out for a second and then remembered that Polasek was still adjusting it.

The *Belligerent* pulled up in Quadrant 48. The Elian line of bombers, cruisers, and dozens of other ship classes already crowded the skies running all the way across the system.

The Imoliv defense force maintained their stance across their own border with the destroyers stationed right inside Elian territory. No way were the Axichis getting through there.

The other pilots from the Command hangar arrived and joined the growing assembly of Elian vessels. They packed in tightly around the bombers until the Elian line became a wall of ships standing off against the Axichis.

The Axichis weren't even in the sky yet. They didn't need to be. They would be hiding out at their bases and stations all over the system. They would only launch when the hammer came down.

LeMaine's gaze drifted back to Ziea, that tiny speck in the far distant corner of the solar system. Who knew such an insignificant planet would play such a pivotal role in this war? The Maczhi battalion deserved the Assembly Medal of Honor if anyone did.

He experienced a rush of pride for them and Buca, but at that instant, the order came down to launch. "We're rolling!' Monk announced. "Strap it up, Hellhounds!"

"Are you sure you don't want to switch places, Captain?" Polasek asked.

"It's a little too late for that now, son. Just tell me you finished reprogramming our placements to protect the battalion."

"All done. You badasses can fire at will."

"God, I love those words!" O'Hara quavered. "Fire at will. I want those words chiseled into my gravestone."

"We can arrange that," Lemon snarled and everyone laughed.

"Get out your scorecards, kids," Peterman added. "Here comes the enemy."

The Elian line started moving forward and the Imoliv defense soared out of position to close the gap. The two fleets flew at an angle to each other making the space between them smaller. One wrong move by the Axichis and they would find themselves trapped.

LeMaine's heart rate quickened as an answering wave of Axichis exploded from all the planets down the line. They launched warships and fighter craft from dozens of stations. Thousands of enemy vessels poured into the skies heading straight for the Elian line.

"Hold the line!" Monk hollered. "Stand your ground!"

"Get ready to make your jump, Monk!" Polasek ordered.

"I'm ready, Lieutenant! I'm just waiting for engagement."

LeMaine adjusted his grip on his cannon. He wanted to start shooting, but he had to keep himself in check, especially when he saw another grouping of Axichis ships launching from Ziea. The Maczhi battalion was in the air.

The instant the battalion launched, another signal came down from Command. "Engage!" Monk bellowed and punched the throttle to the wall.

The *Belligerent* zoomed forward and slammed all the gunners back in their seats. The whole Elian line erupted out of position and the cruisers and Hunters abandoned all formation. They charged the Axichis and the Axichis answered in kind.

The Elian bombers stood firm holding the defensive line to block the Axichis from reaching Elia. The smaller fighter craft rocketed straight for the Axichis and the two armies closed in a hurricane of gunshots.

The Imoliv fighter craft soared in from the side, and at the moment when the Elians and the Imoliv flanked the Axichis from two sides, another signal flashed over the *Belligerent's* controls.

"Frequencies deployed!" Monk hollered. "It's all on, boys and girls! Do your worst!"

All the gunners cheered and opened fire. Shots ricocheted through the Axichis horde and fighter craft exploded along the front. Attack cruisers and Imoliv fighters blasted their way through trying to get to the warships behind.

"Go, Monk!" LeMaine ordered, but Monk was already going at bone-crushing speed.

He plunged into the Axichis horde. "Cannons forward!" he roared. "Blow our way through!"

"What about my score?" O'Hara yelled, but no one answered him.

The whole squad rotated their cannons forward and unloaded. No one took the time to aim. They didn't have to. They just needed to get through this mob without colliding with anything.

Lasers flashed all over the place, but mostly they got mixed up with exploding Axichis ships. Imoliv fighters revolved out of the confusion spitting their phase cannons everywhere. They could destroy the Axichis just fine, now that the frequencies made the Axichis vulnerable to their weaponry.

The *Belligerent* burst through and kept on going into open space before Monk managed to swing the ship around. He turned her nose back toward Elia and the squad observed the battle from behind.

The Axichis were too busy fighting the Elians and the Imoliv to waste their time with the *Belligerent*. LeMaine didn't see the Maczhi battalion anywhere.

"Here we go, gang!" Monk ordered. "You know the drill. You can rack up as many points as you want now."

"What are you going to do, Monk?" Peterman asked.

"I'm just following orders to harass the enemy and drive them into our guns. I don't think. I just do what I'm told."

LeMaine laughed. "Good man. Go to it, Hellhounds."

Monk hit the throttle again. LeMaine swiveled his cannon to target the Axichis when, out of nowhere, a screech of engines distracted him. Thirty more Axichis fighters streaked past his placement, but his targeting system told him the pilots inside were a mix of Maczhi and Cezian.

"Too slow, Hellhounds," a growly voice teased.

"Guza?" LeMaine asked.

"Beat you to it again, Captain," Guza replied. "Try to keep up, Hellhounds."

"You bastard," Heckler growled. "We'll show you how to shoot. Get him, Monk."

Monk responded by diving back into the confusion. Maczhi pilots whirled all around the *Belligerent* and every cannon erupted, but LeMaine didn't have to worry about hitting the Maczhi.

He let his implant off its leash and fired so fast he didn't keep track of the score. He didn't care anymore.

"Basketweave, Monk," Guza told him. "Tie them up with us."

"You got it, brother," Monk replied and hauled the helm hard to starboard.

"What are you doing, Monk?" Lemon roared. "You're giving the other placements all the points."

"Trust me for a second, Sergeant. I promise you'll get your turn."

He spun the *Belligerent* in a complicated intertwined pattern with the Maczhi pilots. They turned somersaults around each other spraying cannon fire everywhere.

The Maczhi battalion confounded the Axichis for a minute and then the plan started to work. The Axichis got so confused between the *Belligerent* and the Maczhi behind them and the Elians and the Imoliv in front of them.

The Axichis kept swiveling front to back and back to the front. They couldn't decide who to hit or which way to face.

Monk and the Maczhi came to the end of the line and separated heading in opposite directions. They raced to the opposite ends of the battle, doubled back, and came hurtling together in another basketweave flight path.

The other side of *Belligerent's* cannon placements got their share of targets, but there were still plenty to go around. LeMaine had long since given up keeping track of his score.

Voices sounded distant in the confusion. He got lost in the Zen of just shooting as many Axichis as he could.

Monk corkscrewed back for another run only to pull up short. "Hold your fire!" Polasek ordered. "We got word coming down from Command!"

"What do they want?" Nunn complained. "We were enjoying ourselves out here."

"Cut it back to Ziea, Monk," Polasek ordered. "Fall in with the battalion."

"What—no!!" Heckler bellowed. "We are NOT falling back."

"Orders, son," Polasek replied. "We're wheeling the battle."

"How?" LeMaine asked.

"I'm not sure, but I think...." Polasek broke off as the Maczhi battalion retreated toward Ziea.

Monk glided into formation with them, and when the Maczhi reestablished their formation in orbit around the planet, the Hellhounds all saw what Command was trying to do.

The battle had escalated even hotter on the front line. The Hellhounds hadn't been able to see it in the confusion, but now it all became clear.

The frequencies worked so well that the Elians and the Imoliv devastated the front line. The alliance had reduced the enemy fighters by more than half and engaged the warships directly. The Axichis fighters couldn't stop the onslaught.

Now Elian attack cruisers and Imoliv fighters surrounded the warships decimating them one after the other. Imoliv destroyers pounded the warships with phase cannons.

The Axichis tried to retreat. They withdrew still trying everything under the sun to defend themselves against the alliance assault, but nothing worked.

The Axichis survivors limped toward their own system. They got nearer to escape with every passing second. That must be the reason Command ordered the Maczhi battalion to pull back. Command wanted to clear a path for the Axichis to leave the system.

"Command is NOT letting these cocksuckers go," Heckler growled. "No damn way."

LeMaine almost said something when, without warning, the Imoliv sprinted out of position. They had only been waiting for the Maczhi to get out of danger.

Imoliv destroyers exploded forward in an unbelievable burst of speed, darted behind the Axichis, and set up another rear flank blocking the Axichis from reaching their own border.

"Yeah!!" Heckler cheered and more voices broke out among the battalion and in all the *Belligerent's* cannon placements. "Hell yeah! Wipe the suckers out! Wipe 'em off the map!"

The Imoliv had the same idea. They unleashed a hellish barrage of phase cannon fire on the Axichis. The Imoliv must have been taking it easy on the Axichis up until now.

Now the Imoliv let them have it with a vengeance. Dozens of warships detonated down the line. Fighter craft wheeled out of the chaos trying to defend themselves and their warships, only to fall to the same fate.

The Elian Military kept driving forward one unstoppable inch at a time. Bombers and cruisers herded the Axichis into the Imoliv guns exactly the way Command ordered the Hellhounds to, but the bombers could do it so much better.

The Imoliv dug in right there inside the Axichis border. The Imoliv didn't move as one warship after another fell into their trap. The two armies kept tightening the noose until every last Axichis ship vaporized into dust.

Chapter 35

The Imoliv fleet stood guard over the Axichis-Elian border for a long time, but no more Axichis vessels came out to challenge the alliance.

Nunn sniffed through the communications system. "I think I'm gonna cry. That was so beautiful!"

Heckler sighed. "The Imoliv have all the fun."

"You got that right," a familiar voice answered.

LeMaine looked around. Four Imoliv fighter craft twirled out of the fleet, buzzed the Maczhi formation around Ziea, and Galo waved through his cockpit window.

"You little shit!" Lemon snarled. "I'm gonna drink you under the table when we get back to Elia."

"And this time, *we'll* bring the liquor," Monk added. "You won't be getting up after this, you lightweights."

The other Hellhounds laughed, but LeMaine interrupted. "Pull your socks up, Hellhounds. We're moving."

"Orders coming down from Command," Polasek announced. "We're falling back to Elia—you, too, Imoliv pilots. You're with us."

"So......" Sindra asked. "What's this drink you're going to give us? Is it toxic to Imoliv?"

"You're about to enter the record books by being the first test subject to find out," Nunn replied. "What are you bringing, Monk?"

"I was thinking a little Nemina firewater," Monk replied.

"Phew!" Hecker exclaimed. "I don't know about that stuff. The last time I drank it, I couldn't see for a week."

"Really?" Lutov asked and his voice trembled. "Is it that bad?"

"If it can put Heckler out, you know it's serious," O'Hara added.

None of the Imoliv pilots answered right away.

"What's the matter?" Lemon jeered. "You aren't scared of a little drink, are you?"

"Of course not," Galo replied. "We just want to make sure it won't kill us."

"You'll never know until you try it," Monk replied. "Besides, you'll go down in history as the first Imoliv to drink it. You'll go down in history whether it kills you or not. What do you have to lose?"

"Um....our lives," Tavon replied and the Hellhounds laughed.

"Do it for science," O'Hara told them.

"Don't come if you're that worried," Lemon added. "No one is going to make you do anything. I'll be drinking Heckler and Monk into an early grave whether you're there or not."

"She will be, too," Polasek replied. "She isn't exaggerating."

Monk turned the *Belligerent* back toward Elia and the ship got swallowed by the rest of the combined Elian and Imoliv forces. No one kept to any formations.

So many vessels gathered around Elia that they couldn't get into orbit at the same time. They had to take turns landing at the Command compound and unloading their crews before more ships could come down.

The Maczhi split off for Ziea long before then. They didn't enter the solar system's inner ring of planets. LeMaine understood why when Monk landed *Belligerent* in her place outside the hangar.

Thousands upon thousands of pilots, mechanics, and military personnel mobbed the runways and airfields all hugging, celebrating, crying, jumping up and down, and talking nonstop about the battle.

Then the Imoliv arrived and the celebration kicked off into an absolute free-for-all. They were supposed to debrief with Command, but it didn't work out that way.

The Imoliv had to hover over the tarmac for a long time before the people on the ground moved out of the way to make room for the destroyers to touch down.

Even then, most of the fighters had to land far away from the Command compound. No one could get near the buildings with so many people packed on the runways.

The Elians stampeded the Imoliv and dragged them into the celebration. No one told these people that the Imoliv wanted to keep their distance from their scumbag alien neighbors.

All of that went down the tubes real quick once the Elians got hold of them. The Imoliv dropped their prejudice and joined the party as food, music, and drink circulated through the gathering crowd.

LeMaine watched from his cannon placement for a long time. He wasn't ready to go out there just yet—or ever, for that matter. He didn't want to have to fight his way through all those people to return to the enlisted mess. The mess would probably be just as packed and noisy as this.

Someone snickered and he glanced behind him to see Lemon smirking. She, Peterman, and Heckler exchanged grins watching the Imoliv living it up side by side with their Elian comrades. They'd all earned the right to celebrate today.

"Are you Hellhounds coming out or what?" Polasek called. "Monk has some serious drinking to do."

The others laughed, climbed out of their placements, and met up in the *Belligerent's* rear compartment. For some reason, they all stopped there and looked at each other.

No one moved for a second and then they all came together in a big, laughing group hug. They all needed a little celebration after everything they'd been going through these last few weeks.

"Let's get the hell out of here," Heckler growled as everyone broke apart. "We don't have to go to the compound. I know somewhere we can go instead...and we can get all the firewater we want there."

"All the firewater Lemon wants, you mean," Kellogg stuck his head back into his placement. "I better bring my kit just in case."

They all laughed and LeMaine popped the hatch. They started to walk down it and stopped when they spotted Sindra, Galo, Lutov, and Tavon coming toward them. All the Imoliv pilots grinned at the sight on the tarmac.

"You Hellhounds should come with us," Sindra offered. "We'll show you somewhere you can have a real good time."

"Better than drinking Nemina firewater?" Lemon asked.

"Come over to my father's ship. We're celebrating there, too. It will be more comfortable than here."

"I'm bringing the firewater anyway," Monk announced. "I don't care where we go."

"All right," Sindra replied. "Bring it."

"Where is it?" Galo asked.

"That's for me to know," Monk replied. "You go on to your ship and I'll catch up."

"I'm going with you," Lemon told him.

He frowned at her and then shrugged. "All right. You can come. No one else."

The others laughed. "It's right over there." Sindra pointed across the airfield.

"I'll find it," Monk replied.

"Don't get lost on the way," O'Hara called after them.

Monk made a rude gesture over his shoulder as he and Lemon walked away. They vanished into the dark. They were the only people for miles in any direction heading away from the Command compound.

The squad crossed the tarmac and entered Sehiri's ship through the hold. It stood open to the rest of the airfield, but no Elians or Imoliv partied in here the way they did at the Command compound. Did the Imoliv even know how to party? The squad could be on their way to the most boring celebration of their lives.

LeMaine didn't argue. The other Hellhounds kept smirking at each other. They were about to be the first Elians ever to see an Imoliv social gathering. What would it be like? Would the Imoliv all stand in a circle in some kind of hypnotic trance?

Sindra led them through the corridors that had become familiar, now that LeMaine and the Hellhounds had spent so much time on this ship. It no longer looked strange or threatening.

Sindra turned off into one of the other holds and the squad stopped dead on the threshold. The hold walls had been removed on both sides to make the space three times as big.

Hundreds of Imoliv occupied the hold and man!—did they ever know how to party. They danced to some kind of strange music and food and drink passed back and forth for everyone to share.

People stood in groups gesticulating wildly with their arms as they relived the battle that defeated the Axichis. The Imoliv crewmen's eyes glowed with delight over their victory.

Colored lights flashed from the ceiling and the crowd enveloped the Hellhounds as soon as the squad showed up. Imoliv strangers pulled the Hellhounds into the hold, talked their ears off about the battle, and shoved food and drink at them.

LeMaine drifted into the crowd trying to figure out where to go or who to talk to. He smiled at everyone and accepted everything they gave him, but he didn't know where he belonged.

He wound up migrating back to the Hellhounds. The crowd had pulled them apart so all the Imoliv could get to know the Elians they'd never seen before.

After a while, all the Hellhounds wound up coming back together. LeMaine didn't want to be anywhere but with them.

Monk and Lemon showed up a little while later. Monk brought out his bottle of Nemina firewater and Sindra's team helped the squad pull a bunch of tables together.

The squad settled down to do some serious drinking. The Imoliv gathered around to see what was happening and the nature of the party changed as word spread through the onlookers.

Someone switched off the music so people could hear the Hellhounds talking to each other. Random strangers approached from the outer spectators' ring to ask questions and make comments on the outcome.

Sindra, Galo, Lutov, and Tavon sat down with the Hellhounds. Someone brought over a bunch of glasses and Monk started pouring out the drinks. "What's the game?" Nunn asked.

"Last man standing," Lemon replied.

"How do you play that?" one of the bystanders asked.

"We drink, glass for glass, until only one person is left," Monk replied. "You light-weights better call a medic now."

"I'm already here," Kellogg replied.

"You're playing, Kellogg," Lemon informed him.

He laughed. "I can't play. I'd be too impaired to pump your stomach after the fact."

"You'll be pumping Peterman's stomach, you mean," she fired back.

"I'm not playing," Peterman countered. "Are you nuts? I feel lightheaded just being in the same room with a bottle of firewater. You won't get me near that table. No way."

"You *are* near the table, Pansy," Lemon told him.

Everyone laughed. "Give Peterman a break," O'Hara chimed in. "He doesn't want to get impaired. He wants to take notes for his book."

"You're damn right," Peterman replied. "This is anthropological gold."

More laughter broke out and some random Imoliv guy stepped forward. "I want to play, too."

"You can't play," Kellogg told him. "You're Imoliv. Firewater might be fatal to Imoliv."

"Sindra and Galo and the others are playing." The guy forced his way to the empty chair that had been set aside for Peterman. The guy sat down. "I'm playing. I want to go in the lieutenant's book."

Laughter answered him and Monk caved. "Fine. What's your name?"

"Buto." The guy slammed his fist into his chest. "I want to be the first Imoliv to beat an Elian in a drinking game."

"You're gonna regret this," Lemon growled.

"We'll see." Buto nodded at Monk. "When do we start?"

Monk glanced around. "Sit down, Captain."

LeMaine stepped forward, but right at that moment, someone touched his arm. He glanced in that direction and froze when he found Sehiri at his side. "Would you mind coming with me for a moment, Captain? It won't take long."

LeMaine was really starting to hate those words. Why did every momentary meeting he had with Sehiri wind up turning into a major life-threatening catastrophe?

None of the Hellhounds said anything when LeMaine and Sehiri slipped away. They were all too used to it.

LeMaine followed Sehiri out of the hold, up the corridor, onto the destroyer's bridge, and into a side compartment LeMaine had never seen before. It was an office. This must be Sehiri's stateroom.

LeMaine froze on the threshold when he saw Colonel Nicholson, Commander Lodge, Captain Hurst, and three other members of the Command staff already inside the room. What the hell were they doing here at a time like this?

LeMaine didn't want to think about how they got here through the crowd of celebrating crewmen out on the tarmac. Whatever these officers were doing here must be serious.

"Come on in, Owen," Colonel Nicholson began. "Thank you for coming."

LeMaine shot a glance from one face to another. "Maybe I shouldn't have."

"Your squad has distinguished itself beyond our wildest dreams," Sehiri remarked. "I had no idea when I first captured you that you would make such a difference to both our peoples."

"What is this all about?" LeMaine asked. "You didn't bring me here to praise me and my squad."

"We need you again, Owen," Captain Hurst told him. "The Hellhounds are famous for getting the job done when no one else can. Now we need you to do the same thing."

"Why?" LeMaine asked. "We just defeated the Axichis. What more is there to do?"

"We only defeated them in one battle of a much larger war," Colonel Nicholson replied. "Sure, it was a decisive battle and it drove the Axichis out of our system, but the war isn't over."

"They're still arming inside their own system," Sehiri added. "They're amassing weapons, ships, cannon stations—all the same infrastructure they moved into Elia in the first place. It's only a matter of time before they try again."

"What do you want me to do about it?" LeMaine demanded. "It isn't like I can go inside the Axichis system and......"

The words died on his lips as all the men present gazed back at him with the same level stare. His blood ran cold.

"No," he whispered.

"You're the only squad we have that can pull it off," Commander Lodge told him.

"This is insane," LeMaine croaked.

"If you don't, our only option will be to take the battle inside the Axichis system ourselves," Colonel Nicholson went on.

"Well, why can't you?" LeMaine heard his voice rising, but he couldn't keep it down. "You have these frequencies. You have the Imoliv and the Maczhi battalion all fighting for you. The Axichis wouldn't be able to stop you from going inside their system and knocking out whatever they're doing in there."

"We can do that anyway, but we need you to go in and weaken them first," Commander Lodge replied.

"How exactly do you propose to get my squad and me inside Axichis space?" LeMaine burst into hysterical laughter at the very thought of it. It all sounded so lunatic impossible that it became ridiculous. "I can't believe I'm actually having this conversation."

"You and Sindra can work that out," Colonel Nicholson replied.

"Sindra!" LeMaine spun around fast and gaped open-mouthed at Sehiri. "You would send your own son into Axichis space?"

"By himself—no," Sehiri replied. "With you and the Hellhounds—yes. I've seen the way your squad and his team work together.....and I've heard the way he talks about fighting under your command. I trust you to do this for the sake of both our peoples."

LeMaine couldn't remember after the fact how he got out of Sehiri's office....or state room....or whatever it was. This wasn't happening.

Going behind enemy lines on Ziea.....or on Evilia.....or anywhere else—the Hellhounds could handle that.

Going behind enemy lines inside Axichis space.....well, that was just plain stupid. Who in their right mind would actually suggest that?

He kept telling himself that he hadn't actually agreed to carry out this mission. He never actually said those words inside that office. He could still back out. He never had to tell the Hellhounds that conversation ever happened. They would laugh him out of the room.

He made it back to the hold without snapping his wire completely. He entered and stopped on the threshold.

All the Hellhounds sat around the table with Sindra, Galo, Lutov, Tavon, and Buto. They all took turns taking shots of the firewater one after the other.

Lemon was already taking the early lead. She might weigh half as much as Heckler and a fifth as much as Monk, but she could hold her liquor like no one LeMaine had ever met.

The five Imoliv were already showing signs of danger. They could barely stay upright in their chairs. Kellogg hovered between them pointing his scanner at their heads and bodies.

He didn't interfere with the game, though. He must have been satisfied that the Imoliv weren't in any immediate danger—no immediate health danger at least.

They *were* in immediate danger of passing out entirely. Their comrades in the crowd laughed and jeered and shouted insults at them every time one of them swayed in his chair.

None of the pilots heard a thing. They didn't even seem to be aware of the crowd or even the Hellhounds in front of them. The pilots were already losing their ability to function mentally.

O'Hara glowed with color and Nunn kept bursting into stupid giggles behind her hand. She pointed at the Imoliv pilots and dissolved in giggles all over again. Her state deteriorated every time she took a shot.

Polasek, Monk, and Heckler weren't holding up too badly. Polasek could carry quite a bit of booze when he wanted to. He was staying alert much better than Monk.

Lemon narrowed her eyes at the three of them, no doubt trying to decide which of them would last the longest. None of them could touch her when it came to drinking. Last man standing was her game. There was no question about that.

LeMaine didn't approach the table. He didn't even enter the hold. He stood back in the shadows so none of the Hellhounds would know he was here.

The instant they saw him, they would realize that something was up—something big. They wouldn't leave him alone until they told him.

Better to let them have tonight. Tomorrow morning, after they all got over their hangovers and Lemon got her bragging rights in by telling them all what a champion she was—then he would tell them—not before.

He propped his shoulder against the wall and crossed his arms to watch. He put the upcoming mission out of his mind and just enjoyed watching them have a good time with their new friends.

They deserved this. There would be plenty of time to take life seriously once they found out they had to do it all over again.

End of Book 3.

Keep Reading

Hellhounds Series: Book 4: The Lost

The final battle for the fate of the free world could be the Hellhounds' last stand when their mission turns against them. The Hellhounds take on their most dangerous mission yet by going deep inside Axichis space. Their objective? To defeat the invasion force in its own territory and stop the Axichis from launching an even more catastrophic conquest of the Elian solar system.

Captain Owen LeMaine and his squad discover a chilling plot to enslave the entire human race, wipe out everyone's consciousness, and turn each and every man, woman, and child into lifeless automatons under Axichis control. The Hellhounds can't do anything to stop the conspiracy after the squad get taken captive and utterly defeated by the same drug they came here to destroy. Is there one last shred of hope or a hidden ally who can come to the rescue at the last minute to save the free world from ultimate annihilation?

You can find it at your favorite book retailer.

Sign Up Once--Get all Theo Mann's free books including brand new releases

S ign Up Once--Get all Theo Mann's free books including brand new releases

Humanity on the brink of annihilation.

A mysterious package, a corrupt officer, and a conspiracy that goes all the way to the top? What could possibly go wrong?

When a routine mission goes horribly wrong, Warrant Officer Ewing Archer and a handful of faithful friends get trapped in a battle to save the last survivors of Earth.

The human race has abandoned the ecological disaster of Earth. Now all that remains is a network of interconnected ships, stations, and satellites surrounding the planet.

But when war breaks out, Archer becomes a firebrand that could destroy it all....or save it.

Sign up at www.theomann.com to read it for free

About Theo Mann

I write 70 books per year—and yes, before you ask, all these books are my original creative work. Nothing written under my name is AI-generated or ghostwritten because I write better than AI and any ghostwriter out there.

People don't read fiction for entertainment or to escape from reality. People read fiction to see their humanity reflected in another person's character and story.

This is my promise to you. When you read my books, you'll see your own humanity reflected in the characters and stories. I take this commitment to my readers very seriously. My books are an intimate form of communication between us. I would never disrespect my readers by turning that over to a machine or another writer. This is my bond between me and you as my reader.

I write 20,000 words per day as my daily work output. If anyone with a public platform would like to challenge me to prove this in a controlled environment, feel free to contact me on this website's contact page.

I worked as a professional ghostwriter for fifteen years. Now I'm on a mission to set a Guinness World Record by writing 700 books over the next ten years and 1400 books over the next twenty years, all originally written by me. See my website for the full book list.

I'm also the author of *Proof for the Existence of God* and the *Crimes Against Fiction* blog. You can find all my nonfiction work at www.crimes-against-fiction.com.

If you have a story idea, or if you would like me to explore a series in more depth, or if you'd like me to explore a character by writing a spinoff series about that character or world, leave me a message on my website's contact page. I answer all reader emails, so ask me anything, tell me what you liked and didn't like, and let me know where you'd like your favorite series to go. I would love to hear your ideas and find out what you'd like to read next.

Find out more at www.theomann.com.

Also by Theo Mann (so far)